"Kirito, Kirito, hang in there!

Asuna Yuuki § Daughter of Shouzou Yuuki, CEO of the electronics manufacturer RCT. She was trapped inside *Sword Art Online* when she played the copy her brother Kouichirou bought.

"Never know until you try, right?"

Kirito § A boy who found himself within a mysterious fantasy realm.

Q

MAY 2017

09

REKI KAWAHARA   ABEC   bee-pee

SWORD ART ONLINE
alicization beginning

SWORD ART ONLINE

"Asuna, sorry."

Kazuto Kirigaya § The Black Swordsman, who saved everyone trapped inside *SAO*, the nightmare MMO. His player name is Kirito. He and Asuna are boyfriend and girlfriend in real life, as well as online.

"You'd be surprised how hard it is. When I was just starting out, I could barely land a hit."

Eugeo § The first resident Kirito met in this new world. He works as a "carver," tasked with felling the demonic Gigas Cedar.

"Just kill them for their meat."

Ugachi the Lizard Killer § The leader of a goblin tribe hiding in the northern pass, a cave that passes through the End Mountains.

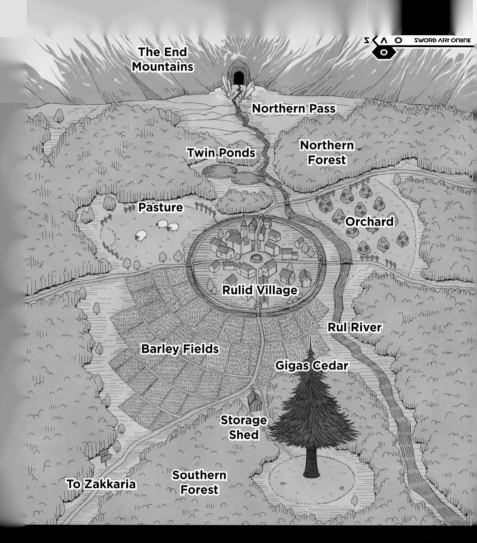

The End
Mountains

Northern Pass

Twin Ponds

Northern
Forest

Pasture

Orchard

Rulid Village

Rul River

Barley Fields

Gigas Cedar

Storage
Shed

To Zakkaria

Southern
Forest

Area Map of Rulid Village

The village of Rulid is home to Eugeo, resident of the Underworld. It exists at the very edge of the Human Empire, at the northern end of Norlangarth, one of the four empires that compose the human realm. The village is three centuries old, but due to the steep mountains surrounding it to the north, east, and west, the standard of living is poor. In order to expand cropland and grazing areas, the Rulidites must develop the forest to the south, but right at the entrance is the demonic Gigas Cedar, which sucks up everything, even the

nutrients of the surrounding area, and blocks all progress. Therefore, through the generations, the village has always had a resident whose Calling is to carve away at the tree with the Dragonbone Ax, which is strong enough to cut iron.

North of Rulid are the End Mountains. Beyond them is the Dark Territory, where no light can reach. To the south is the town of Zakkaria, and farther south is the Human Empire's city of Centoria, which is home to the central Axiom Church.

SWORD ART ONLINE

Alicization beginning

VOLUME 9

Reki Kawahara

abec

bee-pee

YEN ON

NEW YORK

SWORD ART ONLINE, Volume 9: ALICIZATION BEGINNING
REKI KAWAHARA

Translation by Stephen Paul
Cover art by abec

SWORD ART ONLINE
©REKI KAWAHARA 2012
All rights reserved.
Edited by ASCII MEDIA WORKS
First published in Japan in 2012 by KADOKAWA CORPORATION, Tokyo.
English translation rights arranged with KADOKAWA CORPORATION, Tokyo,
through Tuttle-Mori Agency, Inc., Tokyo.

English translation © 2016 by Yen Press, LLC

Yen On
1290 Avenue of the Americas
New York, NY 10104

Visit us at yenpress.com
facebook.com/yenpress
twitter.com/yenpress
yenpress.tumblr.com
instagram.com/yenpress

First Yen On Edition: December 2016

Yen On is an imprint of Yen Press, LLC.
The Yen On name and logo are trademarks of Yen Press, LLC.

Library of Congress Cataloging-in-Publication Data

Names: Kawahara, Reki, author. | Abec, 1985—illustrator. | Paul, Stephen
    (Translator) translator.
Title: Sword art online. Volume 9, Alicization beginning / Reki Kawahara,
    abec ; translation, Stephen Paul.
Other titles: Alicization beginning
Description: First Yen On edition. | New York, NY : Yen On, 2016. | Series:
    Sword art online ; 9
Identifiers: LCCN 2016035665 | ISBN 9780316390422 (paperback)
Subjects: | CYAC: Science fiction. | BISAC: FICTION / Science Fiction / Adventure.
Classification: LCC PZ7.K1755 Swm 2016 Y DDC [Fic]—dc23 LC record available at
    https://lccn.loc.gov/2016035665

10 9 8 7 6 5 4 3 2 1

LSC-C

Printed in the United States of America

"THIS MIGHT BE A GAME, BUT IT'S NOT SOMETHING YOU PLAY."

—Akihiko Kayaba, *Sword Art Online* programmer

Reki Kawahara

abec

bee-pee

PROLOGUE I

JULY 372 HE

1

Squeeze the ax handle.

Lift it up.

Swing it down.

Such simple actions, and yet the tiniest lapse of concentration would cause the ax to miss its mark, sending a tremendous jolt through the arms as the blade struck hard bark. Breathing, pulse, speed, shifting of weight—all these factors must be perfectly controlled for the heavy ax head to properly unleash its power into the tree and create the sound of its famed bite.

But understanding these things did not make them any easier to execute. It would soon be the second summer since Eugeo had been given this job, which was bestowed upon him in the spring of his tenth year. At best, even now, he could produce this perfect strike only one time in ten. Old Man Garitta, who had previously held this position and taught Eugeo the ropes, could strike true every single time. Garitta never looked tired, no matter how often he swung the heavy ax, but it took Eugeo only fifty swings for his hands to go numb, his shoulders to ache, and his arms to stop rising when he commanded them.

"Forty...three! Forty...four!"

He tried counting aloud the ax strikes against the tree as a means of encouragement, but sweat blurred his eyes, his palms slipped, and his accuracy fell further. He swung the tree cutter's ax around madly, putting his entire body into the rotation.

"Forty...nine! Fif...ty!!"

The last swing was wildly off base, hitting the bark far from the sharp, deep rut in the tree and producing an ugly ringing noise. The vibration nearly caused sparks to shoot from Eugeo's eyes; defeated, he dropped the ax, stumbled a few steps back, and plopped down onto the thick moss.

He sat there panting until he heard a joking voice off to his right. "I counted about three good sounds out of your fifty swings. That makes, what, forty-one in total? Looks like the siral water's on you today, Eugeo."

The voice belonged to another boy about his age, lying down a short distance away. Eugeo felt around for his leather canteen and lifted it to his lips. He gulped down the lukewarm water and tightened the cap again, feeling human at last.

"Hmph! You've only got forty-three yourself. I'll catch up in no time. Go on," he said. "It's your turn...Kirito."

"Yeah, yeah."

Kirito—Eugeo's closest, longtime friend and his partner in this gloomy "Calling" since last spring—brushed back his sweaty black bangs, lifted a leg straight up, then hopped to his feet. But rather than pick up the ax, he put his hands on his waist and looked up. Eugeo's gaze traveled to the sky with his.

The mid-July summer sky was astonishingly blue, and in the midst of it, the sun goddess, Solus, unleashed all her light. Yet the tree towering over them spread its branches so thick and wide that nearly none of the light reached Eugeo and Kirito on the ground.

With every passing moment, the great tree's leaves devoured the blessing of the sun goddess and its roots sucked up the favor of the earth goddess, Terraria, healing the damage that Eugeo and Kirito were so painstakingly chopping into it. No matter how hard they tried on any given day, by the next morning the tree had refilled half the damage they'd cut into it. Eugeo sighed and returned his gaze to the tree.

The tree—called by its sacred name of "Gigas Cedar" by the villagers—was a true monster, with a trunk four mels wide and a height of easily more than seventy mels from the ground. Even the bell tower of the tallest church in the village was only a quarter of that height, and to Eugeo and Kirito, who had just grown to a mel and a half this year, the tree might as well be the Titan for which it was named.

As Eugeo looked at the slice cut into the trunk, he couldn't help but wonder if it was even possible to fell the beast with human strength alone. The wedge was just about a mel deep now, meaning the trunk still had three quarters of its thickness intact.

Last spring, Eugeo and Kirito had been summoned to the village elder's home, where they were given the duty of carving the great cedar and told its mind-numbing story.

The Gigas Cedar had spread its roots throughout this land ages before the village of Rulid was founded, and ever since that founding generation, the villagers had ceaselessly put ax to trunk. Old Man Garitta was the sixth-generation carver of the tree, which made Eugeo and Kirito the seventh. Over three hundred years had been spent on the task.

Three hundred years! It was more time than Eugeo could fathom—he had only just turned ten. That hadn't changed now that he was eleven, of course. All he could process was that over his mother and father's generation, his grandparents' generation, and generations even before that, the carvers had put a countless number of swings into the tree, and all that work had combined to produce this slice he was looking at now, less than a mel deep.

The elder told him in grave tones why it was so important for them to fell the great tree.

The Gigas Cedar was so large and its vitality so powerful that it was stealing the blessings of the sun and earth gods over a vast region. No seeds could take root in the land over which its towering shadow reached.

Rulid was at the very northern end of the Norlangarth Empire, the northern of the four empires that ruled over the realm of humanity—in other words, it was literally at the end of the world. Steep mountains surrounded it to the north, east, and west, which meant that the only means to expanding their cropland and grazing pastures was cutting down the forest to the south. Unfortunately, the Gigas Cedar was located right at the forest's entrance, so the village could not grow until it was taken out of the picture.

Yet the tree's bark was as hard as iron; no amount of fire could induce it to smoke, and its roots stretched just as wide and deep as the reach of its branches. So they used the Dragonbone Ax left behind by the founders, a tool strong enough to cut metal, and the task of carving the tree was passed down through the generations.

When the village elder had finished the tale, his voice trembling with the weight and dignity of duty, Eugeo had timidly asked, "If it's so hard, why don't we leave the Gigas Cedar and go around it?"

The elder sternly informed him that cutting down the tree had been the founders' deepest desire, and it was customary for two of every generation to carry on the carver's Calling. Next, Kirito had asked why the founders had bothered to start the village here at all. The elder had been momentarily taken aback before exploding with fury and boxing first Kirito's ears, then Eugeo's for good measure.

Thus, for the last year and three months, the boys had taken turns chopping away at the Gigas Cedar with the Dragonbone Ax. But perhaps because they were still inexperienced at the task, it did not seem like they were making much progress on the existing slice within the tree. Three centuries of chopping had gone into that cut, so it made sense that two children would not produce much in a year's work, but it was nonetheless very discouraging to have so little to show for their labor.

In fact, if they wanted to, they could be discouraged using much clearer and more concrete evidence. Kirito had the same thought as he glared silently at the Gigas Cedar and walked over to it, reaching for the trunk.

"Don't do it, Kirito. The elder told you not to go around constantly reading the tree's life," Eugeo pleaded, but Kirito wore only his usual mischievous grin when he turned around to look at his friend.

"The last time I looked was two months ago. It's not constantly, just every once in a while."

"Oh, you and your excuses...Hang on, I want to see, too," Eugeo added. His panting had finally calmed down, so he flipped up onto his feet like Kirito did and trotted over to his partner.

"I'm going to open it now," Kirito muttered, and held out the index and middle fingers of his left hand, the others tucked away into his palm. Using this brush, he drew a shape like a writhing snake in midair—a primitive version of the sigil of dedication to the goddess of creation.

Once the sigil was done, Kirito struck the trunk of the Gigas Cedar. It didn't make the usual dry bark sound but instead rang out soft and pure, like silverware. A little square window of light appeared, as if shining right out of the tree's trunk.

Everything that existed in the world, whether mobile or stationary, was given "life" by Stacia, the goddess of creation. Insects and flowers had small amounts of life, cats and horses more, and humans even more than that. The forest trees and mossy rocks had many, many times more life than humans. Every being's life grew from its birth until a certain peak point, and then shrank. When that life ran out at last, the animals and people would perish, the plants would wilt, and the rocks would crumble.

A Stacia Window displayed the remaining life in sacred script. Anyone with enough sacred power could call one up by drawing the sigil and striking the target. Just about anyone could bring up a window for little things like rocks and grasses, but it was more difficult for animals, and a background in elementary sacred arts was necessary to open a human's window. Of course, everyone was a bit scared to look upon their own window.

Normally a tree's window would be easier to see than a person's, but the monstrous Gigas Cedar was much more difficult, and it was only half a year ago that Eugeo and Kirito had become skilled enough to see it.

According to rumor, a master of the sacred arts who was elected senator of the central Axiom Church in Centoria once succeeded in opening the window of the earth goddess, Terraria, herself after a ritual lasting seven days and nights. One simple glimpse at the life of the earth was enough to terrify the wits out of the senator, and he fled and disappeared, driven mad by what he saw.

Ever since hearing that, Eugeo was afraid of looking at not just his own window but at other large things like the Gigas Cedar. However, Kirito was not bothered in the least; in fact, his face was pressed up close to the shining window. Eugeo was reminded that sometimes he just couldn't fathom his best friend, but eventually he gave in to curiosity and peered at the window for himself.

The purple rectangle contained a string of odd numerals written in a combination of straight and curved lines. Eugeo could read just the numbers of the ancient sacred script, but writing it was forbidden.

"Umm…" Eugeo murmured, sounding out the numbers one by one as he counted them on his fingers. "235…542."

"Yeah…How much was it two months ago?"

"I think it was about…235,590."

"…"

Kirito threw up his hands in a dramatic gesture of defeat and fell to his knees. He scrabbled his fingers through his black hair. "Just fifty! All that work over two months, and we took it down only fifty out of 235,000! We'll never topple this tree for as long as we live at this rate!"

"Of course we won't." Eugeo smiled wryly. There was no other answer to give. "Six generations of carvers have been working for three centuries and only gotten a quarter of the way through. At that rate, it'll take, um…at least eighteen generations and nine more centuries to finish."

"Don't…even…start," Kirito groaned, looking up balefully at Eugeo. Suddenly, he lunged and grabbed his friend around the legs. Stunned, Eugeo toppled backward onto the local bed of moss.

"Why do you always have to be such a goody-goody?! Try to figure out some way to deal with this unfair duty instead!" Kirito demanded, but he wore a huge smile as he straddled Eugeo and ruffled his victim's hair.

"Ahh! Hey, stop it!"

Eugeo grabbed Kirito by the wrists and pulled hard. Kirito yanked back on his own to avoid being hurled over, and Eugeo took advantage of that momentum to roll upward and take the overhead position.

"There, we'll see how you like it!" He laughed, tugging at Kirito's hair with his dirty hands, but unlike his own flaxen hair, Kirito's black hair already stuck out any which way it wanted, so the attack did little. He was forced to switch to tickling instead.

"Agh! S-stop…n-no fair," Kirito heaved, out of breath, as he struggled against the tickle attack.

Suddenly, a fierce, high-pitched voice broke the grappling stalemate:

"Hey! You're slacking off again!"

Eugeo and Kirito instantly froze.

"Ugh…"

"Oh, crap…"

They both hunched their shoulders sheepishly and turned toward the voice.

Standing atop a rock nearby was a figure with hands on hips and chest puffed out. Eugeo grimaced and muttered, "H-hi, Alice. You're early today."

"I'm not early, I'm exactly on time," the figure snapped in a huff, the long hair on either side of her head throwing off dazzling blond light in the meager dapple that reached through the

leaves. The girl leaped nimbly off the rock, her bright blue skirt and white apron flapping in the breeze. She held a large woven basket in her right hand.

The girl's name was Alice Zuberg, and she was the village elder's daughter. She was the same age as Eugeo and Kirito.

Custom in Rulid—in the entire northern territory, in fact—stated that all children in the spring of their tenth year were given a Calling and entered into an apprenticeship for that job. Alice was the sole exception, as she attended school at the church. She was receiving private instruction from Sister Azalia to capitalize on her gift for the sacred arts, which was the most noteworthy of any child in the village.

But Rulid was not a bountiful enough place to allow an eleven-year-old girl to sit around and study all day, even if she *was* the elder's daughter and had a preternatural gift. Every able-bodied resident needed to work together to combat the Mischief of the Dark God Vecta—drought and flood, pestilence, and anything else that threatened the life of crops or livestock—or there wouldn't be enough to survive the winter.

Eugeo's father, Orick, raised a barley field on cleared forestland to the south of the village that had been in the family for generations. He made a show of being delighted when his third son, Eugeo, was chosen to be a Gigas Cedar carver, but inwardly, he was disappointed. They'd be paid his earnings as a carver from the village treasury, of course, but that didn't make it any easier to replace that extra set of hands to work in the field.

The eldest son of each family typically received the same Calling as his father, with the daughters and further sons of farming families usually following suit. The child of the general store took on the general store, the sons of the men-at-arms grew up to guard the village, and the village elder's child became the new elder. Rulid followed these traditions for centuries after its founding. The adults claimed that this preserved the village and was thanks to the blessings of Stacia, but Eugeo couldn't help but feel something unsatisfying with the explanation.

He couldn't tell if the adults really wanted to grow the village or if they wanted things to stay exactly the same. If they really wanted more farmland, why didn't they just go to the trouble of moving past the accursed tree to the lands farther to the south? But even the village elder, purportedly the wisest of anyone, saw no need to change any of their ancient traditions.

So no matter how much time passed, Rulid was chronically poor, which meant that Alice could study only in the morning, after which she would tend to the livestock and clean the house. Her first task after school was bringing lunch to Eugeo and Kirito.

Alice leaped off the tall rock, basket slung over her arm. Her deep-blue eyes glared at Eugeo and Kirito, locked in mortal combat on the ground. Eugeo hastily sat up and shook his head before those lips could issue another bolt of lightning.

"W-we weren't slacking off! We finished our morning work, promise!" he babbled as Kirito mumbled an affirmation from below.

Alice graced them with another withering stare, then snorted. "If you've got the energy to wrestle after finishing your work, maybe I should ask Garitta to up your number of swings."

"P-please, anything but that!"

"I'm kidding. Come on, let's eat. It's a hot day, so we need to hurry before the food spoils."

She set down the basket and pulled out a large white cloth, which she proceeded to whip open and place on the flattest available bit of ground. Kirito immediately leaped onto the blanket, his shoes already off, followed by Eugeo. The starving laborers watched as more and more food appeared before them.

Today's menu was a shepherd's pie of salted meat and stewed beans; thin sandwiches of black bread, smoked meat, and cheese; several types of dried fruit; and fresh milk that morning. Aside from the milk, they were all long-lasting types of food, but the hot July sun was assuredly doing its best to steal away the meal's life.

Alice held the ravenous boys at bay as though she were ordering dogs to sit, then drew the appropriate sigil in the air to open a window for each item of food, starting with the milk in its bisqueware pot.

"Yikes, the milk only has ten minutes, and the pie, fifteen. And that was after I ran all the way here…You'd better eat all this quickly—just make sure you chew properly."

A single bite of bad food whose life had expired could cause stomach pains and other ailments in all but the extremely hardy. Eugeo and Kirito gave a brief thanks for their food before tearing into their pies.

For a while, all three ate in silence. The two hungry boys were one thing, but it was surprising just how much food Alice could pack away in that tiny body of hers. First went the three slices of pie, then the nine black-bread sandwiches, washed down with the pot of milk. Finally satisfied, the trio sat back for a breather.

"And how was the flavor?" Alice asked with a sidelong glance.

Eugeo answered in as serious a tone as he could manage. "Today's pie was good. I think you've gotten much better at it, Alice."

"D-do you think so? I felt like it was still missing a little something," she said, turning away to hide her embarrassment. Eugeo shot Kirito a glance and they shared a secret smile. Alice had supposedly been making their lunches for the last two months, but it was very clear which days she'd secretly received help from her mother, Sadina. No skill was attained without long years of practice—but Eugeo and Kirito were just old enough to recognize when it was best not to bring that up.

"So anyway," Kirito started, grabbing a yellow marigo from the fruit container, "it's a shame we can't take our time eating such a delicious lunch. Why does the heat make the food go bad so quickly…?"

"Why?" Eugeo scoffed, shrugging. "Because all life drops quicker during the summer, of course. Don't be weird. Meat, fish, vegetables, fruit—it all goes bad if you just leave it around."

"I know that, but I'm asking *why*. During the winter you can leave raw meat outside for several days and it'll still be good as long as it's salted first."

"Because…the winter's cold," Eugeo answered. Kirito's mouth twisted into a childish pout. His black eyes, rare among the northern territory, sparkled with defiance.

"That's right, the food lasts because it's cold—not because it's winter. So if we can keep them cold, our lunches should last longer, even in the summer."

That caused Eugeo to lose his patience for good. He stretched and kicked at Kirito's shin. "You make it sound so easy. How do you make it cold when it's the heat that makes it summer? Are you going to use the forbidden weather-altering arts to bring snow? The Integrity Knights will swoop up from Centoria and take you away the very next day."

"Hmmm…There has to be *some* way…Something simpler than that," Kirito muttered, thinking hard.

Alice, who was twirling her long bangs with her fingertip as she listened to their conversation, interjected, "That's interesting."

"Wh-what? Not you, too, Alice!"

"I'm not suggesting using the forbidden arts. Why go to the trouble of freezing the entire village if all you need is to make the inside of this picnic basket cold?"

It made a lot more sense when she put it that way. Eugeo and Kirito looked at each other and nodded together. Alice, now smug, continued. "Some things are cold even in the summer. Like deep well water or silve leaves. Maybe putting things like that into the basket will cool it down?"

"Oh…good point," Eugeo noted. He crossed his arms to deliberate.

Right out front of the church was an incredibly deep well that had been there since Rulid was founded, and its water was cold enough to bite the skin, even in the summer. The leaves of the rare silve tree that grew in the northern forest emitted a piercing scent and a chill on the skin when plucked, and they were treasured as a treatment for bruises. Now that he thought about it, putting well water in a pot and wrapping the pie in silve leaves seemed like it would be enough to keep the food fresh in transit.

But Kirito shook his head slowly. "I don't think that will be enough. The well water goes tepid just a minute after it's drawn, and silve leaves don't give you more than a brief tingle. That won't be enough to keep the basket cold from Alice's house all the way to Gigas here."

"Are you saying there's a different way?" Alice snapped, unhappy that her idea had been shot down.

Kirito ran his hands back and forth through his raven hair for a while. At last he said, "Ice. If we had a lot of ice, that would keep the lunch cold."

"Oh, come on…" Alice groaned. "It's summer. Where are you going to find ice? There isn't even any in the market at Centoria!" she lectured, like a mother to her stubborn child.

But Eugeo felt foreboding creeping over him, and he watched Kirito in silence. When his best friend had that look in his eyes and spoke in that tone of voice, it always meant he had some dreadful idea in mind. He recalled countless misadventures from the past: the time they went to get emperor-bee honey in the mountains to the east, the time they broke the hundred-years-expired jar of milk they found in the church basement…

"W-well, who cares? All that matters is to eat the food quickly. If we don't get started on the afternoon work soon, we'll be late returning home again," Eugeo urged, trying to divert the topic away as he returned his empty plate to the basket. But the glint in Kirito's eyes told him that his fears were about to become reality, whether he liked it or not.

"…All right, what is it? What have you thought of this time?" Eugeo asked, resigned.

Kirito grinned and said, "Hey…remember that story your grandpa told us ages ago, Eugeo?"

"Hmm…?"

"What story?" Alice asked. She was curious, too.

Eugeo's grandfather, who had returned to Stacia's embrace two years ago, had been an old man with countless old tales stored in his beard that he liked to share with the three children as they gathered around his rocking chair. He had hundreds of stories—mysterious ones, exciting ones, scary ones—so there was no way for Eugeo to guess which one Kirito was thinking about. His friend cleared his throat and held up a finger.

"There's only one story about ice in the summer. 'Bercouli and the Northern White—'"

"Oh, please. You've gotta be kidding!" Eugeo interjected, shaking his head and hands.

Of all the founders of Rulid, Bercouli was the most skilled with the sword, and he served as the first chief guard of the village. Given that he lived three hundred years ago, a number of stories about his exploits had been passed down and inflated in the telling, and the one Kirito mentioned was easily the most fantastical of them all.

One midsummer day, Bercouli saw a large transparent stone rising and sinking in the Rul River, which ran to the east of the village. He fished out the object and was mystified to learn that it was a hunk of ice. Bercouli followed the river upstream until he reached the End Mountains, the very boundary of the human realm, where the river narrowed down until it met the mouth of a massive cave.

Bercouli made his way inside, pushing against the freezing winds that blew out of the cave, and, after braving many dangers, he arrived at the great chamber in the very deepest part. In it, he found an enormous white dragon, which was said to protect all the borders of the human world. When he saw that the beast was sleeping atop an immeasurable mountain of treasure, Bercouli boldly snuck forward and chose a single beautiful sword from the pile. He carefully picked up the sword so as not to wake the dragon and was about to scamper off for safety when, *dun-dun-dun*—so the story went. It was called "Bercouli and the Northern White Dragon."

Even mischievous Kirito couldn't intend to break the laws of the village and cross the northern pass to search for a real dragon, Eugeo prayed. "So…you're going to stake out the Rul and wait for ice to flow down it?" he hedged.

Kirito snorted. "The summer will be over by the time I see anything like that. I'm not going to copy Bercouli and try to find a dragon. Remember how in the story, there were huge icicles right inside the entrance of the cave? Two or three of those should be enough to test out my idea."

"You can't be serious…" Eugeo groaned, then fell silent. He turned and glanced at Alice, pleading her to scold the ne'er-do-well in his stead. But the look of excitement in her blue eyes turned his consternation into despair.

Much to their outrage, Eugeo and Kirito were considered the two biggest troublemakers by the elderly in town, receiving scoldings on a daily basis. But few people knew that the driving force behind their many bouts of mischief was the encouragement of Alice herself, the village's perfect little sweetheart.

Alice put a finger to her plump lips and pretended to think it over for a few seconds, then blinked and said, "That's not a bad idea."

"Come on, Alice…"

"Yes, children are forbidden from crossing the northern pass on their own. But remember the exact wording of the rule: 'Children must not cross the northern pass to play on their own without adult supervision.'"

"Uh…is that how it goes?" Eugeo asked, and shared a look with Kirito.

The laws of the village, officially titled *The Rulid Village Standards*, were recorded on an aging parchment two cen thick that was kept in the village elder's home. When children started going to school at the church, the first thing they did was learn all the laws. Parents and elders always droned on and on about "the laws say this" and "according to the laws that," so by the age of eleven, every child had them thoroughly beaten into his or her head—but in Alice's case, she had memorized the exact wording of each and every law.

She can't have memorized the Basic Imperial Laws as well; those are twice as thick as the village's...Much less that other *thing, which is twice again as thick as that,* Eugeo thought, staring holes into Alice. She cleared her throat and took on a fussy, officious tone.

"Do you see? The law forbids us from going to play. But going in search of ice is not playing. If we can extend the life of our lunches, it will help not only us but the other workers in the barley fields and pastures, won't it? Therefore, we should interpret this to fall under the category of work."

Eugeo and Kirito shared another look. His partner's black eyes seemed hesitant for a brief bit, but that soon melted away like their fabled ice in a hot summer river.

"Yep, exactly. You are correct," Kirito declared, crossing his arms. "It's work, so it doesn't break the village law about crossing the northern pass to the End Mountains. Remember what Mr. Barbossa always says? 'Work isn't just what people tell you to do. If you have free time, find something you can do on your own!' If they get mad, we can just trot out that line in our defense."

The Barbossas had the largest barley fields in the village. Nigel Barbossa was a stout man around fifty years old who, unsatisfied with having over double the income of anyone else in the village, would complain that Eugeo hadn't felled "that infernal cedar yet" every time they crossed paths. Rumor said that he was petitioning the elder to give him first priority on cleared lands after the Gigas Cedar was removed. Whenever he heard it, Eugeo thought to himself, *Your life is going to run out well before that happens.*

Kirito's idea to use Nigel's words against him if they got in trouble was very tempting, but Eugeo was always the first member of the trio to invoke a "but," thereby holding back the others.

"But...it's not just the village laws that forbid going to the End

Mountains…There's that other thing, too, right? Even if we cross the pass, we can only go to the foot of the mountains and not into the cave…"

Alice and Kirito both sobered, if momentarily. What Eugeo mentioned was not *The Rulid Village Standards* or the Norlangarth Basic Imperial Laws but an even more absolute, far-reaching set of laws that covered all the residents of the human world—the Taboo Index.

The Index was upheld by the Axiom Church, residing in its tower in Centoria that stretched nearly to the heavens. The heavy books, bound in pure white leather, were given to every single town and village in not just the northern empire containing Rulid but to those in the east, west, and south as well.

Unlike the village rules and imperial law, the Taboo Index contained well over a thousand entries of forbidden actions, starting with general things like rebellion against the Church, murder, and theft, and going down to specifics like caps on the number of animals and fish that could be hunted in a year or which types of feed were forbidden to give to livestock. Aside from learning letters and numbers at school, the biggest priority was teaching children all the entries of the Taboo Index. As a matter of fact, the Index forbade *not* teaching the Index in school.

But the absolute authority of the Taboo Index and Axiom Church did not extend to all corners of the world. Beyond the End Mountains that surrounded everything was a land of darkness—what was called the Dark Territory in the sacred tongue. Naturally, the entry that forbade going to the End Mountains was listed quite early in the Index, and that was why Eugeo said they could go to the foot of the mountains but not into the cave.

Eugeo stared at his old friend Alice. Surely she would not dare challenge the Taboo Index. Even *considering* such a thing was a taboo.

Alice thought for a while, her long eyelashes dazzling in the sun like fine golden threads. Eventually she raised her head, and her eyes still had that adventurous gleam in them.

"Eugeo, your reading of the Taboo Index isn't entirely accurate, either."

"Huh…? N-no way!"

"Yes way. Here's what the Index says. Book One, Chapter Three, Verse Eleven: 'Thou shalt not cross the End Mountains that encircle the Human Empire.' When it says cross, it means climbing over. Going into a cave doesn't count. Besides, our intention is not to go beyond the mountains but to get ice from *inside* them. There's nothing in the Taboo Index that says, 'Thou shalt not search for ice *within* the End Mountains,'" Alice noted, her crystal voice like the tiniest bell at the church. Eugeo had no response. In fact, what she said was making a certain kind of sense.

But the farthest we've ever been are the twin ponds along the Rul, well short of the northern pass. We don't know what lies beyond that point, and this is the season where the itch-bugs come out along the water…

Kirito roused Eugeo out of his hesitation by slapping him on the back, just softly enough not to damage his life, and shouted, "Alice studies more than anyone else in the village, so if she says so, it's fine, Eugeo! That settles it—next rest day we're searching for that white dra…The ice cave!"

"I'll need to make our lunch with ingredients that last longer."

Eugeo looked at his friends, their faces sparkling with excitement, and could offer only a reluctant "sure" under his breath.

2

The third rest day of July was shaping up to be a beauty.

Even the children over the age of ten who had been given their Calling returned to their younger days and were allowed to go out and play until dinner. Normally Eugeo and Kirito would go fishing or have play swordfights with the other boys, but on this rest day they were out of their houses before the morning dew was gone, waiting for Alice beneath the old tree at the edge of the village.

"She's late!" Kirito grumbled, conveniently forgetting that he had forced Eugeo to wait several minutes, too. "Why do women always put their own preparations ahead of being on time? In two years she'll be like your sister and claim that she can't go into the forest because it'll get her clothes dirty."

"She can't help it; she's a girl," Eugeo said, even as he considered where they would be in two years' time.

Given her status, Alice was still considered one of the children without a Calling yet, so the village tacitly accepted her activities with the boys. But she was also the village elder's daughter, which essentially guaranteed that she would serve as the standard for the other women of the village. It would not be long before she was forbidden from cavorting with boys and forced to learn not just the sacred arts but the proper manners and bearing of a lady.

And what would happen after that? Like Eugeo's eldest sister, Celinia, would she marry into another family? And what did his partner think about this...?

"Hey, stop spacing out. Did you get enough sleep last night?" Kirito wondered. Eugeo nodded vigorously.

"Y-yeah, I'm fine...Oh, here she comes."

He pointed toward the village, where the sound of light footsteps was approaching.

Just as Kirito had groused, Alice appeared through the morning fog with her pristinely combed blond hair tied up with a ribbon and spotless white apron dress swaying. Eugeo looked at his friend and stifled a smile. The boys greeted her in unison: "You're late!"

"No, you're too early. Honestly, when are you two going to grow up?" Alice retorted, handing Eugeo the basket and Kirito the canteen with her nose in the air.

Once they automatically took the items, she turned to the path leading north out of the village, crouched, and plucked a stalk of high grass. She pointed the plump, fuzzy end of it toward the distant mountain and announced, "And now...we head off in search of summer ice!"

Eugeo shared another look with Kirito, wondering how it was that they always ended up being the princess and her two servants, and started trudging after Alice.

The road that ran north to south through the village was well-worn on the southern-heading side with the passage of travelers and horses, but the northern-headed side had long fallen into disuse, littered with tree roots and rocks. Alice stepped nimbly over all these obstacles, humming as she led the two boys onward.

Eugeo thought the way she carried herself was beautiful. A few years ago, Alice could be seen practicing her sword fighting with the other scamps from time to time, and somehow she usually managed to knock Eugeo and Kirito on their backs with even the finest of sticks. Their blunt sticks hit only the air, as though they were clumsily fighting off wind spirits. If she'd kept training, Alice could have been the village's very first woman-at-arms.

"A man-at-arms..." Eugeo mumbled to himself.

It had been a distant dream, a hope that he held onto until he was given the Calling of a carver. If he'd been chosen as a guard (the dream of all the boys in the village), he wouldn't have to use a crude stick yanked off a tree. He could learn actual sword-fighting techniques and use an actual steel sword, even if it was a hand-me-down.

It didn't stop there. The guards from all the villages in the northern territory could enroll in the dueling tournament held in the city of Zakkaria to the south every fall. Ranking highly in the tournament earned a guard the actual title of Sentinel, accompanied by an official sword forged by a blacksmith in Centoria. And not only that—if the sentinel garrison recognized your skill, you could take the test for entry into the venerable Swordcraft Academy in Centoria. If you passed that considerable challenge and graduated from the academy two years later, you could participate in the fighting tournament attended by the emperor of Norlangarth himself. Legends claimed that Bercouli once won that very tournament.

After that, at the top of everything was the Four-Empire Unification Tournament administered by the Axiom Church, which accepted only true heroes from all over the human world. The winner of this event, which was watched over by the gods themselves, stood atop the pinnacle of all warriors. He would be given the holy task of protecting the order of the world itself as a dragon-riding Integrity Knight, swooping into the Dark Territory to battle the demons there...

Eugeo never imagined getting that far, but he once clung to a vision in his head. If Alice left the village not as a sword fighter but as an apprentice of the sacred arts, she might go to school in Zakkaria or even the Artcraft Academy in Centoria. And perhaps, dressed in the green and beige of the official sentinel forces at her side, shining official sword on his belt, would be him...

"The dream isn't over yet," Kirito murmured to him, breaking Eugeo out of his fantasy. That single comment had been enough for Kirito to read every single thought that passed through his head. He grimaced at his friend's perceptiveness and muttered, "No, it's definitely over."

The time to dream of such things had ended. Last spring, it was Zink, the son of the chief man-at-arms, who had received the guard's Calling—despite the fact that his skill with the sword was far below Eugeo's or Kirito's, not to mention Alice's. He felt a momentary surge of anger and even greater resignation.

"Once a Calling is determined, not even the elder can change it."

"With one exception."

"Exception...?"

"When you complete your work," Kirito stated. Eugeo grimaced again, at the stubbornness this time. His partner still hadn't given up on the preposterous goal of felling the Gigas Cedar in their generation.

"If we knock down that tree, our job is done for good. And then you get to choose your next Calling. Isn't that right?"

"It is, but..."

"I'm glad I didn't wind up as a shepherd or a barley farmer. There's no end to those jobs, but there is for ours. There has to be a way to do it. If we cut down that tree in three—no, two years..."

"We can fight in the Zakkaria tournament."

"Well, well, sounds like you're still in the mood for that, Eugeo."

"I can't let you go and hog all the glory, Kirito."

It was strange how just joking about it with his friend made it seem like less of a crazy dream. The boys continued on, grinning at the idea of waltzing back to town with official prize swords to show off to dumb old Zink, when Alice turned around up ahead to glare at them.

"What are you two whispering about back there?"

"N-nothing. We were just wondering if it's time for lunch yet. Right?"

"Y-yeah."

"You're kidding. We've barely just started walking. Anyway, there's the river up there."

Alice pointed her grass stalk at a glittering water surface up ahead. It was the Rul River, which started in the End Mountains and flowed around the east of Rulid and then south to Zakkaria. The road split there, with the right-hand path crossing Rulid Bridge to the eastern forest and the left path continuing north along the riverside. They would follow it north, of course.

At the fork, Eugeo knelt down at the water and sank his hand below the clear, burbling surface. It would have frozen his skin in early spring, but now that it was midsummer, the water was much warmer. It would no doubt feel great to strip off his clothes and jump in, but he couldn't do that in Alice's presence.

"It's definitely not a temperature that will support ice," he reported to Kirito.

Kirito in turn pouted, saying, "Yeah, that's why we're going to the cave where it comes from."

"Fine, fine, just remember that we have to be back at the village by evening bell. Let's see…How about we turn back when Solus reaches the middle of the sky?"

"I guess we have no choice. Let's hurry!" Alice commanded, walking away over the soft grass. The boys hurried to keep up.

The branches of the trees on their left reached overhead like a canopy, blocking the sunlight, and the river on their right brought a cool breeze, so even when Solus was high overhead, the trio walked in relative comfort. The one-mel-wide river path was covered in short summer grasses, and there were almost no holes or rocks to trip them up.

Eugeo found it strange that it was such an easy place to walk, and yet he had never set foot beyond the twin ponds. The northern pass, which the village laws prohibited children from crossing alone, was much farther ahead. So he could have easily walked past the pond without being scolded—yet there was something, a kind of fear of the law itself, that naturally stopped his feet from going farther.

He and Kirito often complained of how stuffy the adults were about rules, but they had never even *thought* about breaking them, much less gone through with it. This tiny little adventure was easily the closest he'd ever come to challenging the Taboo Index.

A belated anxiety visited Eugeo, and he glanced ahead at Kirito and Alice, but they were singing a cheery shepherd's song together. It made him wonder if they'd ever felt afraid or even concerned about anything in their lives.

"Hey, you guys," he called. They looked over their shoulders without stopping.

"What is it, Eugeo?" Alice asked.

He decided to lower his voice to scare her. "We're pretty far from the village now...Aren't there dangerous beasts around here to look out for?"

"What? I've never heard of any such thing," she said, glancing at Kirito.

He shrugged and wondered, "Where did Donetti's grandpa say he saw that long-clawed bear, again?"

"Near the black apple tree to the east. And that was about ten years ago."

"If we see anything around here, it's going to be a four-eared fox. You're such a scaredy-cat, Eugeo."

The pair laughed. Eugeo shot back, "N-no, I'm not scared, I'm just saying...this is the first time any of us has been past the twin ponds, right? Maybe we should be careful, that's all."

Kirito's black eyes sparkled. "You know, I think you're right. Did you know that when this village was founded, the monsters from the land of darkness—goblins and orcs and whatnot—would come over the mountains and steal sheep and children?"

He leered in Alice's direction, but she snorted and then huffed, "Listen to you two, trying to scare me. I know the story—an Integrity Knight came from Centoria and defeated the goblin boss to put an end to it, right?"

"'And ever since then, on clear days, you can see the figure of a knight riding a white dragon over the End Mountains,'" Kirito said, quoting the end of a fairy tale that every child in the village knew. He looked to the north, and Eugeo and Alice followed suit. At some point, the white peaks of the mountains had come much closer, blocking a large swath of the blue sky.

For an instant, they thought they saw a tiny light flash among the clouds, but after blinking and looking harder, there was nothing. The trio looked at one another and laughed awkwardly.

"It's only a fairy tale. I'm sure Bercouli just made up that story about the ice dragon in the cave, too."

"If you say that in town, the elder will put his fist down. Bercouli is the hero of Rulid, after all," Eugeo warned. Alice only gave him another chiding smile and sped up.

"We'll find out once we get there. Better hurry, or we won't reach the cave by midday!"

But Eugeo didn't think they could actually get all the way to the End Mountains in just half a day's walk.

As the name suggested, the End Mountains were the very end of the world, the border of humanity's lands ruled by four empires to the north, south, east, and west. Just because Rulid was at the north edge of the northern territory didn't mean it was close enough for children to make the trip in just a few hours.

So Eugeo was stunned when, just before the sun reached the midpoint of the sky, the narrowed width of the Rul disappeared into a yawning cave mouth cut into the side of the mountain cliff right before them.

The deep forests on either side abruptly stopped, leaving a rough wall of gray stone before them. From here, the white peaks piercing the sky were still faded with distance, but it was undeniable that this rock face was the very edge of the mountain range.

"Did we make it already...? These are...the End Mountains? Wasn't that a little sudden?" Kirito gaped in disbelief. Alice's eyes were similarly wide.

"Then...where was the northern pass? Did we just walk right through it without realizing?"

She had a very good point. The northern pass, the absolute boundary for the village children—and adults, too, perhaps—couldn't have simply passed them by without their notice. There had been a bit of up and down in the terrain about thirty minutes after the twin ponds, but that couldn't have been the pass, could it?

Eugeo turned to look back in disbelief and heard Alice whisper gravely, "If that's the End Mountains...then just on the other side...is the land of darkness? I mean...we walked about four hours, but that isn't even enough to get to Zakkaria. I guess Rulid really is...at the very edge of the world..."

Eugeo was stunned to realize just where in the world his lifetime home was actually located. Was it possible that no one in the entire village realized just how close the mountains were? In three centuries of history, were they the first to pass through the northern forest after Bercouli...?

Something felt *wrong*, he decided. But he couldn't say exactly what.

The adults woke up at the same time every day, ate the same breakfast as the day before, then headed to the same old fields, pastures, smithies, and spinning wheels. Alice claimed that it took more than four hours to get to Zakkaria, but neither she, nor Kirito, nor Eugeo had ever actually been there. They had merely been told by the adults that it took two days of walking down the road south of town to reach Zakkaria. For that matter, how many of the adults had ever actually gone to Zakkaria and come back...?

Before the vague questions floating through Eugeo's head could condense into a proper form, Alice sent them back into oblivion by prompting, "At any rate, now that we're here, we might as well go inside. Let's eat lunch first."

She took the picnic basket from Eugeo's hands and sat down on the soft grass right before it turned to gray gravel. Kirito cheered the imminent end of his hunger, and Eugeo joined them on the ground. The delicious scent of pie was all it took to banish his suspicions for good and remind him how hungry he was.

Alice slapped Eugeo's and Kirito's grasping hands away from the food so she could open the windows of the dishes. Once she was satisfied with their condition, she served the food: fish and bean pie, apple and walnut pie, and dried plums. Lastly, she poured siral water from the canteen into wooden cups and checked to make sure that was good, too.

Once he had permission to proceed, Kirito said a quick grace and tore into his fish pie. Through the food in his mouth, he mumbled, "If we find a bunch of ice in that cave…then we won't have to eat tomorrow's lunch so fast."

Eugeo had the manners to swallow first before responding. "But if you think about it, how will we preserve the life of the ice itself, assuming we find any? What's the point if it all melts by tomorrow?"

"Hmm…" Kirito murmured. Clearly this hadn't occurred to him.

Alice confidently announced, "If we hurry it back and put it in my basement, it should last overnight. I'm appalled that you didn't consider that step first."

Properly scolded, Kirito and Eugeo sheepishly continued eating their lunch. For her part, Alice finished the pie and drank her water faster than usual.

Once she had folded the white cloth and placed it back in the empty basket, Alice stood up. She took the three cups over to the brook and promptly rinsed them out.

"*Yeek!*" she yelped, and trotted back, showing Eugeo the hands she had dried on her apron. "The river water is freezing! It's like the well water in the winter!"

Sure enough, her little palms looked quite red. He reached out to touch them and was surprised to feel that they were pleasingly cool.

"Hey…stop that," she snapped, batting away his hands, though her cheeks were now the same color. Eugeo suddenly realized he had just done something he usually never did, and he shook his head.

"Er…I didn't…I wasn't…"

"All right, you two—shall we go now?" Kirito suggested with a knowing grin. Eugeo stomped lightly on his foot and picked up the water sack, slinging it over his shoulder. He headed toward the cave's entrance without looking back at them.

The clear, narrow brook they had followed was now so small that it was hard to believe it was really the source of the great Rul River. It was barely a mel and a half across. On the left side of the opening in the cliff face from where the water flowed was a rock ledge about the same width across. That would be their walkway inside.

Three hundred years ago, Bercouli the chief guardsman had trod on this very same ground—a thought that urged Eugeo forward into the cave. The temperature dropped, and he rubbed his bare forearms.

Once he heard the other two following, he took another ten steps inside. That was when Eugeo realized his terrible mistake, and he turned to announce, "Crap…I didn't bring any light. What about you, Kirito?"

They were barely five mels inside the cave, and already it was hard to make out one another's expressions. Eugeo was disappointed that he hadn't even considered the obvious fact that it was pitch-black inside a cave. The only response he got from his partner was an oddly confident, "How would I remember something that you failed to remember?!"

"Okay, boys, listen up…"

Eugeo turned toward the faint shine of blond hair, wondering how many times they'd already heard that annoyed tone today. Alice shook her head several times, reached into her apron pocket, and pulled out something long and narrow—the stalk of grass she'd been carrying since they left the village.

She put her left palm to the tip and shut her eyes. Her little lips moved, and she chanted a strange mantra in the sacred tongue. Lastly, she made a quick, complex sigil in the air with her left hand, and the rounded tip of the stalk of grass began to glow. The pale light grew stronger and stronger until the darkness of the cave was kept at considerable bay.

"Whoa!"

"Wow..."

Kirito and Eugeo could not contain their amazement. They knew Alice was studying the sacred arts, but they had hardly ever seen her execute them. According to Sister Azalia's teachings, all the arts that drew upon the power of Stacia, Solus, and Terraria—the dark arts of Vecta's servants excepted—existed only to protect the order and tranquility of the world and were not meant for everyday use.

The only times Azalia and her apprentice, Alice, used the sacred arts was when a villager became sick or injured in a way that herbs could not heal. So the sight of this stalk of grass glowing in the darkness came as some surprise to him.

He asked, "Uh, Alice...are you allowed to do that? You won't get punished, or..."

"Hah. If I was going to get punished for something like this, I'd have been struck by lightning ten times before now."

"..."

Before he could ask what she meant by that, she thrust the glowing stalk of grass toward Eugeo. He took it without thinking, then blanched.

"I-I have to go first?!"

"Of course. Are you going to make the delicate little girl lead the way? Eugeo goes in front, and Kirito in the back. Now let's get going before we waste any more time."

"R-right."

More out of her momentum than any desire of his own, Eugeo held up the tiny torch and started treading farther into the cave.

The flat rock ledge curved here and there but kept a certain width as it went. The dark gray walls shone as though wet, and every once in a while, he felt the sensation of something small moving around in the darkness, out of sight. But no matter how hard he looked, there was nothing resembling ice. Sharp gray protuberances hung from the ceiling like icicles, but they were clearly just rock stalactites.

A few minutes later, Eugeo muttered over his shoulder to Kirito. "Hey...you said the icicles were supposed to be right inside the cave's entrance, right?"

"Did I say that?" his partner replied, playing dumb.

"You did!" he snapped. Alice held out a hand to stop him.

"Hey, bring the light closer to me."

"...?"

Eugeo held out the stalk to Alice's face. She rounded her lips and blew softly toward the light.

"Ah..."

"Did you see that? My breath is white, like in the winter."

"Oh, geez. No wonder it's been feeling colder," Kirito grumbled. Eugeo ignored him and nodded to Alice.

"It's summer outside but winter in this cave. There must be ice," she claimed.

"Right. Let's go in a bit farther."

He turned and resumed his careful progress down the cave tunnel, which seemed to be steadily widening. The only sounds that could be heard were the scraping of their shoes against the rock floor and the streaming of the brook beside them. Even so close to the source, its flow was the same strength.

"If we had a boat, it would be so easy to get back!" Kirito piped up from behind. Eugeo hissed at him to stay quiet. They were already much deeper into the cave than they'd originally planned. So far, in fact...

"What should we do if we really come across the white dragon?" Alice whispered, reading Eugeo's thoughts.

"I guess...we'll just have to run away..." he whispered back, but it was drowned out by Kirito's next oblivious comment:

"It'll be fine. The dragon chased Bercouli because he was stealing the sword, remember? Well, I'm sure the dragon won't mind if we're only taking icicles. But then again...if possible, I sure would like one of its old scales..."

"What in the world are you thinking?"

"I mean, just think of what'll happen if we bring back proof that we saw a real dragon. Zink and the others'll die of jealousy!"

"That's not funny! And just so you know, if you get chased around by a dragon, the two of us are running off and leaving you behind."

"Don't shout so loudly, Eugeo."

"That's your fault for talking nonsense, Kirito..."

Eugeo fell silent when he heard a strange sound at his feet. It was a cracking sound, like he had stepped on something and broken it. He brought down the light and checked under his right foot, then gasped.

"Oh! Look at this."

Alice and Kirito leaned down to peer at where his toe was pointing. A little puddle of water pooled on the smooth gray rock had a thin layer of ice over its top. He reached out and plucked free a piece of the clear film.

Within seconds, the ice melted into water in his palm, but it was enough to bring smiles to the trio's faces.

"That's ice, sure enough. There must be more ahead," Eugeo said, holding out the light. A number of other frozen puddles reflected it back. And up ahead, much farther into the darkness of the cave...

"Oh...there's a lot shining up there," Alice pointed out. When Eugeo moved his hand, countless tiny sparkles flickered ahead. They forgot all about the dragon and trotted farther down the tunnel in that direction.

After what felt like another hundred mels, the walls on either side suddenly vanished.

And the trio was faced with a breathtakingly fantastical sight.

It was huge. A vast chamber that seemed impossible for a subterranean cave. It was at least twice as large as the square in front of the church.

The chamber's walls, which curved in a spherical shape, were not the damp gray of before but were covered by a thick, pale-white film. The floor itself was an enormous pond—no, a lake. It perfectly explained how the Rul River came to be, except that the surface was completely still. It was frozen solid from the banks all the way to the center.

Out of the misty lake jutted oddly shaped pillars here and there, easily taller than the three children. They were hexagonal, with pointed ends. Eugeo was reminded of the crystal that Old Man Garitta had shown him once, years ago, only these were much larger and more beautiful. The numerous pure-blue pillars absorbed the holy light that Eugeo's grass stalk emitted, then sprayed it all around to reflect off the other surfaces, such that the entire domed space glowed with light. The number of pillars increased toward the center of the lake, making it impossible to see to the middle.

Ice. The walls around them, the lake below them, the strange looming pillars—everything was made of ice. The blue walls stretched up to form a rounded top far above, like the ceiling of the chapel.

They stood still for minutes, breathing out white mist, forgetting the chill that stung their skin. Eventually, her voice trembling, Alice mumbled, "I think there's enough ice here to chill all the food in the village."

"More like enough to turn the village to winter on its own. C'mon, let's go in farther," Kirito suggested, and took a few steps forward to test out the lake ice. He carefully added more and more weight until he was standing on it with both feet, but the ice was so thick that it didn't even creak.

Normally it was Eugeo's job to reel in his partner's reckless ideas, but curiosity won out in this case. He couldn't help but wonder if there really was a white dragon up ahead.

Eugeo held up the holy light, and he and Alice followed after Kirito. Carefully, silently, they traveled toward the center of the lake, moving from the shadow of one giant ice pillar to another.

This is amazing. What if I see a real dragon? Will our story be told for centuries, like the others? And if we're able to do what Ber-

couli couldn't...and bring home a piece of the dragon's treasure, will the village elder rethink our Calling and give us a new one...?

"Mmph!" Eugeo had been so wrapped up in his fantasies that he smacked his nose right into the back of Kirito's head after the other boy came to a halt. "Hey, don't just stop like that, Kirito!"

But his partner did not respond. He heard only a low moan.

"...What is this...?"

"Huh...?"

"What the hell is this?!"

Curious, Eugeo and Alice both peered around Kirito's sides to see what was ahead.

"What's the big idea, Kiri..." Alice started—and then she saw what Eugeo saw.

It was a mountain of bones.

Bones made of blue ice. The fierce shine coming off them made the bones look like carved crystal. The vast collection held a variety of bones of all shapes and sizes, all of which were far larger than a human. Together, they formed a pile that easily dwarfed the three children, and resting at the top was an especially large piece that told them exactly what kind of bones these were.

Eugeo understood at once that it was a skull. It had empty sockets and long, narrow nostrils. At the back were jutting growths like horns, and the gleaming jaw featured many, many fangs the size of swords.

"The white dragon's...bones?" Alice whispered. "It's dead...?"

"Yeah...but it didn't just *die*," Kirito answered, calm once again. Eugeo could tell, through his intense familiarity with the boy, that there was an emotion present that he rarely exhibited.

Kirito took a few steps forward and picked up an enormous claw that once may have been the dragon's forearm. He lifted the heavy thing with both hands and showed it to the others.

"Look...see how damaged it is? And the end is chipped clean off."

"Was it fighting with something? But what could possibly kill a dragon…?" Alice wondered. Eugeo had the same question. The white dragon of the north made its home in the mountains that surrounded the world, one of the great ultimate guardians that protected mankind from the forces of darkness. What kind of creature could kill such a beast…?

"These wounds aren't from fighting an animal or another dragon," Kirito muttered, tracing the blue claw with the thick of his thumb.

"Huh…? Then what was it…?"

"These are blade marks. A human being killed this dragon."

"B-but…but even Bercouli the hero, champion of the tournament in Centoria, could only run away from the dragon. How could any swordsman achieve such a…?" Alice started, then fell quiet as a thought occurred to her. Silence settled on the icy lake, now revealed to be a massive grave.

Seconds later, tiny lips unleashed a fearful whisper.

"…An Integrity Knight…? Did an Integrity Knight from the Axiom Church slay the white dragon…?"

3

An Integrity Knight, the ultimate realization of law and order and symbol of goodness, killed a white dragon that served as protector of the human world. In eleven years without ever doubting the way of the world, Eugeo had never considered a concept as difficult as this. He agonized over a suspicion he could neither swallow nor chew, and he shot his partner a pleading glance.

"...I don't know," Kirito muttered, no more certain than Eugeo. "Perhaps...there was an incredibly strong knight from the land of darkness who came and killed the dragon...But if that was true, then it doesn't make sense that the armies of darkness never once crossed the End Mountains to attack. And it certainly doesn't seem like whoever did it was after treasure..."

He walked over to the dragon's remains and placed the claw back on the pile, then reached down and dragged out something long from the bottom.

"Whoa...this is really heavy..."

He unsteadily dragged the object about a mel and showed it to Eugeo and Alice.

It was a longsword with a white leather sheath and platinum pommel. There were fine inlaid patterns of blue roses here and there on the handle, making it clear from a glance that it was more valuable than any sword in the village.

"Oh…could that be…?" Alice wondered, eyes wide. Kirito nodded.

"Yeah. It's got to be the Blue Rose Sword that Bercouli tried to steal from the sleeping dragon. I wonder why whoever killed the dragon didn't take it with them…"

He crouched down and, grabbing the grip with both hands, tried to lift it, but the best he could do was get the tip a few dozen cens from the surface of the ice.

"…I can't!" Kirito shouted, and dropped the sword. It clattered heavily to the ice, causing fine cracks to form in the thick layer. It had to be unbelievably heavy for such a slender weapon.

"What do we do with it?" Eugeo asked. His partner shook his head as he stood up straight again.

"It's no good. We couldn't get this back to town even if the two of us carried it together. All it takes is a few swings of that ax to get us wheezing, remember. But it does look like there's other kinds of treasure down under the bones…"

"Yes…but I don't feel in the mood to go taking it out of here," Alice murmured gravely. The boys shared her opinion.

They wanted a tiny little prize from a sleeping dragon to show off to the other children, but taking treasure from this place would be little more than grave robbing. The taboo in the Index about stealing applied only to other humans and not here, but just because something was not in the Taboo Index did not mean it was justified.

Eugeo looked again at his friends, then nodded. "Let's just take the ice, as we planned. I'm certain that the white dragon would have allowed us to do that, if it were alive."

He walked over to a nearby icicle and kicked at one of the countless ice crystals growing from its base like plant buds. It cracked off cleanly, and he picked it up and offered it to Alice, who lifted the lid of the empty basket and tossed it inside.

For the next few minutes, the trio gathered up shards of ice to put into the basket. When the base of that pillar was clean, they moved on to the next one to repeat the process. Before long,

the large basket was completely full of little blue ice crystals that sparkled like precious stones.

"There…we…go." Alice grunted as she lifted the basket. She stared down at the mass of twinkling light in her arms. "It's so beautiful. It seems like a shame to take it home and have it all melt."

"I don't care, as long as it keeps our lunches fresher," Kirito opined crassly. She made a face at him, then held out the basket.

"What? I have to carry it back, too?"

"Of course you do. It's quite heavy."

Eager to stop them before they started bickering like usual, Eugeo suggested, "I'll take turns carrying it with you. We need to get going back to the village or we won't make it by the evening. It's been nearly an hour since we entered the cave, wouldn't you say?"

"Yeah…It's hard to tell the time when you can't see Solus. Can't you use a sacred art that will tell us the time or something?"

"There's no such thing!" Alice snapped, and turned her head away in a huff to glance at the exit to the side of the vast ice lake.

Then she turned to the opposite wall to look at another exit. She frowned.

"Umm, which one did we come through, again?"

Eugeo and Kirito both pointed confidently—at different exits.

Once they had exhausted the other possibilities—that there should be footprints (the smooth ice surface left no marks), that the exit the water flowed through was the right one (it was flowing out of both), that the direction the dragon skull looked was the exit (it wasn't pointed toward either)—Alice finally suggested an option that seemed promising.

"Remember how Eugeo stepped on that little puddle and broke the ice? We should find it a short distance down the correct tunnel."

It was a good point. Eugeo cleared his throat to hide his embarrassment that he hadn't thought of that himself and said, "Okay, let's check the nearer tunnel first, then."

"I still think it's the other one," Kirito grumbled. Eugeo pushed him on the back, held up the glowing stalk, and walked forward toward the water-carved tunnel.

Once they were out of range of all that reflective and refractive ice, the formerly steadfast sacred light seemed weak and unhelpful. It hastened their pace down the tunnel.

"…Getting lost so we can't find the way back. Who are we, the Berrin brothers from the old tale? We should have left a trail of nuts behind us. No birds in the cave to eat them," Kirito groused, but it was an empty attempt to hide his worry. Oddly enough, Eugeo found it reassuring to learn that his best friend could actually *be* worried in this situation.

"Don't be silly, we didn't have any nuts with us to start with. If you want to start making use of our lessons, why don't you leave a piece of clothing at every branch in the path?"

"No way, I'll catch a cold," Kirito complained, and mimed a sneeze.

Alice smacked him on the back and said, "Stop being stupid and start watching the ground. We don't want to miss the puddle. In fact…" She paused, then frowned, her brows arching. "We've walked quite a long ways, and I haven't seen any broken ice. Do you suppose it was the other direction?"

"No, I think it's farther ahead…Oh, hey, quiet."

Kirito put a finger to his lips, and Eugeo and Alice clamped their mouths shut. They listened carefully.

Beneath the quiet trickling of the brook next to them was a different sound. It was wavering between higher and lower pitches, like a mournful flute.

"Is that…the wind?" Alice wondered. Eugeo thought it did sound quite a bit like the wind rustling through branches.

"We're nearly outside!" he shouted in relief. "We picked the right way! Let's go!" He took off at a trot.

"Don't run, or you're going to slip and fall," Alice warned, but she was skipping, too. Kirito took up the rear, his expression suspicious.

"But…is that the sound the summer breeze makes? It sounds more like…the rattle of winter…"

"It'll blow that hard in the canyons. Let's just get out of this cave already," Eugeo said. He sped through the cave at an easy run, the light in his hand jiggling wildly. The desire to get back to the village and his comfortable home was rising within him. If he got some of the ice from Alice and showed his family, they would be stunned.

But ice melts so fast. Maybe we should have taken one of those old silver coins instead, he thought, just as a little light appeared in the darkness ahead.

"It's the exit!" he cheered, only to immediately sour. The light was reddish. They'd gone inside just after noon and could have spent only an hour inside—but maybe it had been much longer than he realized. If Solus was already descending to the west, they might not make it back to the village by dinner unless they rushed the entire way.

Eugeo sped up. The high-pitched whistling was now loud enough that it overpowered the sound of the river, bouncing off the cave walls.

"Wait, Eugeo, wait! Something's wrong! It's only been two hours; it shouldn't be so…" Alice called out, but he did not stop. He'd had enough adventure. All that mattered now was getting home.

He turned right, then left, then right again, and the red light filled his vision. The exit was just a few dozen mels ahead. He slowed down as he shielded his dark-accustomed eyes, then finally stopped.

There was the cave mouth.

But the world through it was not the one Eugeo knew.

The sky was entirely red, though not from the setting sun. In fact, he couldn't see Solus anywhere. It was just an endless expanse of a dull, dark red, like the juice of overripe grapes or lamb's blood.

Meanwhile, the ground was black. The eerie mountain range in the distance, the bizarrely shaped rocky outcroppings closer up—even the water surfaces here and there were as black as cinders. Only the trunks of the gnarled dead trees were white, like polished bone.

A cutting wind set the dead branches to whistling, a mournful howl that droned on and on. It was clearly the source of the sound they'd heard within the cave.

This world, so forsaken by all the gods, could not possibly be the human world that Eugeo knew. Which meant that the landscape before them was…

"The Dark…Territory…" Kirito rasped, only for it to disappear among the whistling of the trees.

The place beyond the light of the Axiom Church, the land of evil dedicated to the dark god Vecta, the world that existed only in the old stories told by the village elders—just a few steps ahead of them. The thought froze Eugeo's mind, leaving him helpless to do anything but stare. It was as if all this new information flooding into a part of his mind he'd never needed to use before robbed his brain of the ability to process it.

Against the plain white background of his mind, Eugeo saw one thing sparkling fiercely—a verse from the very start of the Taboo Index. Book One, Chapter Three, Verse Eleven: "Thou shalt not cross the End Mountains that encircle the Human Empire."

"We can't…We can't go…any farther," Eugeo struggled to say through numb lips. He held out his hands, trying to motion Kirito and Alice back.

Just then, there was a heavy, sharp sound from above. Eugeo flinched and looked up at the red sky.

Against the bloodred color, he saw something white and something black, locked in a fierce grapple. They were like tiny grains, so they must have been flying extremely high—but they were clearly far larger than a human. The two objects dashed back and forth, closing in on each other and then breaking apart, the clashing of metal sounding each time they crossed each other.

"They're dragon knights," Kirito muttered.

As he said, the two combatants were huge flying dragons, with long necks and tails and triangular wings. Barely visible on their backs were knights with swords and shields. The knight on the white dragon wore white armor, while the one on the black dragon was clad in all black. Even their swords matched their color—the white knight's shining bright, while the black knight's trailed a dark miasma.

With each collision of their swords came a blast like thunder and a shower of sparks.

"I suppose the white one…is one of the Church's Integrity Knights," Alice murmured.

"Yeah, I bet you're right," Kirito added. "And the black one must be a dragon knight for the forces of darkness…He seems to be about as tough as the Integrity Knight…"

"No way…" Eugeo murmured, shaking his head. "The Integrity Knights are the strongest people in existence. They'd never fail to beat a dark knight."

"I don't know. From what I can tell, their sword skill is about even. Neither one is breaking down the other's defense," Kirito noted. Just then, as if hearing what they were saying, the white knight pulled back on the dragon's reins to open up the distance between them. The black dragon swept forward, trying to close the gap.

But before the distance closed between them, the white dragon pulled into a sharp turn and lowered its head, appearing to tense and summon its strength. Its neck shot forward and its jaws opened wide. A line of brilliant white fire shot from between its fangs, covering the black dragon knight.

An explosion drowned out the sound of the howling wind in Eugeo's ears. The black knight writhed in pain and lurched to the side in midair. The Integrity Knight took the opportunity to switch out his sword for a giant bronze-colored bow and loose a similarly long arrow.

It flew through the air with a faint trail of fire behind it and landed smack in the middle of the black knight's chest.

"Ah...!" Alice let out a little shriek.

The black dragon, the film of its wings mostly burned away, began to plummet. The knight tumbled from the dragon's back, spraying blood as he fell directly toward the cave where the children stood.

First came the black sword, sticking blade-first into the gravel nearby. Next was the knight, landing barely ten mels away from the trio. Lastly, the black dragon struck the rocky mountain a considerable distance away, shrieking one last time before it fell silent.

The three children watched in silence as the black knight struggled painfully to sit up. They could see the deep hole torn into the shining breastplate. The knight's head, covered with a heavy helmet that hid the wearer's features, turned to face them.

A trembling hand stretched out, pleading for help. Then an eruption of blood spilled from the throat of the helmet, and the knight collapsed to the ground with a clatter. Red liquid continued to pool beneath the still body, spreading along the black gravel.

"Ah...ah..." Alice continued to gasp at Eugeo's side. She stumbled forward, as if compelled, out of the mouth of the cave.

Eugeo couldn't even react. On his other side, Kirito hissed, "No!!" Alice twitched and tried to stop, but her foot stumbled and she toppled forward. Both Eugeo and Kirito reached out on instinct, trying to grab Alice's dress.

Their fingers just missed and touched only empty air.

Alice tumbled to the cave floor, her blond hair flying, and grunted.

She just fell over. That was all. It wouldn't have affected her life more than one or two points, if they checked her window. But that wasn't the problem. When she fell forward, the fingers of her right hand landed about twenty cens over the very clear boundary line between the bluish gray of the cavern rock and the cinder-black ground. Her white palm brushed the black gravel. The surface of the Dark Territory.

"Alice!" the two boys cried together, reaching down to grab their friend's body. It was the kind of thing that she would scold them for under normal circumstances, but they were too desperate to drag her back into the cave to think about consequences.

When they lifted her back up, her eyes were still fixed on the fallen knight. Eventually they fell to her hand. The puffy palm had a number of little pebbles and grains of sand stuck in it. They were as black as a brand.

"…I…I…" she stammered. Eugeo reached out both hands to hers in a trance. He rubbed away all the grit and desperately tried to reassure her.

"D-don't worry, Alice. You didn't actually leave the cave. You just brushed it with your hand. That's not a taboo, right? Right, Kirito?"

He looked up at his partner, pleading. But Kirito wasn't looking at either Eugeo or Alice. He was down on one knee, focusing hard on their surroundings.

"Wh-what is it, Kirito?"

"…Don't you feel it, Eugeo? Someone…something…"

Eugeo frowned and looked around as well, but there wasn't even a bug in the cave with them, much less another person. All he saw was the black knight ten mels away, presumably dead. The victorious Integrity Knight was nowhere to be seen in the sky.

"It's just your imagination. Come on, let's…"

Take Alice back down the other path of the cave, Eugeo was going to say, but Kirito grabbed his shoulder. Eugeo grimaced and followed his partner's gaze, then froze solid with terror.

There was something near the ceiling of the cave.

A purple circle, rippling like the surface of water. On the other side of the fifty-cen-wide circle was the vague image of a human face. The face was simplistic, so much so that it was impossible to say if it was male or female, young or old. The skin was pale, without a single hair on the entire head. The wide-open eyes contained no visible emotion. But Eugeo knew instinctively that it was not looking at him or Kirito but at the stunned Alice between them.

The face's mouth opened and spoke odd, unintelligible words through the purple portal.

"*Singular Unit Detected. Tracing ID...*"

The marble-like eyes blinked, followed by that strange voice again.

"*Coordinates Fixed. Report Complete.*"

The purple window abruptly vanished. Eugeo belatedly realized that the thing's words resembled the mantra of sacred arts, and he looked first at Kirito and Alice, then at his own body. Nothing had changed.

But the incident was much too bizarre to ignore. Eugeo shared a look with his partner, then they helped Alice up and cradled their trembling friend as they proceeded back into the cave. The group began to run in the direction from which they'd come.

Eugeo couldn't exactly remember how they'd made their way back to Rulid.

When they got back to the lake where the dragon's bones slept, they crossed right through it to the exit on the other side. They ran back through the long cave in a fraction of the time it had taken them originally, tripping and sliding on the wet rock many times, and by the time they leaped out into the light again, the afternoon sun was still pouring down from above.

Yet Eugeo's unease could not be forgotten. The thought of that eerie white face poking out of the purple window behind them spurred him onward without rest.

The birds chirped peacefully in the forest branches and the schools of little fish darted here and there in the brook beside them, but the trio marched on in resolute silence. They crossed the hill that was supposed to be the northern pass, then the twin ponds, and finally reached the north end of Rulid Bridge.

When they at last reached the foot of the ancient tree where they'd met in the morning, relief was palpable. They looked at one another and managed weak, nervous smiles.

"Here, Alice, look," Kirito said, holding out the heavy basket. It was full of the summer ice that was the goal of their little adventure—and Eugeo suddenly realized that he'd forgotten all about it.

He tried to hide his sheepishness by advising, "You should put that in the basement as soon as you get back. Then it might last until tomorrow."

"...Okay, I will." She nodded obediently, taking the basket and looking at the two boys. At last, her confident smile returned. "Look forward to tomorrow's lunch. I'm going to make sure you get a proper reward for all your hard work."

Neither of the boys was cruel enough to point out that it was Sadina who would be treating them to a good meal. They shared a look, then nodded.

"...What was that pause for?" she asked suspiciously.

They patted her shoulders from either side and chimed, "Nothing! Let's go home!"

They walked back to the center of town under the true sunset now. Kirito headed for the church where he lived, and Alice went to the village elder's house. Eugeo arrived at his home on the west side of the village just seconds before the bell rang six.

All throughout dinner, Eugeo was silent. He was certain that his older siblings had never had such an adventure—not even his parents or grandparents—but for some reason, he didn't feel like boasting about the events of his day.

He didn't know how he would describe that land of darkness he had seen; nor the battle between the Integrity Knight and the foe on the black dragon; nor, most of all, the bizarre face that had appeared from nowhere. In fact, he felt afraid of how his family would react when they heard the story.

That night, Eugeo went to bed early, hoping to forget everything he had seen at the end of his adventure. If he couldn't, the awe and respect he felt for the Axiom Church and Integrity Knights might turn into something else altogether.

4

Solus sank and rose, and the usual schedule of life returned.

Normally, Eugeo would return to his work on the morning after a rest day with a gloomy outlook, but today, he was more relieved than anything. He'd had enough adventures for now—chopping at the tree was just fine, thank you very much. He headed out the south gate of town and met up with Kirito at the barley field next to the forest.

Eugeo spotted a tinge of relief in his partner's features, as well as recognition of the same in himself. They shared bashful grins for a moment.

They retrieved the Dragonbone Ax from the shack a short ways down the forest path, then continued on for a few minutes to reach the Gigas Cedar. The sight of the slit carved into the massive trunk would normally remind them of the unchanging nature of their lives ahead, but today that was a reassurance.

"Okay, the one who gets the least number of good hits has to buy the siral water again."

"Really? Aren't you tired of always having to pay, Kirito?" Eugeo teased, continuing their ritual as he lifted the ax. The first blow struck loud and true, a good sign for the day ahead.

All morning they delivered stout blows to the tree with uncanny accuracy. Neither one wanted to admit that the reason for his unusual concentration was a desperate attempt to keep the visions of yesterday out of his head.

When they had finished nine sets each of fifty consecutive swings, Eugeo's stomach rumbled. He looked up to the sky, wiping the sweat from his brow, and saw that Solus was nearly to its apex. One more set of swings, and Alice would come by with their lunch. Only this time, they'd be able to take their time eating the pie and drinking ice-cold milk. The thought brought a twinge of pain to his empty stomach.

"Whoops…"

If he thought too hard about food, his aim would slip. Eugeo rubbed his sweaty palms with his towel and took careful grip of the ax handle.

The sunlight abruptly dimmed.

Great, not a passing shower, Eugeo thought, looking up.

Through the expanse of the Gigas Cedar's branches, he could see blue sky, and at a significantly low elevation, a fast-moving black shadow. His heart wrenched up into his throat.

"A dragon?!" he yelled out. "Hey, Kirito! That was—!"

"Yeah, the Integrity Knight from yesterday!" his partner cried, frozen with fear.

Before their eyes, the platinum-clad knight on the dragon brushed over the branches of the tree and vanished in the direction of Rulid.

What is he doing here? Eugeo wondered amid complete silence. Even the birds and insects seemed to be holding their breath.

Integrity Knights were the guardians of order who purged the enemies of the Axiom Church. Given that there were no rebellious groups threatening the four cardinal empires that made up the realms of man, the only enemies for the Integrity Knights to battle were the forces of darkness. So all the tales said they always fought beyond the End Mountains, a sight Eugeo had witnessed for himself the day before.

That was the first time he'd ever seen a real Integrity Knight.

One had never actually come to the village in his life. So why now…?

"You don't think…Alice…?" Kirito murmured.

Suddenly, the sound of that eerie voice from yesterday filled Eugeo's mind again. The strange arts spoken by the person with the bizarre features sitting behind the purple window. His spine went as cold as if someone were dripping freezing water down it.

"You're kidding…They wouldn't…Not for just that…" he gasped, looking to Kirito for reassurance, but the other boy was staring grimly in the direction of the knight. After a few moments, he looked back into Eugeo's eyes and said, "Let's go!"

He grabbed the ax from Eugeo's hand and raced northward.

"H-hey!"

Something bad was going to happen. Eugeo could feel the dread seeping into his skin as he took off after his partner.

They made their way down the familiar path around tree roots and rocks until they joined the main road into town through the farm fields. There was no sign of the dragon flying overhead. Kirito slowed slightly and called out through the green shoots to a farmer who was staring agape at the sky.

"Mr. Ridack! Which way did the dragon rider go?!"

The farmer turned toward them with a start, as though waking from a dream. He blinked several times, then answered at last, "Oh…oh, yes…It went and landed in the center of the village, I think…"

"Thanks!!" they shouted briefly, and resumed their sprint.

Here and there on the road and in the fields, villagers were grouped together to stare. No doubt even the elderly in the village had never seen a real Integrity Knight before. They all just stared in the direction of the village, uncertain of what to do. Eugeo and Kirito continued running through their midst.

They sprinted through the south gate, paced the short lane of shops, then ran over the little stone bridge, and finally came within view of it. The boys stopped still, the breath catching in their throats.

The long, curving neck and tail of the dragon occupied the northern half of the square outside the church.

Its massive wings were folded on either side, nearly hiding the church building from view. The beast's gray scales and occasional piece of armor reflected the light of Solus, making it look like an ice sculpture. Its bloodred eyes stared down impassively at the village square.

And standing before the dragon was the platinum-clad knight, shining even brighter.

He was taller than anyone in the village. Every inch of the knight was covered in thick plate that shone like a mirror and fine silver chain to cover the joints. The helmet, fashioned to look like a dragon's head, sprouted one decorative horn at the forehead and two backward from either side of the skull, with a heavy faceplate hiding the knight's face.

At the knight's left side hung a longsword with a silver handle. On his back, an enormous brown bow a good mel and a half in length. It was undoubtedly the very same Integrity Knight they had seen kill the black dragon rider from the mouth of the cave yesterday.

The knight stared silently through the cross-shaped slit in the faceplate toward the south end of the square, where a few dozen villagers had their heads hanging toward the ground. When he saw a girl carrying a picnic basket toward the back, Eugeo felt his shoulders ease with relief. It was Alice, wearing her usual blue and white apron dress, watching the Integrity Knight through the crowd of adults.

Eugeo nudged Kirito with his elbow, and they crouched down as they snuck up right behind Alice and softly called her name. Their friend spun around, her blond hair waving, about to say something to them in alarm. Kirito put a finger to his lips to silence her. "Quiet, Alice. You should get away from here at once," he whispered.

"Huh...? Why?" she whispered back. Apparently she had no inkling of the danger she was in. For his part, Eugeo hadn't realized it until Kirito had brought it up, either.

"Well…I think Integrity Knight is…" Eugeo started to explain, and then paused. A few soft murmurs from the villagers filled the silence. He looked over and saw a thin, tall man striding from the town hall toward the square.

"Oh…Father," Alice mumbled.

It was the elder of Rulid, Gasfut Zuberg. His slender frame was covered in a simple leather tunic, and his black hair and whiskers were neatly trimmed. Despite having inherited the Calling of village elder only four years ago, the sharpness of his gaze earned him the respect of all the inhabitants of Rulid.

Gasfut proceeded before the knight, alone and unafraid, then clasped his hands in front of him and bowed in the manner of the Axiom Church. Then he straightened up and said in a crisp, loud voice, "I am Zuberg, the elder of Rulid Village."

The Integrity Knight, standing a full two fists taller than Gasfut, nodded with a faint clank of metal armor, then spoke at last.

"I am the Axiom Integrity Knight overseeing the northern Norlangarth territory, Deusolbert Synthesis Seven."

The voice had an unnatural ring to it, a quality that identified the speaker as something other than a mortal human being. The metallic sound echoed across the square, silencing all the residents of the village. Over twenty mels away, Eugeo grimaced as he felt the knight's voice pierce his forehead rather than his ears, burrowing into his mind.

Even Gasfut stumbled back half a step, overwhelmed by its force. But he quickly recovered, regaining his posture and proclaiming, "It is the utmost of honors that an Integrity Knight, protector of all human lands, should set foot in our humble, distant village. We wish to offer you a feast of welcome, however meager it might be."

"That will not be necessary. I am here on official duty," the knight boomed, the gaze from the slit of the helmet as cold as ice. "I am here to apprehend and escort Alice Zuberg, daughter of Gasfut Zuberg, for her crimes against the Taboo Index, so that she may be judged and her sentence carried out."

Alice's body shook. But neither Eugeo nor Kirito could move a muscle, much less say anything. The knight's words were echoing, repeating in their heads.

The elder's body also lurched. What could be seen of his facial features from his distant profile were skewed with emotion.

After a long silence, Gasfut spoke again, his voice no longer smooth with authority. "My lord knight…what crime is it that my daughter has committed?"

"She has broken Book One, Chapter Three, Verse Eleven of the Taboo Index: venturing into the Dark Territory."

The villagers listening to the exchange abruptly broke into uneasy murmuring. The children's eyes bulged, and the adults muttered sacred mantras and made sigils to ward against evil.

At last, instinct pushed Eugeo and Kirito into motion. They muscled Alice out of the way and stood shoulder to shoulder, blocking her from the view of the other villagers. But they could do no more than that. If they moved too quickly, they would draw the attention of the adults just in front of them.

The only thing in Eugeo's mind was a question that repeated over and over: *What do we do?* Terror bubbled in his chest, demanding immediate action, but he had no idea what action that should be.

All he could do was watch as Gasfut the elder stood, still and silent, his head hung low. *It's all right, he'll do something,* Eugeo thought. He hadn't spoken much with Gasfut, but among the people of the village, the elder was most respected by all, after perhaps Old Man Garitta.

However…

"In that case, I will call my daughter here. I wish to hear her story for myself," the elder said when he raised his head at last.

No! You can't let the knight see Alice, Eugeo thought wildly. The Integrity Knight lifted a heavily armored hand. Eugeo's heart leaped into his throat when he saw that the index finger was pointing directly toward them.

"That will not be necessary. Alice Zuberg is right there. You and you…" He pointed at two men in the midst of the crowd. "Bring the girl to me."

The villagers parted before Eugeo's eyes. Only he and Kirito stood between the knight and Alice now.

Two familiar villagers walked up through the empty space. Their skin was pale and lifeless, their eyes oddly empty. The men pried apart Kirito and Eugeo and pushed them aside, each grabbing one of Alice's arms.

"Ah!" she yelped, then bravely clamped her mouth shut. A weak grin dimpled her usually rosy cheeks, and she nodded to the boys to indicate that she was all right.

"Alice…" Kirito mumbled, right as the men roughly yanked her forward and the basket fell from her arm. The lid opened, spilling the contents onto the cobblestones.

The men dragged Alice away toward the Integrity Knight before she could scoop it up. Eugeo looked down at the toppled basket.

All the pie and hard bread was wrapped in white cloth, with the rest of the basket completely packed with fine ice chips. Some of the ice had spilled out to glitter in the sunlight. Within moments, it began to melt atop the hot stones, fading away into dark little stains.

At his side, Kirito sucked in a sharp breath. Eugeo raised his head and watched them drag Alice away. He gritted his teeth and tried to force his immobile legs into action.

The two men released Alice next to the village elder, then stepped back and knelt. They clasped their hands and hung their heads in a gesture of obedience to the knight.

Alice looked to her father, her face pale. Gasfut briefly gave his daughter a pained look, then lowered his head again.

The Integrity Knight nodded, then pulled an odd tool from the back of his armor. It was a thick metal chain with three parallel strips of leather attached, ending in a large ring.

The knight handed the tool to Gasfut with a heavy clank.

"I command the village elder to punish the guilty."

"..."

The elder stared at the shackles, dumbfounded. Just then, Kirito and Eugeo reached the knight. The imposing helmet turned slowly to face them.

The cross-shaped slit in the front of the helm was entirely dark, but Eugeo felt the power of that gaze on his skin. He automatically looked away and tried to say something to Alice, who was just ahead of them, but his throat was scorched, incapable of speech.

Kirito was similarly downcast, breathing rapidly, but then his head shot up and he spoke in a loud but tremulous voice. "Sir Knight!!"

He took another breath. "A-Alice did not enter the Dark Territory! Her hand merely brushed the surface! That was all!"

But the knight's response was brief. "And what else is necessary?"

He waved to the kneeling men, commanding them to take the boys away. They stood up and grabbed Kirito's and Eugeo's collars, pulling them off. Kirito struggled helplessly. "Then...then we're guilty, too! We were in the same place! If you're going to take her away, take us with her!"

But the Integrity Knight did not heed them.

That's right...If Alice broke a taboo, then we ought to be punished with her, Eugeo thought. With all his heart.

But the words would not come out. He tried to shout like Kirito, but all he could do was emit rasping exhaust, as if he had forgotten how to speak.

Alice looked back at him. She gave a small smile and nodded, as if to say it was all right.

Her stone-faced father slipped the menacing restraints over her body. She grimaced as the three leather straps wrapped tightly around her shoulders, stomach, and hips. When the last was tightened, Gasfut took a few unsteady steps back. The knight approached Alice and picked up the chain dangling from her back.

Eugeo and Kirito were dragged to the center of the square and pushed to their knees. Kirito pretended to wobble toward Eugeo so that he could whisper into the other boy's ear. "Listen, Eugeo…I'm going to attack the knight with this ax. I'll try to hold him off for a few seconds, and you take Alice away to freedom. If you rush to the barley field to the south, you can hide among the stalks and slip into the forest. That should give you good enough cover."

Eugeo glanced down at the Dragonbone Ax still clutched in Kirito's hands and found his voice at last.

"B-but…Kirito…"

You saw the way that Integrity Knight used his sword and bow yesterday. He'll kill you in no time…just like that black knight.

Kirito read Eugeo's unspoken thoughts on his face and continued. "It's all right. The knight didn't execute Alice on the spot. I don't think he can kill someone without a trial or whatever. I'll look for my chance to escape. Besides…"

He turned his burning gaze upon the knight, who was checking that the restraint straps were on tight. With each tug of a strap, Alice's face twisted in pain.

"…Besides, if we fail, so what? We'll get hauled in with Alice and wait until we have a chance to escape. All that matters is that if Alice gets taken away on that dragon, we'll never see her again."

"I…don't…"

He had a point. But it was so brash and reckless it didn't even qualify as a "plan." Wasn't that just rebellion against the Church? The very greatest of crimes, outlawed in Book One, Chapter One, Verse One…

"Why would you hesitate, Eugeo?! Who cares about taboos?! Are they more important than Alice's life?!"

Kirito's impassioned but restrained voice lashed his ears.

And he was right.

Deep down, Eugeo's mind screamed at him.

The three of us were born in the same year, and we decided we'd die in the same year. We swore to always help one another. Each of us lives for the other two. So there's no reason to hesitate. Which is more important, the Axiom Church or Alice? The answer is obvious. It should be obvious. It's...it's...

"Eugeo...What's wrong, Eugeo?!" Kirito nearly screamed.

Alice was looking at them, distraught. She shook her head.

A strange, unfamiliar voice broke from his throat. "It's...it's..."

But he couldn't finish the sentence. He couldn't even formulate the words that came next into his head. A sharp pain winced behind his right eye. An odd itching that refused to go away was blocking his thoughts. *Wince, wince.* Bloodred color covered his vision. The sensation of his limbs faded.

The village elder noticed the change in Eugeo and weakly waved his arm to the two men standing behind the boys, commanding, "Take them out of the square."

Hands grabbed their collars and resumed pulling.

"Damn...let go! Elder! Mr. Gasfut! Do you really want him to take Alice away?! Are you fine with that?!" Kirito raged, knocking away the man's hand. He prepared to charge with the ax.

But his simple leather shoes would not take a single step forward. Something impossible had happened.

Having finished checking Alice's restraints in the distance, the Integrity Knight merely glanced at Kirito, and the Dragonbone Ax gripped tightly in the boy's hands clanged and flew high into the air. The knight hadn't touched his sword or his bow. He hadn't even moved a finger. Yet as though his own will were a physical blade, he had struck the ax from Kirito's hands, sending it flying to the edge of the square.

Kirito fell onto his back with the momentum of that strange collision. A number of villagers immediately set upon him and held him down.

His cheek forced into the cobblestones, Kirito screamed, "Eugeo! Please, you have to go for me!"

"Ah...uhh..." Eugeo grunted. His body shuddered.

Go. You have to go. You have to steal Alice from the knight's hands and run into the forest, a tiny voice commanded in his head. But then came that stabbing pain behind his right eyes again, robbing him of his agency. Another voice clanged inside his head along with the pulsing red light.

The Axiom Church is absolute. The Taboo Index is absolute. Disobedience is forbidden. No one is exempt from the law.

"Please, Eugeo! At least get them off me! Then I can—!"

The Integrity Knight did not watch what was happening in the square. He fixed the end of the chain to another chain connected to his dragon's saddle. The creature lowered its head, and the knight swung up to straddle it. The silver armor shone again.

"Eugeo!!" Kirito screamed at bloodcurdling volume.

The white dragon rose, stretched it wings, and beat them. Again and again, it pounded the air.

Alice was tied directly to the dragon's saddle. She stared at Eugeo and smiled, her blue eyes seeming to be saying good-bye. The updraft of the beating wings brushed her golden hair, which sparkled just as brightly as the knight's armor in the sun.

But Eugeo couldn't move. He couldn't speak.

He couldn't budge an inch, as though his feet were rooted right into the ground.

PROLOGUE II

1

Shino Asada took a sip of cold-brewed iced coffee with just a dab of milk, allowing the rich flavor to seep back into her throat before she let out a long breath.

Through the faded glass window was an assortment of colored umbrellas moving in different directions. Shino hated the rain, but it was rather relaxing to sit at a table in the hidden, alley-side café and watch the damp gray city move. The interior devoid of technology and the nostalgic smells wafting from the kitchen behind the counter made her feel like she'd fallen into some gap between the real world and the virtual world. Just an hour ago, she'd been in class, but that felt like it had happened in a distant dimension now.

"It's really coming down."

She didn't realize at first that the baritone from beyond the counter was directed at her. But of course it was; there were no other customers. Shino turned to look at the barista polishing drinking glasses, his skin the shade of a latte.

"It's the rainy season," she replied. "It's supposed to rain until tomorrow."

"And here I thought it was the work of an undine mage," the stern-faced man said flatly. She snorted.

"No one's going to understand that you told a joke if you don't at least make the right expression, Agil."

"Hrm…"

Agil, owner of the café/bar Dicey Café, wriggled his eyebrows and mouth in search of the "right expression," prompting Shino to burst into laughter when each face he made looked more likely to bring small children to tears. She lifted her glass to her mouth and drowned out the laughter with coffee.

Satisfied, he put on an even fiercer look, just before the bell on the door jingled. A new guest stopped dead in his tracks in the doorway when he saw the proprietor's face, and he shook his head.

"Listen, Agil, if you greet all your customers that way, your place is going to go out of business very quickly."

"N-no, it's not that. This is my joke face."

"…It's not that, either," the customer snapped, putting his umbrella in the whiskey barrel near the door once he'd shaken off the drops. When he saw Shino, he waved to her. "'Sup."

"You're late," she scolded, glaring at Kazuto Kirigaya as he winced in apology.

"Sorry, it's been so long since I rode the train…" He sat down across from Shino, opening his collar.

"You didn't ride your motorcycle?"

"I wasn't up for riding it in the rain…I'll have a caffé shakerato, Agil," said Kazuto, trying a new drink. The collarbone peeking through the top of his shirt was as thin as that of his virtual avatar. His skin color wasn't particularly healthy, either.

"…Have you lost more weight? You really need to eat more." Shino grimaced, but Kazuto just waved his hand.

"I was back at my base weight for a while. I just lost a bit more over this long weekend…"

"Why, were you training in the mountains?"

"Nope, just sleeping."

"How do you lose that much weight?"

"Probably because I wasn't eating anything."

"...Huh? Are you trying to reach enlightenment or something?" she asked, baffled. Just then, a light clattering came from the counter. The owner of the café was working a silver shaker with (rude as it was to admit) surprising dexterity for his size. Agil poured the contents of the shaker into a wide coupe glass and set it on a tray, and Shino was reminded that the place turned into a bar at night.

He set down the glass in front of Kazuto, the contents light brown with a fine layer of froth on top.

"So this is a...caffé shakey-something?" she asked. Kazuto pushed the glass over to her. She lifted it and put her lips to the rim to take a sip. The creamy texture of the head gave way to a pleasantly chilly coffee flavor, followed by a sweet aftertaste. It wasn't anything like the cans of iced milk-coffee from the vending machine at school.

"...It's good," she murmured.

Agil tapped his bulging bicep happily. "You can't get that much head on it unless the bartender really knows what he's doing."

"We hear enough bragging about your skill levels without you having to do it in real life, Agil. And what's that smell?" Kazuto wondered, his nose twitching.

The bartender cleared his throat and announced, "Boston baked beans. They don't come out right unless the cook really knows what she's—"

"Oh, a taste from home from your wife, huh? I'll take an order of those, too."

Agil retreated to the kitchen, scowling at being cut off. Kazuto grabbed the glass back from Shino and took a big gulp. He exhaled, sat up straight, and stared right at her.

"...How is he doing?"

Shino understood at once what he meant. But rather than answer, she snatched Kazuto's glass back again and downed a big swig. The thick froth slid past her tongue, filling her nose with rich flavor. The coffee's stimulation jolted the fragments of memory into the form of a proper response.

"Yeah…He seems to have settled down a lot."

Half a year ago, at the end of 2025, these two were involved in the "Death Gun" incident.

One of the three culprits in that case and Shino's only real friend at the time, Kyouji Shinkawa, underwent an extraordinarily long trial for a case involving a minor and was finally sent to a juvenile medical facility last month.

He maintained total silence throughout the trial and hardly said a word to the experts brought in for a psychological evaluation until, at last, six months after the case, he finally began to answer the counselor's questions bit by bit. Shino had a rough suspicion of why it took exactly that long. Six months—180 days—was the length of time until an unpaid subscription in the VRMMO game *Gun Gale Online* forced the automatic termination of the account. Only when that much time had passed and Kyouji's alter ego, Spiegel, was gone forever from the *GGO* server did he summon up the determination to face reality.

"I plan to request a meeting again after a little while. I think he might agree to see me this time."

"Uh-huh," Kazuto grunted, then turned to look out at the rain. After a few seconds, Shino decided to put on a facetiously unsatisfied face.

"Isn't that normally the spot where you'd ask if I'm sure about that?"

"Er, oh, r-right. Umm…how do you feel about it, Sinon?"

She grinned, secretly satisfied that she'd managed to rattle the normally aloof young man. "I watched all the movies in that old action-flick collection you lent to me. The one I liked the most was where they twisted around the gun bullets to strike behind cover and stuff. I'll have to use it as a practice model—I think I can probably pull it off in *GGO*."

"Ah…okay. Well, great…Just go easy on us…" He grimaced, cheek twitching. She had to hold back her laughter.

The fear of guns that had tormented Shino for over five years wasn't entirely gone yet. She'd learned to enjoy shoot-out movies, but the unexpected sight of guns on street corner posters or models in shop windows caused her heart to skip a beat in a nasty way. By this point, she'd started to rationalize it as a proper response to a deadly weapon and a sign of healthy caution. After all, there was no guarantee that she would never again encounter a criminal waving an actual gun in real life.

Besides, just the fact that she no longer fainted or vomited at mere images of guns was more than enough for Shino to feel like her life had been saved. She no longer felt like an outcast at school—she even had a few friends to eat lunch with. On the other hand, it wasn't the easiest thing to deal with, the fact that she and the young man sitting across from her had started hanging out in the first place after he'd driven his motorcycle to the front gate of her school and waited for her there.

Meanwhile, Kazuto just smiled benignly across the table and said, "So I guess that means the Death Gun incident is finally over and done with...at last."

"Yeah...I guess so," she said, then fell silent. It felt like there was something in the back of her mind that refused to go away, but before she could figure out what it was, the kitchen door opened and the proprietor emerged with two steaming plates for the table.

The sight of gleaming brown kidney beans and thick chunks of bacon brought a violent growl to her stomach, which hadn't had anything to do since digesting lunch. She automatically picked up the spoon, then came to her senses and put it back, waving her hand.

"Oh, I didn't order any."

The towering owner put on a mischievous leer. "Don't worry, the meal's free. It's on Kirito."

Kazuto's mouth dropped open in exasperation, while Agil retreated gracefully behind the counter. Shino felt a chuckle rise in her throat, then grabbed the spoon again and waved it at Kazuto.

"Thanks for the grub."

"…Well, that's all right. I just got paid, so I've got some cash to burn."

"Oh? What kind of job are you doing?"

"The one that involved three days of fasting. But we can talk about that after we clear up the main business here. Plus, we've got to eat this while it's hot."

He picked up the bottle on the table and squirted a dollop of mustard on the rim of the plate, then passed it to Shino. She followed his lead, then scooped up a spoonful of beans to her mouth.

The beans were boiled to a fluff on the inside. The soft, gentle sweetness filled her with a simple nostalgia, despite the food's foreign origin. The thick pieces of bacon weren't too oily, and they crumbled in her mouth.

"This is…really, really good," she mumbled, while Kazuto stuffed his cheeks across the table. "Why are they called Boston baked beans? I wonder what they're flavored with."

"Umm…I forget what it's called, but it's some kind of by-product of refining sugar. What's it called again, Agil?"

The owner looked up from polishing glasses and said, "Molasses."

"Yeah, that's it."

"Ohhh…I thought American food was nothing but hamburgers and fried chicken," she said, dropping down to a whisper for the latter part. Kazuto made a face.

"That's a stereotype. In fact, all the VRMMO players I've met from over there are pretty cool, once you get to know them."

"Yeah, that's true. The other day I went on the international *GGO* server and talked with a girl from Seattle about sniping for almost three hours. Then again…I don't know if I'll ever see eye to eye with *him*…"

"Who?" Kazuto asked, already half-done with his plate of food.

"That's what I was going to talk to you about today. You know they held the fourth Bullet of Bullets individual competition last week."

"The BoB" was the name of the battle royale tournament to determine the greatest player in *Gun Gale Online*.

Kazuto nodded. "Yeah, we all watched the stream. Actually, I didn't congratulate you yet…but I'm guessing you weren't happy about the result. Congrats on coming in second, though."

"Uh…thanks," she said awkwardly, not expecting the compliment. To hide her embarrassment, she quickly went on. "Then you saw it on the stream. Subtilizer, the player who won first… That's his second time being champion."

Kazuto blinked several times, then looked up, consulting his memory.

"Now that you mention it…I think I remember you saying that while we were together in the third BoB. An American player who completely dominated the first tournament with just a knife and handgun…But didn't he get shut out the second time because they split the servers into US and JP, so he was on the other side?"

"Supposedly, yes…He didn't register for the second or third tournament. But somehow he either got around the IP block this time, or he had a connection with the game management…In either case, I was happy. I always wanted a chance to face the legendary Subtilizer."

"Yeah, even on the feed I could tell you were really pumped," he said with a smirk. She pouted.

"I-it wasn't just me. All thirty people in the final…well, all twenty-nine aside from him were excited. A couple of them had fought him and lost in the first one. America might be ground zero for FPS games, but we were ready for the battle royale to show our pride in Japan, home of the Seed Nexus that *GGO* uses…And once we got the chance…"

"It ended up being a repeat of the first tournament, huh?"

Shino nodded, frowning. She scooped up the last piece of thick bacon and savored the rich, homemade flavor to reset her emotional compass, hoping to view her memories of the past week in a more objective light.

"Yes, that might have been the result…but in fact, it was even more of a blowout than the last one. This time, he started off the battle totally unarmed."

"What...? Bare-handed?"

"Yes. Instead of a weapon, he had the Army Combative skill. He took his first target unawares and beat him with some hand-to-hand moves, then took his victim's weapon and used it on the next one...over and over. He couldn't reload the guns he picked up, so there were a few fights where he had to go back to fighting bare-handed. All you can say is that his talent for combat is on another level entirely," she lamented.

Her companion crossed his arms and grunted. "On the other hand...Subtilizer plays an ultra-close-range build, right? Couldn't anyone have taken him out at mid- or long-range? In fact, aren't the majority of *GGO* players like that...?"

"You saw what happened when he beat me, right?"

"Yeah, I was watching from within *ALO*. On the screen, you were heading straight for the spot where Subtilizer was hiding three minutes earlier, so everyone was screaming, 'Don't go there!' and 'Sinon, behind you!' and all that stuff."

"Yes, that part," she said, snorting to drive away the shock and humiliation of that moment before they could visit her again. As calmly as she could, she explained. "After the tournament, I talked to the other eleven people he beat hand to hand, and they were all taken down the same way. He couldn't have had more than the briefest of data on all of us, but the way he went from sneak attack to mortal blow before we could fire a single shot, it was like he knew ahead of time what we were going to do. I don't know how things are on the American side, but on the JP server, there are barely even any knife fights, much less bare-handed combat..."

"...Well, from what I heard, there were a lot more players using lightswords after the third tournament," he noted awkwardly. She scowled.

"It's no surprise, after the show you put on with it. There were a lot of players practicing cutting bullets with lightswords right around the start of the year, but I don't think anyone's made the training stick."

Despite her distant tone, Shino herself had bought a small lightsword in secret and attempted similar training against soldier mobs. After a month of painful work, she'd gotten good enough to get the first and maybe second bullet in a hail of assault-rifle fire, but the skill was useless unless you could fully stop a three-bullet burst in a proper battle. So she dismissed as a dream within a dream ever stopping a ten-bullet volley like Kirito, and she kept the lightsword hidden in her inventory as a good-luck charm.

But if only she'd taken it out and kept it at her waist, she might have been able to strike one blow on Subtilizer...Shino shook her head. She hadn't had the presence of mind for that. She decided to change the topic.

"At any rate...Not a single JP player was able to even point their rifle at him, much less hit him with a bullet. Perhaps Subtilizer's greatest skill isn't his close combat but his predictive abilities in battle."

"Hmm, I see...I just don't know if that's possible...A beginner is one thing, but these are veteran players, finalists of the BoB. Could you really predict their actions with one hundred percent certainty?" Kazuto wondered aloud.

She shrugged. "If over ten people lost the same way, you can't claim it's a fluke. But I suppose it's possible that veterans are more predictable *because* they know the most efficient actions to take. There's a general understanding of where to set up in what terrain and what exact routes to take to get around fastest."

Just saying that aloud brought her a belated realization, and she gasped.

The moment at the very end of the final.

Shino had chosen the very top floor of a half-crumbled building as her sniping spot to take down the last remaining foe, Subtilizer. By her prediction, she should have had a good shot at him with her Hecate II from that particular window as he crossed the road below.

But her foe predicted that prediction, snuck into the building before her, and lay in wait close to her final sniping position. He just waited until she set up the rifle on its bipod and got into firing position…then pounced on her from behind like a feline hunter.

However, Shino had originally planned to use the second floor from the top. It still had enough altitude to give her a good view. The reason she changed her mind was because that floor was an archive. She was afraid it would distract her by reminding her of the old middle school library that had served as her sanctuary, so she spent a few precious seconds to rush up one more floor. It just so happened that the foe she was rushing to shoot was hiding in the shadows of that very floor…

In other words, Subtilizer predicted that Shino would snipe from the very top floor, not the archive floor below. But the reason she changed her spot wasn't based on sniper-specific theory but a totally illogical personal rationale. He could predict the actions of Sinon the sniper, but he couldn't know that Shino Asada loved books in the real world. So was it just a lucky guess that Subtilizer chose the top floor to hide? Or did he see the archive and somehow know that Shino would avoid it…?

If it was the latter, his prediction wasn't based on data or experience. It would be beyond the scope of simple VRMMO player skill—the ability to read minds…

"—non. Hey, Sinon."

Someone's fingers pressed against the hand she held in midair, and she looked up with a start. There was Kazuto, looking at her with concern in his eyes.

"Oh…s-sorry. What were we talking about?"

"The patterns and strategies of veteran players or something."

"Ah, r-right. So, um…yeah. I was just thinking, maybe a player who didn't fit into a pattern and acted in ways that ran counter to theory could actually catch Subtilizer by surprise…"

Only once she had said that aloud did Shino realize that she'd hit on the precise reason that she'd called Kazuto here today. She picked up her glass of water, all the ice melted by now, and chugged it in a vain hope of snapping her mind out of its funk, but the chill clinging to her back did not want to leave.

It was the memory of what Subtilizer had whispered in the second before her HP gauge ran out, following the brief struggle in which he incapacitated her from behind. It was so quiet, and spoken in English, that she didn't understand what he'd said at the moment, but hearing the memory now, she grasped its meaning.

"Your soul will be so sweet."

It couldn't mean much. Many players had their own little catchphrases they liked to say when they seized victory online. Just a bit of role-playing. That's what she told herself.

Eager to move onward, she adopted a falsely cheery tone and said, "So, speaking of players who ignore common sense and do the improbable, the absurd, and the impossible, I can only think of one other. While it's a bit early, I figured I would recruit him for the fifth BoB at the end of the year..."

She made a gun gesture with her hand and pointed it at Kazuto.

"...and that's why I called you."

"Wh-what...? Me?" he gasped, stunned.

She smiled and delivered her preprepared line: "I know you'll have to convert your character back from *ALO* to *GGO* again, so I understand if you refuse, but on the other hand, I feel like you still owe me one. How's that legendary weapon working out for you?"

"Urk!"

The golden longsword Excalibur that Kirito (Kazuto) used in *ALfheim Online* would have been lost in a bottomless hole if it weren't for Shino. She'd happily presented him with the ultrarare weapon, which was utterly unique on the server, so she had the right to call in a favor. And Kazuto would no doubt salivate at the chance to face a worthy foe.

Sure enough, he cleared his throat and said, "Well, sure, I'd like to try fighting this Subtilizer...but I think a big reason for how far I got the last time was because nobody else was used to a guy with a sword. And from how you describe it, Subtilizer's a vet in both close combat and guns. I don't know if I stand a chance..."

"I don't think I've ever heard you sound so weak-willed. Yes, he's very tough, but he's just another VRMMO player like the rest of us. You don't have to act like it's an amateur versus pro thing..."

"That's the thing," he said, leaning back in the old wooden chair and placing his hands behind his head. "Is Subtilizer really an amateur...? Is he really just a normal VRMMO player?"

"What's that supposed to mean? What else would he be?"

"A professional. Someone who fights with guns not for play but for work. A soldier...or a special-ops police guy."

"What?! Oh, come on," she snorted, assuming he was joking, but Kazuto's expression was deadly serious.

"I only know what I read in news articles...but from what I hear, certain militaries, police forces, and private security firms are already using full-dive tech for training. I think it's quite possible that a real professional with skill in that arena could have entered the BoB to test himself."

"...I suspect you might be..."

Overthinking this, she was going to say, but stopped. She recalled Subtilizer's remarkably sharp instincts and the smoothness of his motions. He fought like a robot soldier, well beyond what she would expect from an amateur gamer.

But assuming he *was* a real soldier or policeman, would he really say something like "your soul will be so sweet" when he dispatched his target? In terms of professionals, that was less of a soldierly action and more like a straight-out killer...

She had to stop herself there. *GGO* and all other virtual worlds existed for the sole purpose of enjoyment. It didn't matter what sort of person Subtilizer was in real life. She just had to hit him with her .50-caliber rifle next time, that was all.

"No matter who he is, all players come into *GGO* on equal conditions! I'm not going to lose multiple times to the same guy, so I'll do whatever it takes to win next time!" she swore.

"And 'whatever it takes' happens to be…me?"

"You're just one of the means, technically."

He looked confused by that, so Shino grinned and explained. "I don't feel too confident with just you for a close-range expert, so I called on someone else, too. Something like a control system—a set of brakes to keep you in line."

"C-control system?" he repeated. The term set off something in his mind, and the chair rattled as he sat up straight. He pulled his ultrathin phone from a pocket and slid his finger across the screen. A moment later, he looked up and fixed Shino with a look. "Aha, I see."

"…What do you see?" she asked. He set down his phone and slid it across the table to her. On the high-definition four-inch monitor was a map of the Okachimachi area, centered on the café. There was a blinking blue dot en route to them from the train station.

"What's this blip?"

"Your next guest, Sinon. Only a hundred yards to go."

As he said, the dot was heading right to the café. It crossed an intersection, entered the alley, and reached the center of the map.

Just then, the bell on the door clanged, and Shino looked up. There was a person folding an umbrella at the door. She swiped her chestnut-brown hair aside, looked at Shino, and smiled brightly enough to drive away the gloomy rain.

"Hiya, Shino-non!"

2

It was the first nickname she'd had in five years. Shino couldn't help but smile as she got to her feet.

"Hi, Asuna."

Asuna Yuuki strode across the natural wood floor so that they could clasp hands and share in the delight of reunion. They sat down in adjacent chairs, and Kazuto asked in surprise, "When did you two get to be so close?"

"Oh, I stayed at Asuna's house last month."

"Wh-what? Even I've never been to her house."

"And whose fault is that?" Asuna chided, fixing Kazuto with a glare. "Who keeps claiming he needs more time before he's ready?"

His response was to sulk and sip at his drink. Still, Asuna smiled at him with kindly understanding, and when she noticed Agil approaching with water and a damp towel, she stood up to greet him.

"It's nice to see you again, Agil."

"Welcome. This reminds me of the time you two stayed upstairs at my place."

"You'd better watch out, or we'll crash your current store in Ygg City, too. Now…let's see what I want today…"

Asuna, who was old friends with the imposing-looking café

owner, looked over the corkboard menu. Shino, meanwhile, peered at the phone Kazuto had left on the table. The little blue blip was fixed right on the café.

"...I think I'll go with the ginger ale, spicy," Asuna decided.

When Agil went back to the counter to get her drink, Shino smiled and said, "You guys track each other's GPS? You really *must* be close."

Kazuto waved his hand with a straight face to indicate the contrary. "What you see there is technically the coordinate of Asuna's phone, and she can make it invisible if she wants. Mine is nowhere near that friendly. Show her, Asuna."

"Okay," she said, and pulled her phone from the bag slung over the back of the chair, presenting it to Shino with the welcome screen activated. It was set to display a cute animated background.

In the center of the screen was a pink heart with red ribbons, pulsing regularly once a second. There were two numbers on the bottom of the heart, but she wasn't sure what they meant at first. On the left was the number 63 in a large font, while smaller and on the right was 36.2. As Shino watched curiously, the left one rose to 64.

"What is...?"

Kazuto sheepishly asked her not to stare at it. At last, she figured out what the numbers represented.

"Wait...this is your pulse and body temperature in Celsius, Kirito?"

"Bingo. You catch on quick, Shino-non," Asuna said, clapping. Shino looked back and forth from the phone to Kazuto's face a few times, then asked the first question that came to mind.

"B-but...how?"

"Under the skin, right here," Kazuto said, pointing to the center of his chest with his thumb. He reached out toward Shino and made a gap with his fingers less than a quarter of an inch wide. "There's a tiny sensor about this big stuck in there. It measures my heart rate and temperature and sends it to my phone through

Bluetooth. From there it goes through the Net to Asuna's phone, giving her a real-time status update on me."

"What? A biometric sensor?" Shino squawked. Two seconds later, she wondered, "B-but why...? Oh, is it an anti-cheating system?"

"N-no, no!"

"It's not that!"

Both Kazuto and Asuna shook their heads with perfect synchronization.

"Actually, when I started my new job, the client recommended having it implanted," he explained. "It beats having to stick the electrodes to my chest each and every time I go in. When I told Asuna about it, she strongly recommended that I send her the vital data. So I put together a little app and installed it on Asuna's phone."

"I mean, I don't want some company to monopolize Kirito's body data. In fact, I was against him getting that weird object put in him in the first place."

"Oh, really? Who was it who happily said she liked to check the monitor when she had a moment to spare?" he prodded. Asuna's cheeks went just a bit red.

"I don't know...it just calms me down, I guess. The thought that I'm seeing your heart beating just...sends me on a little trip, I guess..."

"Whoa, that sounds kinda creepy to me, Asuna." Shino laughed, looking down at the phone again. Kazuto's pulse had gone up to 67, and his temperature was rising, too. Outwardly, Kazuto wore a poker face as he crunched on his ice, but the data faithfully showed that all the attention had made him a bit bashful.

"Aha, I see...On second thought...this is kinda nice," she mumbled, then looked up with a start. Kazuto and Asuna were staring at her. She shook her head. "Er, uh, I mean, not in a serious way or anything. I mean...in *GGO* there's a heartbeat sensor, but it's for use when fighting in poor visual conditions. It's not as...romantic as this, that's all."

She hastily handed the phone back to Asuna and babbled on. "Oh, r-right. I forgot about why I brought you here. Anyway, I already asked Asuna through e-mail about the next BoB. Do you think you can compete? I'm not going to demand it if you don't want to convert your characters."

"Oh, that's fine. I have an alt account for *ALO*, so I can stash my house and items with that one while I'm in the other game," Asuna said with a gentle smile.

This eased Shino's bout of agitation, and she took a deep breath before continuing. "Thanks. Having your help will be huge, Asuna. You're the machine gun to my pillbox! I'm pretty sure that you'll have the knack of the photon sword after a few days of practice."

"I'll convert about a month before the tournament. You'll show me around the city, right?"

"Of course. In fact, the food in *GGO* isn't that bad. So, um...I know this is getting a bit ahead of ourselves, but...Put 'er there."

She held out her right hand, which Asuna took ahold of with willowy fingers. Once they'd shaken hands, Shino disengaged and rapped on the tabletop.

"That ends the business discussion. Now..." She turned to Kazuto, who was still crunching his ice across the table. "Let's hear more details. What is this fishy job you're doing? Knowing you, it's probably just an alpha test for some new VRMMO or something."

He stared at her for a long moment, then clarified her suspicion: "Well, you're not right, but you're not wrong."

Kazuto smirked and traced the center of his chest where the microsensor was embedded. "Yes, it's true that I'm a tester. But what I'm testing isn't a new game, but the brain-machine interface of an entirely new full-dive system."

"Ohh!" Shino exclaimed. "So they're coming out with a new generation of the AmuSphere? Are you testing it for Asuna's dad's company?"

"Nope, RCT has nothing to do with it. In fact...I'm not really sure what the whole scope of the company is. It's a venture I'd never heard of before this, but their development funding is massive. I wonder if they've got some huge investment fund backing them," he said, putting on an enigmatic expression.

Shino tilted her head and asked, "Oh...what's the company's name?"

"It's called Rath."

"No surprise, I've never heard of it, either. Hmm, is that an English word...?"

"I wondered the same thing. Asuna knew the answer."

Next to Shino, Asuna finished her sip of ginger ale and nodded. "It's from the poem 'Jabberwocky' within the text of *Through the Looking-Glass*. The raths are fictional creatures within the poem. Some say they're supposed to be like pigs; others say they're like turtles."

"Ohhh..." Shino had read the book years ago, but she didn't remember that word at all. She tried to imagine a pig's head sticking out of a round shell. "Rath, rath...And they're going to sell their own next-gen full-dive console? Rather than doing a joint development with a bunch of other companies like with the AmuSphere?"

"Well, I don't know," Kazuto said, still maddeningly vague. "The actual body of the machine is kinda huge. Combined with the control console and cooling system, it would probably fill this entire room...From what I hear, the very first full-dive prototype was that big, and it took them five years to get it down to the size of the NerveGear. And they say RCT's pushing to get the AmuSphere's successor out next year...Wait, was that supposed to be a secret, again?"

Asuna laughed and said, "It's fine, they're going to announce it at the Tokyo Game Show next month."

"Oh, RCT's got a new one, too? I hope it's not that expensive," Shino opined, throwing an innocent look at Asuna, who nodded gravely.

"I know, right? They won't even tell *me* the price, though...But

I'm really enjoying *ALO*, so I'm not in any hurry to upgrade. It's tempting when they talk about how much better the graphical power is, though. They said it's going to be backward-compatible."

"Whoa, really? Maybe I should look into a job, too," Shino said, consulting a mental spreadsheet of her finances. She looked over at Kazuto and asked, "Does that mean that huge full-dive machine Rath is working on isn't for commercial use? Is it industrial?"

"I think it's still before that stage of development. In fact, if you're going to be specific, it's a completely different thing from the current full-dive system."

"Different...? But it's still a virtual 3-D world that the user dives into, right? What's it like on the inside?"

"I don't know," he said, shrugging. Then he matter-of-factly dropped the most shocking detail yet. "It's probably for the purposes of secrecy, but I can't actually bring the memory of what happens in the VR world back to real life. I've completely forgotten everything I saw and did during the test."

"Wh-what?!" Shino shrieked, then lowered her voice to ask, "You...can't bring out your memory with you? How is that even possible? Do they put you under hypnosis at the end of your shift?"

"No, it's a purely electronic measure. Or...quantum measure, I guess," he said distractedly, then glanced down at his phone on the table. "It's four thirty. How are you two on time?"

"Fine."

"I've got time, too."

With that settled, Kazuto leaned back against the antique wooden chair. "Then I'll start by explaining the broad picture. What the Soul Translation tech is all about," he said slowly.

The unfamiliar name sounded like a spell in a game, Shino thought. Something about it didn't seem to fit the concept of cutting-edge technology. Next to her, Asuna wondered, *Really...? "Soul"...?*

"Yeah, I thought the name was pretty overblown the first time

I heard it, too," Kazuto said, shrugging. Then he abruptly asked, "Where do you think the human mind is?"

"The mind?" Shino asked, taken aback. The answer seemed obvious. She cleared her throat and said, "Inside the head...the brain."

"Then if you zoomed in and looked at the brain in detail, where would you find the mind?"

"Where...?"

"Well, the brain is just a mass of brain cells. Like this..."

He held out his left hand toward Shino, fingers extended, then used his right index and middle fingers to trace a circle in his palm, then a larger one around it.

"You've got a nucleus in the middle, then a cell body that surrounds it..."

He tapped his five fingers in order, then drew a line from wrist to elbow.

"You've got dendrites, and an axon, then the connection to the next cell. Which part of this brain cell contains the mind, do you suppose? The nucleus? The mitochondria?"

"Umm..." Shino mumbled.

Asuna spoke up. "You just mentioned that it's connected to the next cell, Kirito. Isn't it the network of all those neurons tied together that makes up the mind? It's like if you asked someone what the Internet is—you can't explain the answer if you only look at individual computers."

"Yes," he said, satisfied. "At present, the neural network is the mind, in my opinion. But...I feel like the question of what the Internet is, for example, would get you a lot of different answers. I mean, it's a construct of computers all over the world connected through a common protocol..."

He pointed to his own phone on the table, then to Asuna's. "In terms of making up that network, you can say that these individual computers are the Internet. You might even claim that the users operating those computers are part of the Internet. All these things together make up what we know as the Internet."

Kazuto took a breath there and asked for a sip of Asuna's ginger ale. He swallowed and closed his eyes. "Wow...the ginger ale here really is sharp."

"It's not at all like the stuff they sell at the store. It's supposed to be for mixing cocktails, but I like drinking it straight. You really taste the ginger."

Shino's first experience with the Dicey Café ginger ale was half a year ago, when Kazuto first invited her to the place. If she'd never met him in *GGO*, she would never have set foot in this odd establishment. The way your life could change from the smallest things...

"So...what does the human mind have to do with the Internet?" she prompted.

Kazuto gave the glass back to Asuna and made a spherical gesture with his hands. "Well, the *shape* of the Internet is this giant net of servers, routers, computers, and mobile phones."

"The shape..."

"So what is its *essence*?"

Shino thought it over and asked, "You mean...what flows through that network? Electronic bits and bytes...?"

"True, but the electric and light pulses are just the medium. The essence of the Net is what is passed through the medium: information put into words. Let's use that definition here."

He stopped gesturing and steepled his bony fingers on the tabletop. "Now, let's return to the network made up of tens of billions of brain cells. If we view this as the shape of the mind, then what is the essence we should be looking for?"

"The stuff being transferred through the medium...through the electric pulses in the brain cells. So...information?"

"Actually, the pulses are more like," Kazuto said, forming a fist with his right hand and pushing it toward his open left palm, "a trigger that releases a transmission substance into the synapses between neurons. Just the consecutive firing of cells along a particular route can't be called the essence of the mind, I think."

"Umm…so…" Shino mumbled, frowning, and Asuna stepped in at last.

"This isn't really fair, Kirito. After all, even modern science doesn't have a clear answer about what the mind is, does it?"

"That's true," he said, grinning.

"Wh-what?! You set me up into racking my brain over something I could never figure out!" Shino fumed.

Kazuto merely looked away at the rainy neighborhood through the window and said gravely, "But there is one person who approached the answer, while working on a particular theory."

"A…theory?"

"Quantum mind mechanics. It was originally proposed by an English scholar toward the end of last century and treated like fringe science for years. Now Rath is building that monstrous machine based on it…First of all, let me clarify that I barely understand everything after this point. But anyway, remember how I described the structure of the brain cell?"

Shino and Asuna nodded.

"Inside the cell is a frame that supports the whole structure. They're called microtubules. The thing is, those little 'bones' don't just support, they're also like a skull. For the brain inside the brain cell."

"Huh…?"

"They're tubules. Hollow tubes. Just very, very small ones… nanometers in diameter. But they're not empty. There's something stored inside those tubes."

Shino looked over at Asuna, then they both looked at Kazuto. She asked, "What's inside them?"

"Light," he said. "Photons. Evanescent photons, they call them. A photon is a quantum of light. Their existence is indeterminate in nature and fluctuates constantly in a probabilistic manner. According to this theory in question, this fluctuation is, in fact… the human mind."

Those words sent an instantaneous, inexplicable chill across Shino's back and upper arms. *The human mind is flickering light?*

The image was mysterious, beautiful, and, in her opinion, eerily holy in nature.

Asuna's brown eyes wavered nervously as she considered the same concept. In a hoarse voice, she said, "Earlier, you said the name of the new full-dive machine is...the Soul Translator. Are they claiming the aggregate of all that light is the human soul?"

"The Rath engineers call it a quantum field instead. But given what they named the machine, I'm certain that's how they feel about it...That this quantum field is the soul."

"So what does that mean? That the Soul Translator is a machine that connects not to the human brain but to the soul itself...?"

"When you say it that way, it sounds less like a machine and more like a magic item in a game." He grinned, trying to lighten the mood. "But it's not powered by magic or holy miracles. To explain how it works a little more: It records a microtubule photon as a unit of data called a 'cubit,' based on its spin and vector. So the brain cell isn't just a gate switch that allows signals through but a tiny little quantum computer all its own...And even that surface explanation is beyond my understanding..."

"Don't worry, you lost me ages ago."

"Me, too..."

Shino and Asuna signaled their resignation, and Kazuto heaved a sigh of relief.

"So this amalgamation of photons acts as both a processor and memory, and it might just be the true form of the human soul... Well, Rath decided to give it their own special name. It's based on the term *fluctuating light*, which is combined as..."

He paused.

"Fluctlight."

"...Fluct...light," Shino mumbled, repeating the strange word. If everything he'd just told them was correct, then one of these fluctlights was inside her own head. In fact, it was what she was using to think... Her own consciousness...

That shiver returned, and she rubbed at her bare arms where they emerged from her short summer sleeves.

Asuna was also cradling her own body, and she mumbled, "And reading…er, translating that fluctlight is what the Soul Translator does. Which means…it's not just a one-way translation, right?"

Shino didn't understand at first. She gave her friend a probing look, and Asuna's eyes were full of worry.

"Think about it, Shino-non…The AmuSpheres we use don't just intercept the movement commands our brains give our bodies. They send images, sounds…all kinds of sensory information back *into* the brain to make us experience a virtual world. That's the core of the full-dive experience, you know? Which means the Soul Translator wouldn't be a follow-up to that device if it couldn't do the same thing."

"Meaning…it writes information into the user's soul…?"

They both looked at Kazuto. The black-haired boy was uncertain for a moment, then eventually indicated a confirmation.

"The Soul Translator, which Rath refers to with the acronym STL, has a bidirectional translation capability. It takes the billions of cubits of data the human fluctlight possesses and translates them into words we can understand, and it also retranslates information written in our words in order to record them. Otherwise it wouldn't be a full dive into another world, as Asuna said. Essentially, it accesses the part of the fluctlight that stores and processes sensory information and gives it the information the machine wants the person to see or hear."

Asuna leaned forward. This was what she'd been waiting for. "Are you saying…this even works on memory within the soul? You just said you don't have any memory of what happens after you come out of a dive. Are you saying the Soul Translator—the STL—can erase or overwrite memories?"

"No," he said, brushing her hand reassuringly and shaking his head. "The parts that manage long-term memory are so wide-ranging and have such a complex archiving system that

it's beyond their grasp at the moment. The reason I don't have memories of the dive is just because they shut off access to those parts, they say. So it's not that the memory was erased after it happened—I just can't remember it, I guess."

"But still…I'm concerned, Kirito. I mean, memory manipulation…" Asuna said, her face downcast and worried. "And wasn't it Chrysheight…I mean, Mr. Kikuoka from the government who brought you that job offer? I don't think he's a bad person, but I feel like I don't fully understand his motives. He's like the guild commander, somehow. I just get the feeling…that something bad is going to happen again…"

"You're right that he's not someone you can fully let your guard down with. I still don't know his exact position or job duties. But…"

Kazuto paused, and his pupils focused on someplace far away.

"I took the very first morning train on the day the original industrial full-dive machine was first put on display at the amusement park in Shinjuku. I was only in grade school…but I knew that was it. That was the world that had always called to me. I saved up all my allowance to buy the NerveGear the day it came out…and spent countless hours on all kinds of VR games. At the time, I couldn't have cared less about the real world. Eventually I got selected to the *SAO* beta test, and everything went wrong from there…All those people died. Even after we finally got out after two years, there was Sugou, and Death Gun after that. I just…want to know. Where full-dive technology is taking us…What all those incidents truly meant…The way the Soul Translator functions is entirely new, but the basic architecture is modeled after the Medicuboid they use in hospitals."

Asuna's shoulders twitched when she heard that. But his quiet, steady voice continued to fill the room.

"I just have a feeling. There's something within the Soul Translator. Something more than just an amusement…Yes, there might be risks involved. But…" He mimicked grabbing a sword and swinging it. "I've come back from all those worlds before.

I'll be back from this one, too. Even if I am just a wimpy, under-weight gamer in real life."

"You'd be totally helpless without me there to watch your back." Asuna laughed, then sighed and looked over at Shino. "I wonder where he gets this confidence."

"Hmm, I don't know. He *is* the legendary hero, after all."

Shino understood some of the things Asuna and Kazuto were talking about and didn't know others, so she chose to keep her distance from the conversation as it was happening. Now she tried to break the chilly mood by saying, "I read that *Full Record of the* SAO *Incident* book that came out last month. I'm still having a hard time reconciling that the Black Swordsman in there is *this* guy."

"H-hey, don't say it like that," Kazuto complained, waving his hands dismissively as he leaned back.

Asuna giggled. "I know, right? The leader of a pretty big guild among the active members of the game put the book together, so it's pretty accurate about most stuff, but there's a heavy bias on how they represent the people. Like the scene where Kirito fights the orange player…"

"'When I pull out my second sword, no one can withstand me!'"

The girls burst into laughter and Kazuto sank sullenly into his chair. Relieved that Asuna was smiling again, Shino decided to deliver a follow-up.

"I hear the book's going to be translated into English for America. Then the great hero will be an international figure."

"…Just when I was trying to forget…They really owe me some royalties, I figure," Kazuto grumbled to another round of laughter.

Shino decided she'd get back on topic by asking something that had been bothering her. "But Kirito, does this STL just end up doing the same thing as the AmuSphere? If it's just going to generate a virtual polygonal world and send the images and sounds to the brain like before, why go to the lengths of this elaborate new system?"

"Aha! Good question," he said, sitting up straight again. "You said 'generate a virtual polygonal world.' Well, a polygon is just a series of coordinates and a plane connecting them. It's digital data. Modeling is so high-res nowadays that trees and furniture and all that are indistinguishable from the real thing, but at its core, they're no different from this."

He flipped through the phone on the table and booted up one of the preinstalled mini-games. The futuristic race car that rotated slowly on the demo screen had a primitive interior design and somewhat blocky angles. It wouldn't fool anyone.

Shino looked up and noted, "Sure…even in *ALO* and *GGO*, if you get enough players in one place, the system sometimes starts to chug as it draws objects. But there isn't really a fundamental difference between the AmuSphere and STL in that regard, is there? They're both showing their users things that don't exist so that they can see and touch them. Those things still have to be created as a 3-D model from scratch."

"That's the thing. Umm…how do I explain this…?"

Kazuto paused, then picked up the empty caffè shakerato glass and showed it to Shino. "This glass exists in reality, right?"

"…Yes," she replied drily. Kazuto pushed it closer to her face. His next words were somewhat difficult to understand.

"Listen. At the same time that this glass is being held in my fingers…it's also in your mind, in what Rath would call your fluctlight. Technically it's just the light reflecting off the glass that your retinas are catching and converting into nerve signals that allow you to visualize it as a glass in your mind. Now if I do this…"

He reached out and covered her eyes with his other hand. She automatically shut her eyelids, reducing her vision to solid gray with a hint of red.

"Did the glass within you disappear instantaneously?"

She wasn't sure what he was getting at but gave him an honest answer anyway. "I'm not *that* forgetful. I was watching it for so long, I remember the color and shape of the glass. Oh…but it is getting a bit more vague…"

"Exactly."

He took away his hand, and Shino opened her eyes to glare at him.

"Exactly, what?"

"Get this…When we look at the glass, or the table, or each other, we're *holding that data* in a form that can be stored and replayed within the visual processing center of our fluctlights. It's not just a copy that disappears the moment we close our eyes. So when I hide this glass from sight and your memory of it fades…"

He slipped the hand holding the glass under the table.

"And then I input into your fluctlight vision center a perfect copy of that data from when you were looking at the glass earlier, you will be seeing a glass that isn't actually on the table right now. Something far more vivid than just a 3-D model…The glass will be absolutely identical to the real thing."

"Okay…maybe that's true in theory…but when you're talking about data that the human mind saves, that's just memory, right? You can't just hypnotize people into recreating their memories from an external source. How do they…"

Shino stopped. Just a few minutes ago, Kazuto had told her about a machine that could do that very thing. Asuna broke her long silence to chime in for Shino.

"The same way the AmuSphere shows the user's brain 3-D data…the STL writes in short-term memories to the user's mind. In other words…it's not a creation. The virtual world and everything in it that the STL builds…is essentially real, as far as our brains can process it…?"

Kazuto dipped his head and put the glass back on the table. "Rath calls the images in our minds 'pneumonic visual data.' I still remember what happened in my first few test dives…and it was different. It was nothing at all like the VR worlds that the AmuSphere creates. It was just a small room I was in, but I…"

He paused and adopted an awkward, deliberate grin that dimpled one cheek.

"…I didn't realize it was virtual at first."

3

A virtual world that was indistinguishable from reality.

It was a theme that numerous fictional stories had covered for decades. Shino could name right on the spot at least five books or movies based on the idea.

When the age of full-diving, NerveGears, and AmuSpheres in every home had arrived, the media was overrun with thought pieces and blog articles wondering if the time had finally come when we'd lost track of whether or not our reality was truly real life. Shino remembered being nervous about the concept before she took her first dive.

But once she tried it, for better or for worse, that concern vanished. The AmuSphere's VR experience was a true miracle of cutting-edge technology. The full sensory experience of the virtual world was brilliant and beautiful—which only highlighted its difference from the real world. The sights, sounds, and textures of everything were too pure, too…simple. There was no dust in the air, no clothes fabric fraying with wear, no scratches or dents in the tables. Every 3-D object that was coded had a hard limit in terms of the designing company's manpower and the CPU power of the device displaying it. That might change in the future, but in 2026, technology could not create a virtual world that was indistinguishable from the real one…

Or so Shino had thought, until she heard what Kazuto Kirigaya had to say.

"But Kirito...that means that you could be in the...STL, they call it? Right at this very moment. They could be feeding you memories of Asuna and me," Shino said with a teasing smile, trying to hide the shiver crawling over her skin. She figured he would just laugh it off, but even worse, he frowned and stared at her.

"H-hey, stop that! I'm real!" she protested, waving her hands, but Kazuto looked even more suspicious.

"If you're the real Sinon...you'd remember the promise you made to me yesterday."

"P-promise?"

"You said that as thanks for coming out here to meet you, I could have as many Dicey Cheesecakes as I want. It's the most expensive dessert on the menu."

"Wh-what?! I never made that deal with you! Oh...b-but that doesn't mean I'm a fake! Come on, Asuna, tell him I'm real!"

She looked to her friend for help. Asuna grabbed her hands and whispered, "Shino-non...did you forget? You promised *me* I could have as many Berry-Cherry Tarts as I wanted..."

"Whaaat?!"

Maybe she was the one who was trapped in a virtual world and having her memory manipulated. Then both Kazuto's and Asuna's cheeks puffed out, and they burst into laughter. Shino finally realized that she was not the teaser but the teased.

"How dare...Not you, too, Asuna! I'm going to hit both of you with a hundred homing arrows each next time I see you in *ALO*!"

"Ha-ha-ha! Sorry, Shino-non, forgive me!" Asuna laughed, hugging the girl. The simple friendliness of that gesture filled her heart with warmth, which she tried to hide by turning away in a huff. Still, she couldn't keep a smile away for long, and she soon joined in the laughter.

Kazuto added a slow comment to the more relaxed atmosphere. "The tech sounds really creepy when you hear all these terms like *fluctlight* and *pneumonic visuals*…but I think I actually connect with the world the STL creates more than the Amu-Sphere's. When you get down to it, it's basically more like a waking dream…"

"A…dream?" Shino said, not expecting that word to come up. Rather appropriately, the boy who played a spriggan fighter with a penchant for putting others to sleep in *ALO* continued. "Yeah. You're calling forth objects that exist as saved memories, creating a world by combining them together, then doing stuff in it…Doesn't that sound like how dreams work? In fact, they say the brain patterns of people in the STL are very close to those of being asleep."

"So your job is basically to dream? You slept for three whole days and made a bunch of money doing it?"

"Th-that's what I told you right at the start. I didn't eat, didn't drink, just slept. I mean, I had an IV for water and nutrition."

Now that he mentioned it, she did remember him saying that just after he'd shown up at the café. But she figured he was just lying on a gel bed, not literally engaged in a very, very long dream.

Shino looked up and murmured, "A three-day-long dream… You could do all kinds of things in that time. And you wouldn't have to worry about waking up before you get to eat that delicious piece of cake."

"Sadly, I don't remember what sort of things I ate on the other side. Let's just say I had cake for every meal…" he joked, but let the words trail off. Shino looked down and saw that his eyebrows were pensive under those long bangs.

"…What's wrong, Kirito?" Asuna asked, but he didn't respond. He made the motion of grabbing something and bringing it to his mouth.

"…It wasn't…cake…Something harder…and salty…but it was good. What was it…?"

"Y-you remember? What did you eat in the virtual world?"

"…Nope. Can't remember. It was something I've never eaten in reality…I think…"

He scrunched up his face for several more seconds, thinking hard, but eventually exhaled and gave up. Shino couldn't hold back the question that popped into her head.

"Wait, is that even possible, Kirito? Eating something in the STL that you've never tasted in real life? I thought you said the STL creates a virtual world constructed from parts that it finds in the user's memory. So in a basic sense, it can't show you things you've never seen or feed you things you've never eaten, right?"

"Oh…yeah, right. Good point, Shino-non. Wouldn't that mean the STL's virtual world is extremely limited in nature, despite its realism? You couldn't create a true fantasy realm like they did for Aincrad or Alfheim."

He acknowledged her point with a nod and smiled to dispel the awkward atmosphere he had created. "That's very sharp of you two. As a matter of fact, I didn't recognize that limitation the first time I heard about pneumonic visuals. I only realized it just before this long-term experimental dive, and I asked the Rath staff about it, but I guess it went right to the heart of the STL's tech, and they wouldn't tell me too much about it. The one thing I can say is…the staff described the virtual world as being built from memory but did *not* say that it came from the memory of the diver."

"Huh…? What does that mean…?" Shino asked, but Asuna sucked in a short breath.

"You mean…other people's memories? Or…or that they can create memories that belong to no one, right from scratch…?" she asked in a half whisper. Shino understood at last.

What if these pneumonic visuals were saved in a format that other human beings could process? What if they'd already cracked that format itself? That would fundamentally make this idea possible. New objects, new tastes, scenery that had never been imagined…The creation of a truly "real" dream.

Kazuto confirmed her suspicions. "It's been a little over two months since I started working at Rath…There was no memory limitation on the first few tests, so I remember a couple of those VR worlds. One of them was just a big room that happened to have a couple hundred cats hanging out in it."

"...So many cats..."

Shino let a smile play across her features as she imagined that paradise, then shook her head to dispel the image. She nodded to Kazuto to continue, and he made a face as he tried to recall the others.

"From what I remember...there were a bunch of cats in there from breeds I didn't recognize. And not just that...Some of them had wings and flew around, and others were all round and poofy and bounced off the walls. I couldn't have 'remembered' things like that."

"And they couldn't have come from anyone else's memory, either," Asuna added. "I mean, no one's ever seen a cat with wings in the real world. Either someone on the staff created that flying cat to show you...or the STL system generated it from scratch."

"If it's the latter, that would be a major feat. If the system is capable of doing that much for one object, it could ultimately create an entire world."

They sat on his words in silence.

A virtual world created without human input or labor.

Something about that concept caused Shino's heart to soar. Recently she'd found a growing alienation within her toward the arbitrary design of VRMMOs like *GGO* and *ALO*.

Naturally, all existing VR games had to be created by game designers from a development team. While the buildings, trees, and rivers all looked like they just existed on their own, all of them were modeled and fashioned according to the whims of an artist, of another human being.

Every time she was reminded of this fact while playing the game, a deep part of her woke from a reverie. It was the recognition and acknowledgment of the fact that they were all dancing on the palm of the "gods" who developed the game for them to play.

Shino hadn't even started *Gun Gale Online* for the purpose of having fun. Even though she'd overcome some of her emotional baggage, she still believed there was a real-life meaning to what she experienced in the virtual world. She didn't share the sentiments of those squadrons who collected model guns in real life and wore their uniforms with matching medals in the game. No, she believed that the perseverance and self-control that Sinon developed in the game might in some way transfer over to Shino Asada in the real world. If not, then why had she been spending so much time and money on this activity?

The fact that such a shy person could get to be so friendly with Asuna after just a few months was a sign of major progress, Shino thought. The other girl always carried a hint of a smile, but Shino was certain that they shared the same views. VRMMOs weren't an escapist pleasure but a tool to improve herself in the real world. Asuna was like that, too. And Kazuto...well, it needn't be said.

Which was exactly why she didn't want to think that a VR world was just a construction, and that everything that happened inside of it was fiction. She didn't want to think it, but someone, of course, built every one of them.

On the night she'd stayed at Asuna's house last month, Shino had clumsily revealed in the darkened bedroom this sense of alienation. Next to her in the large bed, Asuna thought it over. Then she said, "Shino-non, you could say the same thing about the real world. Everything about the environment we live in, from our homes and cities, to our status as students, to the structure of society itself, was designed by people...For the purpose of getting stronger or being able to pursue the path that we want, I think."

She paused, then smiled and continued. "But I'd kind of like to see a VR world one day that wasn't designed by anyone. If that was an actual thing, I kind of feel like it'd be an even realer world than the one we live in..."

*   *   *

"A realer world," Shino muttered without realizing it. Asuna glanced at her and nodded, clearly remembering the same conversation.

"Kirito, are you saying…that if you use the STL, you could create a reality that is subjectively the same or greater than the real world? A true alternate world without a human designer?"

"Hmmm," he mumbled, then slowly shook his head. "No…I think that would be very unlikely right now. You might be able to generate natural terrain like forests or fields, but I think it'd be impossible to create complex cities in a logical manner without the involvement of a human mind. As far as other possibilities… I guess that if you get a couple hundred testers and make them build a town or a culture itself on empty plains, *that* might be considered a world without a godlike Creator…"

"Wow, that sounds like a real long-term project."

"It would take months for the map to be finished."

The girls laughed at Kazuto's joke. But the furrow between his brows stayed put as he continued to ponder the idea. Eventually he muttered, "So it's a culture-development simulation? That might not actually be far off the mark. If the STL's FLA function evolves further…but that'll require a limit on the memory you bring inside…"

"S to the F to the L to the what now?" Shino asked, lost in the string of acronyms.

He looked up in surprise. "Oh…right. It's the second magic power of the Soul Translator. I said the STL's virtual world is like a dream, yeah?"

"Yeah."

"Do you ever have a really long dream, and when you wake up, you're just exhausted? Especially when it's a nightmare…"

"Oh, sure," she said, scowling. "It's like you're running and running from something, and you know it's a dream partway through, but you can't wake up. Only after you've been running all night do you wake up—and then it turns out you're still in the dream."

"How long does it feel like those dreams go?"

"How long? Two hours...three, maybe."

"That's the thing. When you measure the brain waves, even the times that people feel like they've been dreaming forever, the actual period of dreaming is just for a few minutes before they wake up," Kazuto said. He held out his hands and covered the phone screens lying on the table. Then he impishly asked, "Sinon, if we started talking about the STL at four thirty, what time do you think it is now?"

"Uh..."

She wasn't expecting that question. It was just past the solstice and there was plenty of light outside, making it impossible to tell the exact time just from the amount of light coming through the windows. She had to guess.

"Umm...about four fifty?"

He pulled away his hands and turned the screen toward Shino. The clock said it was well after five.

"Whoa, it's been that long?"

"See, the flow of time is very subjective, not just in our dreams but in the real world as well. When there's an emergency and you get a rush of adrenaline, time goes slowly. On the other hand, when you're relaxed and enjoying a nice chat, you look up and it's hours later. In their study of fluctlights and human consciousnesses, Rath put together a rough theory of why this happens. At the center of your mind there's a pulse they call a 'thought-clocking control signal,' though they don't know much about its source yet."

"Clocking...?"

"Yeah, like a computer. How they measure the number of giga-hertz of your CPU and stuff."

"The number of calculations per second?" Asuna prompted. Kazuto tapped his finger on the table.

"They always list the maximum value for the catalog, but it's not constantly going that fast. Usually it goes at a fairly slow pace to keep it cool and conserve power, but as you ask it to process more and more..." He increased the speed of his tapping. "It pulls up the processor clock to increase the speed. The photon computer recreating a fluctlight acts the same way. In an emergency, when the amount of data to process gets much greater, it speeds up the thought-clock in response. Don't you feel like the bullets in *GGO* slow down when you're concentrating really hard?"

"Well, when I'm in a really good rhythm, yeah. But I can't do that bullet-dodging stuff you pull off." She pouted. He frowned and shook his head.

"I couldn't do that right now, either. I've got to retrain before the next BoB...Anyway, the thought-clock affects your perception of time. When the clock is running fast, your perception of the passage of time will slow down. This becomes especially pronounced while sleeping. The fluctlight speeds up quite a lot to process all that memory data, and you end up having several hours' worth of dreams within a few minutes."

"Hrmm..."

Shino crossed her arms. It was already crazy enough that they were talking about a computer that read her mind with light—all this stuff about the act of thinking causing her mental speed to go up and down had to be taken with a grain of salt. But Kazuto was grinning as though there was even more to the story.

"So extrapolate from there. Wouldn't it be awesome if you could do your homework or your job in your sleep? In just minutes of real-world time, you could do hours of work."

"Th-that's crazy."

"Exactly. You can't control your dreams to do exactly what you want," Asuna protested.

But Kazuto's smile did not falter. "The reason actual dreams are so scattershot is a by-product of the memory filing process. The dreams you see in the STL are far clearer—in fact, it's basically just a VR world that works on dream logic. When you're inside that world, it interferes with the mind's thought-clocking pulse and speeds it up. Then it synchronizes the passage of time within the virtual world to speed it up, too. As a result, the amount of actual time the user experiences within the virtual world is multiplied. That's the greatest function of the STL: Fluctlight Acceleration, or FLA."

"...This all...just..."

Doesn't seem real, Shino thought. It was more than "just a little" different from the AmuSphere.

Just the introduction of regular access to full-dive tech had brought about significant social change. In the almighty search for cost-cutting measures, businesses began holding virtual presentations and meetings. Multiple fully 3-D shows and movies came out each day, offering the viewer the ability to inhabit the scene from any angle. Seniors loved the tourist software that specialized in highly accurate recreations of popular destinations. And as Kazuto mentioned earlier, it was also finding use in military training.

The sudden increase in the range of interests that could be enjoyed indoors led to a predictable counter-surge in "Walkers" who insisted on going outside and strolling the town without a destination. Bizarrely enough, that led to a very successful line of Virtual Walking Simulators. Even the big fast-food chains had gotten into the business with virtual locations you could visit.

So society wondered where exactly the virtual world would send the real world that we live in. What would happen once the Soul Translator appeared and people could speed up their consciousnesses? Shino felt something chilly run across her skin.

Meanwhile, Asuna repeated, "A long...dream..." then looked up at Kazuto and smiled. "I suppose I should be grateful that *SAO* happened before the Soul Translator was developed. If we were playing it on the STL, Aincrad instead could have been a thousand floors and taken twenty years to beat."

"Ugh...spare me," he groaned, shaking his head.

Asuna smiled again and asked, "So all this week, you were just having one long dream?"

"Yeah. It was a function test for long-term consecutive use—

three days in a dive without food or water. I think I did lose some weight..."

"More than a little! There you go, getting yourself into crazy business again," she said, putting on a cutesy tantrum and crossing her arms. "I'm visiting Kawagoe tomorrow to cook you some food! I'd better ask Suguha to stock up on plenty of veggies."

"J-just go easy on me."

As Shino watched the two banter with a grin on her face, a sudden question occurred to her. "So, um...does that mean that during the three-day-long dive, that thought accelerator was working? How much time did you actually experience in there?"

He tilted his head, trying to remember, and said, "Well...like I explained earlier, my memories of the dive are limited...but I recall them saying that the current maximum amplification factor of the FLA is a bit over three..."

"So...nine days?"

"Or ten."

"Hmm...I wonder what kind of world it was and what you were doing. If you can't take out the memories, could you at least bring your memories in with you? Were there other testers?"

"Honestly, I have no idea about any of that. They said having advance knowledge will affect the test results. But even if they block memories from within the dive, I don't know if they can limit your existing memory...At any rate, the place I go in Roppongi only has one experimental STL in it, so I'm guessing I was the only one diving. They wouldn't tell me anything about the inside. What's the use of being a beater if you can't get an advantage as a beta tester? All they would tell me was the code name of their test world."

"And what is that?"

"The Underworld."

"Like...an underground world? I wonder if that's the design theme."

"I don't even know if it's meant to be realistic, or fantasy, or sci-fi. But with a name like that, I'm guessing it's dark and subterranean…"

"Hmm. It doesn't really stick out to me," Shino murmured.

Meanwhile, Asuna put a finger to her slender chin and said softly, "Maybe…that has to do with Alice, too."

"Alice…?"

"Like I said with the source of the name Rath, maybe this one comes from *Alice in Wonderland*. Well, the original manuscript title was *Alice's Adventures Under Ground*."

"Oh, I didn't know that. The more I hear, the more this company sounds like it came from a fairy tale," Shino noted giddily. "In fact, both Alice books were big, long dreams in the end, right? I wonder if that means you were having tea parties with rabbits and playing chess with a queen while you were under, Kirito."

Asuna giggled at the thought. But Kazuto himself was staring at a fixed point on the table, lost in thought.

"…What's wrong?" Shino asked.

"…Oh, uh…"

He looked up, still squinting, then blinked in obvious confusion. "When you said 'Alice'…I felt like I was about to remember something…It was just one of those things, you know? Where you're on the brink of recalling something huge, but you can't remember what it was, so it just sits there on your shoulders like this big ball of anxiety?"

"Oh, yeah. It's kinda like when you have a nightmare and wake up from it, but you can't remember what it was about."

"There's something…something I'm forgetting that I was supposed to do right away," Kazuto lamented, scrunching up his hair.

Asuna looked at him with concern and asked, "Is it a memory from the test…?"

"But you already said that all the memory from the virtual world gets deleted," Shino reminded him. He shut his eyes and groaned, then gave up and slumped his shoulders.

"Well, it was ten days of memories. Maybe there are little fragments here and there that they couldn't block out entirely…"

"I see…If that's the case, if you still had the memory, you would be a whole week older than us compared to before, mentally speaking. That's…kinda scary to think about."

"I don't know…I kind of like that," Asuna said. She was a year older than him. "It's like it closes the gap a bit."

Kazuto gave her a weak smile. "Speaking of which, from the end of yesterday's dive to about the middle of school today, I got this weird feeling. It was like…all the familiar parts of town and TV shows and everything were all fresh, like I hadn't seen them in forever. And when I saw people in class, I was like…'who is that again?'"

"Oh, don't be dramatic. It was only ten days," Shino snapped.

"Yeah, you're going to make me worry," Asuna complained. "You have to stop participating in that dangerous experiment, Kirito. It's definitely going to affect your health, for one thing."

"Right. The long-term consecutive diving test was a major success, and all the big hurdles as far as the fundamental construction have been passed. Next comes the stage where they shape it into a functional machine, but I can't begin to guess how many years it will take to shrink that enormous thing down to a commercial level…I'm not going for any side jobs anytime soon. I've got finals next month, anyway."

"Ugh," Shino said, grimacing. "Don't remind me. You two are lucky; you barely even have any paper tests. We still have to use Scantrons. I wish they would get with the times."

"Hee-hee! Well, we should have a study session sometime soon," Asuna suggested. She looked up at the wall behind Shino and gasped. "It's almost six! Time really does fly when you're chatting."

"I guess we should wrap it up. I feel like we only talked about the main point of the meeting for about five minutes," Kazuto said, smirking.

"Well, the BoB is way far ahead, and we can decide on character build and finer strategy once you've converted," Shino suggested.

"Good idea. I won't use anything but a lightsaber, though."

"You have to call it a photon sword!"

He laughed and picked up the bill, offering to pay it with the seventy-two straight hours of wages he'd just earned, and took it to the counter. Shino and Asuna loudly chimed in their thanks for the meal and started for the door.

"We'll be back, Agil."

"Thanks for the baked beans; they were great," Shino called out to the owner, who was busy preparing for the night traffic, as she took her umbrella from the whiskey barrel. The door bell clattered when she opened the door, letting in the sounds of bustle and rain.

It wasn't yet sundown, but the heavy clouds blocked most of the light, so it felt as dark as night along the wet street. She opened her umbrella and took one step down the small staircase, then stopped. She quickly scanned the area.

"What's wrong, Shino-non?" Asuna asked behind her. Shino came back to her senses and rushed down into the street, then turned around.

"N-no, it's nothing," she said shyly. She wasn't going to admit that the sniper sense on the back of her neck had just crawled. The possibility that her instinct for sensing a sniper while out in the open had transferred into real life was not something she wanted to confront right now.

Asuna was still curious, but then the door bell jangled again, prompting her to continue down the steps.

Kazuto emerged, stuffing his wallet back into his bag. As he descended to the street, he muttered, "Alice..."

"Are you still going on about that?"

"Well...now that I think about it, I must have heard something from the staff talking among themselves before the STL dive on Friday...A, L, I...Arti...Labile...Intelli...Hmm, what was it again...?" he muttered, mostly to himself.

Asuna extended her umbrella over him and chuckled. "Once he gets his mind on something, he can't stop. If you're that curious about it, just ask them the next time you go there."

"Yeah, good point," Kazuto said. He shook his head a few times to clear his thoughts and finally opened his own umbrella. "Well, Sinon, we'll meet again to plan out this *GGO* conversion."

"Roger that. We can meet in *ALO*, too. Thanks for coming."

"So long, Shino-non."

"Bye, Asuna."

She waved to the couple as they headed off to their JR train, then turned the opposite direction to walk to her subway station. She peered out from under her umbrella again, but the prying gaze she'd felt just moments earlier was gone, as if it had never been there.

INTERLUDE I

Body temperature is such a strange thing, Asuna Yuuki thought.

Beneath the navy sky, its clouds curling with orange after the end of the rain, they walked along hand in hand. Kazuto Kirigaya had been lost in thought for the last several minutes, looking down in silence at the brick tiles on the pedestrian path.

Asuna lived in Setagaya and Kazuto had to get back to Kawagoe, so they normally took their separate trains at Shinjuku Station, but for whatever reason, Kazuto had said he would escort her closer to home this time. It was almost an entire hour extra for him to get home from Shibuya, but she sensed something different in his look this time, so she accepted the offer.

After they got off at her stop, Miyanosaka Station on the Setagaya Line, they naturally wound up holding hands.

There was something about the experience she found reminiscent. It was a memory that was as painful and frightening as it was sweet, so she normally didn't allow it to surface, but every once in a while she felt it when she was holding his hand.

It wasn't a memory of the real world. It happened in Grandzam, the city of iron towers on the fifty-fifth floor of old Aincrad.

At the time, Asuna was the vice commander of the Knights of the Blood guild and had a greatsword-wielding personal guard named Kuradeel at her side at all times. Kuradeel held a fanatical obsession toward her, and when Kirito (Kazuto) prompted her to consider quitting the guild, he tried to use a paralyzing poison to kill her friend.

With two fellow guildmates dead and Kirito nearly gone as well, Asuna drew her rapier with rage. She tore away at Kuradeel's HP bar, but at the point where one more hit would have finished him, she hesitated. Kuradeel used that moment of weakness to strike back, and he was stopped only when Kirito recovered from his paralysis.

The pair returned to the KoB headquarters on the fifty-fifth floor, announced their departure from the guild, then walked through Grandzam without a destination, hand in hand.

She'd played it cool at the time, but underneath, her heart was swirling with disappointment in herself for hesitating, and guilt for having forced that burden onto Kirito. Just as she was feeling that she didn't have the right to be considered a member of the elite front line or to walk at Kirito's side, she heard his voice telling her that he would do whatever it took to get her back to her old world.

In that instant, a powerful drive overtook her. The next time, *she* would protect him. Not just that time, but every time. In any world.

She still vividly remembered how the hand that had been so cold the entire time she held it suddenly erupted with warmth like a furnace. Even now, after the flying fortress fell and she escaped from the land of fairies, the memory of that skin temperature came back to her when she held his hand.

Body temperature truly was a strange thing. It was merely the by-product of the expenditure of energy to keep the body running, but the sharing of that heat through touch also seemed to impart some kind of information. As evidence of that, Asuna knew that Kazuto was silent because he was hesitant to tell her something important.

Kazuto had just said the human soul was photons trapped in the microtubules of brain cells. Could that light exist not just in the brain but throughout all the cells in the body? A quantum field made from fluctuating motes of light in the shape of a human being, connected through their palms...Perhaps that was what she was truly feeling when she felt his body temperature.

Asuna closed her eyes and said a silent reassurance.

It will be all right, Kirito. I will always be watching your back. We're the greatest forward and backup in the world.

Kazuto came to a sudden stop, and so did Asuna at the exact same moment. When she opened her eyes, the striking of seven o'clock caused an old-fashioned wrought-iron streetlamp to flicker to life.

There were no other people to be seen on the residential walkway in the dusk after the day's rain. Kazuto slowly tilted his head to look at Asuna with those dark eyes of his.

"Asuna..."

He took a step forward to drive away his hesitation.

"...I think I'm going to go."

Asuna knew that he had been weighing a decision about his future path. She asked, "To America?"

"Yeah. I spent a year doing a lot of research, and I think the brain implant chip they're studying at a university in Santa Clara is the proper next step in the evolution of full-diving. I think that's the way that the brain-machine interface is going to go. And I really, really want to see when the next world is born."

She looked directly back into those eyes and nodded.

"It wasn't all just fun times...There were hard times and sad times, too. You want to find out why you were called to that castle, and where it's been taking you."

"I could live hundreds of years, and I'd still never see the end of that road," Kazuto quipped with a grin. However, he soon fell silent again.

Asuna sensed that he couldn't bring himself to say that they'd be living far apart. She was going to keep that smile on her face and tell him her own answer that she'd been incubating within her for so long—but Kazuto found his voice then, his expression the exact same one she remembered from when he proposed to her in Aincrad.

"So, I...I want you to come with me, Asuna. I just—I can't do it without you. I know this is an impossible request. I'm sure you have your own ideas for your future. But even still, I..."

He hesitated—Asuna's eyes had bulged, and she snorted.

"Huh...?"

"S-sorry, I shouldn't laugh. But...is that seriously what you've been worrying about all this time?"

"W-well, of course."

"Oh, sheesh. My answer's been decided for ages before all this."

She reached over and enfolded Kazuto's hand with both of hers. She gave him an even bigger bob of the head and said, "Of course I'm going with you. I'll go anywhere to be with you."

He stared at her, blinked several times, then gave her a dazzling smile of the sort he rarely ever showed. He lifted his other hand to her shoulder. She let go and circled her arms around his back.

Their lips were chilly when they first touched, but they soon melted into warmth. Asuna imagined the light that made up their souls trading infinite information. She knew for certain that no matter what world, no matter how long they traveled, their hearts would never be apart.

In fact, their hearts had been connected long ago. Since the moment they disappeared in a rainbow aurora above the collapse of Aincrad, or perhaps even before that—as lonely solo players who met deep in a dark labyrinth.

"So does that mean," Asuna wondered aloud several minutes later as they resumed their walk through the neighborhood, "you don't think the Soul Translator you've been testing is the proper evolution of full-diving? The brain chip is a connection on the cellular level like the NerveGear, but the STL goes further to interface on a quantum level, right?"

"Hmm..."

Kazuto tapped the metal end of an umbrella against the bricks.

"Yes, it might be true that the scope is much more advanced than the brain chip. But it's just...*too* progressive. It won't just be a few years until they can downsize that tech for home usage. It'll take at least ten or twenty. I feel like the STL I've been working with isn't meant for the purpose of simply allowing a person to full-dive into a virtual world..."

"Huh? What's it for, then?"

"I think it might be a tool to understanding the fluctlight, the human consciousness..."

"Hmm..."

So the STL wasn't the goal but the means. Asuna tried to imagine what knowing a person's soul would gain you, but he resumed talking before she could fathom such a thing.

"Besides, I think the STL is more like...an extension of Heathcliff's ideas. I don't know why he created the NerveGear and *SAO*, why he victimized thousands of people, why he fried his own brain and unleashed the Seed into the world...or if there was even a reason for those things. But I can't help but feel like the STL possesses some part of his essence in it. I do want to know what it was Heathcliff sought, but I don't want that to be *my* destination. I don't want to feel like I've been dancing in the palm of his hand all along."

For a moment, Asuna envisioned the long-gone man's face and nodded.

"I see...Hey, is the guild leader's mind—or thought-mimicking program or whatever—still alive on some server somewhere? You mentioned that before, didn't you?"

"Yeah, just once. The machine he used to commit suicide was a primitive prototype of the STL. In order to read the fluctlight, it had to use a high-powered beam that fried all his brain cells. I think it was probably an hours-long process and far more painful than when the NerveGear destroys a brain...Whatever reason he went to those lengths to make a copy of himself, I think there has to be a connection to what Rath is trying to do with the STL. The only reason I took Kikuoka's offer…might be due to something in my heart that still wants to see an end to that…"

He looked up to the sky, where the last vestiges of red were vanishing. Asuna gazed at his profile for a while, then squeezed his hand harder and whispered, "Just promise me one thing: that you won't do anything dangerous."

He turned back to her with a grin. "Of course. I promise. Now that I know I get to go to America with you next summer."

"Well, you need to study hard and get a good SAT score if you intend to do that, remember?"

"Ugh," he grunted, then cleared his throat to change the topic. "At any rate, I ought to at least introduce myself to your parents once. I've exchanged an occasional e-mail with your father, Shouzou, but I'm a bit afraid of what your mother thinks…"

"Oh, don't worry, she's become much more understanding. Oh, right…If you're coming this far, why don't you just stop in?"

"What?! I-I don't know…Maybe I'll visit once the term finals are over. Yeah."

"Good grief…"

Eventually they reached a small park that was fairly close to her house. It was customary for them to part here when Kazuto walked her "home." She came to a hesitant stop and turned to face him. He looked her in the eyes.

Right when they were only inches apart, heavy footsteps thudded in their direction, and Asuna instantly pulled away.

Trotting toward them from the T-intersection behind her was a figure, a short man wearing dark clothing. When he spotted Asuna and Kazuto, he approached, apologizing in a high-pitched voice.

"Excuse me, which way is the station?" the young man asked, bowing profusely.

Asuna pointed to the east. "Just go straight down this road, then turn right at the first ligh…*Ah!*"

Kazuto had abruptly reached out and pulled her shoulder back. He stepped forward and moved her behind him.

"Wh-what's...?"

"You. *You* were outside Dicey Café. Who are you?" he demanded. Asuna sucked in a sharp breath and looked closer at the man.

He sported long hair with the occasional highlight. His sunken cheeks were thick with stubble. There were silver earrings in his ears and a thick silver chain around his neck. He was wearing a faded black T-shirt and black leather pants with a metal chain that jangled at his waist. Despite the hot season, he wore heavy lace-up boots. Weirdly enough, he seemed to be covered in dust.

Narrow, mirthful eyes peered out between shaggy bangs. The man tilted his head in apparent confusion at Kazuto's accusation, but that suddenly gave way to a dangerous look, his pupils glinting.

"...No use trying a sneak attack, then," the man lamented, drawing back one corner of his mouth in what couldn't be distinguished as either snarl or grin.

"Who are you?" Kazuto commanded again. The man shrugged, shook his head a few times, then sighed theatrically.

"Oh, come on now, *Kirito.* You forgot my face already...? Well, I guess I did wear a mask before. But I haven't forgotten yours for a single day since then."

"You..."

Kazuto twitched. His back went straight. He pulled back his right leg and dropped his weight.

"You're Johnny Black!" he accused, and his hand shot like lightning to grab empty space over his shoulder—the exact same spot where Kirito the Black Swordsman once reached for the hilt of his beloved Elucidator.

"Bwa-ha! Heh-ha! Ha-ha-ha-ha-ha-ha-ha! You got no sword there, bud!" The man named Johnny Black cackled, writhing with high-pitched laughter. Kazuto slowly lowered his hand, though it wasn't a relaxed gesture.

Asuna knew that name. It belonged to one of the more famous red players of old Aincrad, the ones who eagerly and intentionally killed other players. He had formed a partnership with Red-Eyed Xaxa within the PK guild called Laughing Coffin, and they were responsible for more than ten deaths between them.

...Xaxa. That name had come up just half a year ago, too. He was the ringleader of the horrendous Death Gun incident.

Xaxa (Shouichi Shinkawa) and his younger brother had been arrested, but their companion got away, according to the report just after the incident. They assumed he had been caught long ago. But that meant the third man, named Kanamoto, must be the man before them now...

"You're still on the lam?" Kazuto rasped. Johnny Black, real name Kanamoto, grinned and pointed his index fingers at them.

"Of course, baby. Xaxa's locked up now, so I gotta do the heavy lifting, right? The last member of the Coffin. It took me five months to track down that café, then another month of staking out the place...They were hateful days, man."

Kanamoto grunted and tilted his head back and forth. "But Kirito, without your swords...you're just a weak little kid, ain'tcha? You look the same, but you sure ain't the swordsman who crushed us all so badly."

"Speaking of which...what can *you* do without those cheap poisoned weapons?"

"Y'know, only an amateur judges a weapon by what he can see."

With snakelike quickness, Kanamoto swung his right hand behind his back and grabbed something from his shirt.

It was a strange item. A toylike grip jutted out of a smooth plastic cylinder. Asuna thought it was just a water pistol at first, but the way Kazuto tensed caused her to hold her breath. Her confusion turned to fear when she heard his voice.

"That's...the Death Gun...!"

He pushed out backward with his right arm to further distance Asuna from the man, meanwhile pointing the end of his folded umbrella toward Kanamoto.

Even as she unconsciously took a few steps back, Asuna's eyes were glued to the plastic "gun" the whole while. She knew that was not a simple plastic gun but an injector using a high-pressure gas, loaded with a terrifying chemical that would stop a human heart.

"As it happens, I *do* have a poison weapon. Too bad it's not a good old knife, though."

Kanamoto hissed with laughter as he waved around the tip of the injector, the only metal part on the tool. Kazuto kept the umbrella pointed carefully at him and shouted, "Asuna, run! Go and get someone!"

After a moment's hesitation, she spun and raced away. As she ran, she heard Kanamoto say, "Hey, Flash! You'd better tell everyone you know…that it was Johnny Black who finally took down the Black Swordsman!"

It was about a hundred feet on a straight line to the intercom of the nearest house.

"Someone…somebody help!!" she shrieked at maximum volume as she ran. She wondered if it was a mistake to run and leave Kazuto behind, if it would have been better for them both to leap on him and subdue the weapon. She was halfway to her destination when she heard the sound.

It was the short, sharp sound of depressurization, like the bottle cap of a carbonated drink or a blast of hair spray. But the knowledge of what it meant in this context was so terrifying that Asuna's legs faltered, and she slipped and put a hand to the wet bricks.

She turned slowly to look over her shoulder.

It was a ghastly scene.

The prod of Kazuto's umbrella was jammed all the way into Kanamoto's right thigh.

And Kanamoto's injector was pressed against Kazuto's left shoulder.

They both lurched over and toppled onto the street.

The next several minutes were as surreal as a black-and-white movie.

Asuna worked her disobedient legs until they took her to Kazuto's side. She pulled him away from the agonized Kanamoto, who was clutching his leg, and urged her boyfriend to hang in there as she pulled out her cell phone.

Her fingers were as cold as ice. She fumbled across the touchscreen, and her voice quavered as she called the emergency center, relating to the operator their location and status.

Belatedly, onlookers appeared. Someone had called it in, because a police officer soon shoved his way through the crowd. Asuna answered his questions briefly and merely clung to Kazuto's body after that.

His breathing was short and shallow. He could say only two words through the pain: "Asuna, sorry."

After an eternity of several minutes, two ambulances arrived. They loaded Kazuto into one, and Asuna rode in it with him.

The paramedic examined Kazuto, who was lying unconscious on the stretcher, making certain that his airway was clear, then promptly turned to his assistant and shouted, "He's in respiratory failure—get me the ambo bag!"

They produced a breathing device, a clear mask that went over Kazuto's nose and mouth. Asuna nearly screamed in terror, but through a near-miracle brought about by the severity of the situation, she was able to tell the paramedic the name of the drug.

"Um, he was hit with a drug called…succinylcholine! In the left shoulder."

The paramedic looked briefly stunned, then barked out new orders.

"He needs epinephrine…no, atropine! I've got the vein!"

They removed Kazuto's shirt, stuck an IV needle in his left arm, and plastered heart-rate electrodes on his chest. Voices shouted back and forth. Sirens rent the air.

"Pulse is dropping!"

"Prepare the CPR machine!"

Under the LED light of the ambulance interior, Kazuto's face was alarmingly pale. It took quite a long time for Asuna to realize that the voice saying, "No, no, Kirito, you can't," was coming from her own lips.

"Flatline!"

"Continue the massage!"

This can't be real, Kirito. You're not going to leave me behind and go somewhere else. You said...we'd always be together.

She glanced down, and her eyes caught the screen of the phone clutched in her hands.

The pink heart on the screen shuddered once, then fell still.

The digits on the readout dropped to zero with cruel precision, then stayed there.

CHAPTER ONE

1

The air had a certain scent.

That was the first thing I noticed, through the fragmented thoughts I had just before awakening.

The air coming into my nostrils brought a wealth of information. The smell of sweet flowers. The smell of fresh grass. The bracing, cleansing smell of trees. The tempting smell of water to a parched throat.

Next I focused on my hearing and was overwhelmed by an instant deluge of sound: The rustling of countless leaves. The cheerful twittering of songbirds. The soft hum of insect wings. The distant trickling of a creek.

Where was I? Certainly not in my home. There were none of the usual features of waking there, like the sunny smell of dried sheets, the AC's dehumidifier's growl, or the distant traffic over on the Kawagoe Bypass. Plus, the shifting patterns of green light on my eyelids weren't coming from the reading light I forgot to turn off, but from the shade of branches.

I pushed aside the lingering temptation of sleep and opened my eyes.

Countless bits of light leaped into my sight, and I blinked rapidly. I had to lift the back of my hand to rub at the welling tears, and I sat up.

"…Where am I…?" I wondered.

The first thing I saw was clumps of light-green grass. Little white and yellow flowers appeared here and there, and brilliant pale-blue butterflies wandered among them. The carpet of grass ended just fifteen feet ahead, replaced by a thick forest of gnarled, decades-old trees.

I squinted into the gloom among the trunks, but as far as the light allowed me to see, the trees continued. The flowing, textured bark and ground were covered in thick moss that shone golden-green where the sunlight caught it.

Next I glanced to the right, then rotated my entire body. The ancient trees greeted me in every direction. Apparently I had fallen asleep in a little grassy opening in the middle of the forest. Lastly, I looked up and saw, among the reaching branches all around, blue sky and trails of white.

"Where...am I?" I wondered aloud again. No one answered.

No matter how hard I tried to remember, I had no memory of coming to a place like this and taking a nap. Was it sleepwalking? Amnesia? I shook my head to dispel the disturbing possibilities.

My name was Kazuto Kirigaya. Age seventeen and eight months. Living in Kawagoe in Saitama Prefecture with my mother and sister.

The easy recollection of that personal data brought me some relief, so I reached for more.

I was in my second year of high school. But I would reach the credits necessary to graduate in the first semester of next year, so I was preparing to move on to college that fall. In fact, I had been talking with someone about that. The last Monday of June—it had been raining. After class, I went to Agil's Dicey Café in the Okachimachi neighborhood to talk with my friend Sinon—Shino Asada—about *Gun Gale Online*.

After that, Asuna Yuuki met up with us and the three chatted for a while, then left the café.

"Asuna..."

I spoke the name of my girlfriend, the partner in whom I placed all my trust when my back needed watching. But the memory of her face and figure was nowhere to be seen here. There was no one at all on the grassy enclosure or among the trees.

Struck by a sudden loneliness, I continued my recollection.

Asuna and I said good-bye to Sinon and got on a train. We took the Ginza Line subway to Shibuya, then got on the Setagaya Line that would take us to Asuna's neighborhood.

When we got off, the rain had stopped. We walked down the brick sidewalk, talking about college. I revealed that I was thinking of going to school in America and made a desperate plea for her to join me. She showed me that usual smile, brimming with gentle love. And then…

The memories ended there.

I couldn't remember what Asuna had answered, how we had separated, if I'd gone back to the station, what time I'd gotten home, or how many hours of sleep I had gotten—nothing.

Somewhat stunned by this realization, I tried desperately to summon the memory.

But Asuna's smile merely blotted away, as if being submerged in water, and no matter how hard I tried, I couldn't draw out the next part of the scene. I clenched my eyes shut and dug as hard as I could into that heavy gray void.

Blinking red light.

A maddening shortness of breath.

Those were the only two images I could surface, meager as they were. I sucked in a lungful of sweet air instead. The thirsty dryness in my throat resurfaced, stronger than before.

I was certain of it. I had been in Miyasaka of Setagaya Ward just last night. So what brought me here to sleep in this mysterious forest, all alone?

But was it really yesterday? The breeze playing on my skin felt nice. There was none of the humid misery of late June here in this forest. This time, a true thrill of horror ran down my back.

Were the "memories from yesterday" actually real? I was clinging to them as if to a life raft in the open sea, after a storm. Was I really me…?

I rubbed my face all over, pulled my hair, then lowered my hands to stare at them closely. As I remembered, there was a little mole near the base of my right thumb and a childhood scar on the back of my left middle finger. This brought me some amount of relief.

At that point, I belatedly realized that I was wearing an odd outfit.

It wasn't the T-shirt I used as nightwear, or my school uniform, or any of my personal clothes. In fact, they didn't look like any kind of clothes you would buy at the store.

My top was a half-sleeve shirt of crude cotton or linen, dyed pale blue. The consistency was uneven and rough. The sewing along the sleeve was clearly done by hand, not a machine. There was no collar, just a V-cut in the front, tied with a brown string. By touching it, I could tell that the string was not corded fabric but a piece of finely cut leather.

My trousers were the same material as the top, but an unbleached cream color. There were no pockets, and the leather belt around my waist was fastened not with a metal buckle but with a long, thin wood button. My shoes were also hand-sewn leather, and the thick leather sole was studded with a few cleats for slip resistance.

I'd never seen clothes or shoes like these before. In real life, at least.

"…Oh, okay," I muttered, exhaling.

They were otherworldly clothes and yet quite familiar as well. They were Middle Ages European garments—in short, "fantasy" wear: a tunic, cotton pants, and leather shoes. This wasn't the real world but a fantasy one. Just another virtual realm.

"What the hell…"

I craned my neck again. I had fallen asleep while in a full dive? But why couldn't I remember what game I had logged in to and when?

In any case, I'd find out by logging out. I waved my right hand.

A few seconds passed, and no window appeared. I tried with the left hand instead. No results.

With the ceaseless rustling of leaves and chirping of birds in my ears, I did my best to dispel the growing prickle rising up my midsection.

This was a virtual world. It had to be. But it certainly wasn't familiar Alfheim. In fact, it couldn't be any of the AmuSphere's VR worlds fashioned from the Seed engine.

Actually, I had just moments ago confirmed the moles and scars of my real body. I didn't know of any VR games that re-created the body to such a degree of detail.

"Command. Log out," I ordered without much hope. There was no response. Sitting cross-legged, I examined my hands once again.

There were fine swirls on my fingertips. Wrinkles on the skin of my joints. Fine body hair. Little droplets of cold sweat seeping forth.

I brushed them aside with my tunic, then examined the fabric again. The rough thread was primitively sewn into the cloth. Even the fraying of the textile into little puffs was clearly visible.

Any machine that could generate a virtual world this detailed had to be frighteningly powerful. I gazed forward into the trees and swung my arm to snatch up a blade of grass and bring it before my eyes.

The detail-focusing system that all Seed-based VR worlds used would be unable to handle that sudden action, creating a brief lag before the fine texture on the grass could load. But the very instant my eyes caught the blade, they made out fine veins, jagged edges, even a droplet of moisture hanging from the torn end.

That meant that every visible object here was being consistently generated down to the millimeter in real time. This blade of grass alone had to represent a few dozen megabytes of data. Was that even possible?

I had to stifle that line of thought before I followed it any further. Instead, I parted the grass between my feet and used my hand to shovel through the dirt.

The damp soil was surprisingly soft, and featured the occasional tangle of fine roots. I spotted something wriggling through the lattice and picked it out.

It was a little earthworm, maybe a tenth of an inch long. It writhed desperately in its dangerous new surroundings, gleaming and green. I wondered if it was a new species, and abruptly the end that appeared to be its head split open to emit a tiny screech. I put it back in the soil, feeling dizzy, and pushed the dirt back over the hole. My palm was black with dirt, and I could make out the individual grains under my nails.

After most of a minute sitting in stunned silence, I reluctantly formulated three theories to explain my circumstances.

First was the possibility of a virtual world that was an extension of today's full-dive tech. After all, waking up alone in a forest was a stereotypical opening scene for any fantasy RPG.

But as far as I knew, there was no supercomputer capable of generating such a vibrant wealth of ultra-detailed 3-D scenery. That would mean that in the time I had blanked out, years—perhaps decades—had passed in real time.

Next was the possibility that this was a place in the real world. I was the target of some crime, or illegal experiment, or vicious prank, dressed in these strange clothes and taken somewhere unfamiliar—perhaps Hokkaido or the southern hemisphere—and released in a forest. But I didn't think there were any metallic-green worms that screeched in Japan, and I hadn't heard of any such thing elsewhere in the world.

Lastly was the possibility that this was a true alternate dimension, alternate world, or life after death. It was a common trope in manga, books, and anime. Dramaturgy suggested that I would soon rescue a girl being attacked by monsters, fulfill the village elder's requests, and eventually rise as the hero to vanquish the dreaded sorcerer lord. Yet I didn't see that rudimentary bronze sword I was supposed to start with.

I just barely overcame a sudden urge to belly-laugh and naturally ruled out the third option. If I lost sight of the boundary between reality and unreality, I would truly be losing my grip on sanity.

That left two possibilities: the virtual world or the real world.

If it was the former, no matter how ultrarealistic, there would be ways to identify this. Just climb the nearest tree to the top, then jump off headfirst. If you logged out or were revived at the nearest holy temple at a save point, it was VR.

But if this was the real world, that test would have disastrous consequences. In a suspense novel I read years ago, a criminal organization decided to put together a video of a real game of death by kidnapping ten or so people, taking them into the remote wilderness, and forcing them to kill one another for survival. It was hard to imagine that happening in real life, but then again, the *SAO* Incident was just about as unlikely. If this was a game taking place in the real world, committing suicide right at the beginning was a poor choice.

"In that sense, the other one was better..." I muttered aloud without realizing it. At least in Akihiko Kayaba's game, he had done us the courtesy of appearing at the start for a detailed explanation.

I stared up at the sky through the branches and called out, "Hey, GM! Say something if you can hear me!!"

But there was no enormous face that appeared in the sky or hooded figure that popped into existence next to me. Just in case, I searched again over the little grassy opening and all over my outfit, but I found nothing that might be a rule book.

Whoever had thrown me into this place wasn't going to answer any calls for help. Assuming the current situation wasn't the result of some accident, at least.

With the oblivious twittering of the birds in my ears, I dedicated my mind to considering my next actions.

If this was all a real-world accident, then rushing around too much probably wasn't a good idea. There could be rescue crews heading for my location as I sat here.

But that raised the question: What kind of accident could produce this baffling situation?

If you had to come up with whatever seemed the least unlikely, I could have been on a vacation or traveling in a vehicle—airplane or car—that suffered some malfunction, throwing me into this forest, knocking me out, and jarring my memory. It wasn't that far-fetched—if not for the strange clothes I was wearing and the lack of any scrapes or bruises.

Perhaps it was an accident with a full dive. Some trouble arose with the transmission route, and I logged in to a place I shouldn't be. But again, that failed to explain the tremendous fidelity of the simulation.

It seemed more and more likely that someone had designed this situation for me. In which case, I had to assume that nothing would change unless I took some kind of action.

"In either case..."

Somehow I had to find out whether this was the real world or a virtual world.

There had to be some way. It was often said that a nearly perfect VR world was indistinguishable from reality, but I didn't believe it was possible for absolutely every aspect of the real world to be represented in perfect accuracy.

For nearly five minutes, I sat among the short grass, pondering the possibilities. But ultimately, I did not come up with a simple idea that I could test on the spot. If I had a microscope, I could examine the soil for bacteria. If I had a plane, I could try flying to the ends of the earth. But with only my own two hands and feet, the best I could do at the moment was dig in the dirt.

If only Asuna were here, she could tell me some simple, unexpected way to ascertain the nature of the world, I lamented. Either that or she would get me off my butt and taking action.

Loneliness set in again, and I bit my lip.

I was paradoxically both surprised and unsurprised by how helpless I felt, not being able to contact Asuna. Nearly every decision I had made in the last two years was made through discussion with her. Without her thought process to guide me, I was like a CPU missing half of its cores.

As far as I knew, I had been talking with her for hours at Agil's place just yesterday. If I'd known this was going to happen, I wouldn't have wasted my breath on Rath and the STL but asked her about ways to distinguish the real world from a highly detailed virtual...

"Oh..."

I leaped to my feet. The sound of the clearing grew faint.

What in the world? I have to be crazy not to have thought of that until just now.

Of course I knew. I was quite familiar with the technology to create a VR world that far surpassed what was available today, a type of "super-reality." Which meant this world had to be…

"Inside the Soul Translator…? Is *this* the Underworld?"

No one responded, of course, but I barely registered the lack of an answer as I stared around, dumbfounded.

Knotted, ancient trees, indistinguishable from the real thing. Waving grasses. Fluttering butterflies.

"So this…is the artificial dream it wrote into my fluctlight…"

On the very first day of my stint with Rath, I got an explanation (more like bragging) about the rough working of the STL and the realness of its world from research/operator Takeru Higa.

On my first test dive, I realized that his words were not hyperbole in the least—and all I saw was a single room. While the desk, chair, and various items were all indistinguishable from reality, the space itself was much too small to be considered a "world."

But the size of the forest around me now had to be miles wide in terms of real-world scale. In fact, if the faint outline of mountains in the far distance were real, then it was tens, hundreds of miles in scope.

You'd have to scour together all the data space in the entire Internet to create and run such an environment using existing technology. It would have to be an entirely new form of tech… something possible only through the STL's pneumonic visuals system—but even I'd never imagined that it would be like *this*.

And if my supposition that this was the Underworld, the STL's virtual realm, was correct, then it would be essentially impossible to confirm that through any kind of user action from within.

After all, every object I could see was no different from the real thing, as far as my consciousness perceived it. If I pulled out every blade of grass, my fluctlight would receive the exact same information as if I did that action in real life. Discerning the difference from real life was fundamentally impossible.

If the STL was ever going to be put to a functional use, it would definitely need some kind of notable marker that identified its VR world as such, I noted to myself as I got up to my feet.

So I didn't have any certain proof yet, but it was reasonable to assume for now that I was in the Underworld. Meaning that in the real world, my body was lying in the STL test unit in Rath's Roppongi lab, making two thousand yen an hour.

"But wait…is that right?" I wondered, after my momentary period of relief.

I could have sworn that Higa had told me my memories as Kazuto Kirigaya were blocked during testing to prevent data contamination. But the only part of my memory that was blank was the single day between seeing Asuna off and then getting into Rath's STL. That was too narrow to qualify as a memory block.

Plus—yes, that was right! I'd decided not to visit Rath for a while so I could study for my finals. Sure, the pay was tempting, but I didn't want to think that it would take only a single day for me to break a promise to Asuna.

So if this was an STL test dive, I had to assume that some issue had arisen. I looked up at the sky through the branches and shouted, "Mr. Higa! If you're monitoring this test, call off the dive for a bit! I think there's a problem!"

More than ten seconds passed.

Countless leaves shook in the breeze beneath the pleasant sun. Butterflies flapped their wings sleepily. Nothing changed.

"Man…I don't know about this…"

A possibility suddenly occurred to me. Was this situation actually a test I'd elected to undertake?

Perhaps they'd blocked only the brief bit of memory before the dive and tossed me into the STL's ultrarealistic world to collect data on what a person would do if he wasn't able to discern if his setting was the real world or a virtual one.

If that was true, I wanted to smack my head for agreeing to such an unpleasant experiment. If I had assumed that I would easily escape my predicament through quick thinking and action, then it was a breathtakingly thoughtless decision.

I used my fingers to list a number of possibilities that explained my situation, along with totally arbitrary percentages.

"Let's see…Chances that this is somewhere in the real world:

three percent. Chances that this is an existing type of VR world: seven percent. Chances that this is a voluntary STL test dive: twenty percent. Chances that there was a spontaneous accident during the dive: 69.9999 percent. Which means..."

There's a 0.0001 chance I got summoned to a real alternate world, I added mentally. Racking my brain for an answer wasn't going to get me much further. If I wanted to be more certain, I had to brave danger to interact with another person, be it game player or test diver.

It was time for action.

The first step was to quench my thirst, which was reaching persistent levels. I did a full 360-degree turn in the middle of the grass. The sound of flowing water was coming from what I estimated to be east, based on the position of the sun.

Before I started off, I reached behind my back just in case, but there was no sword or even a stick there, of course. I strode forward before I could start to feel lonely about that, and in less than ten steps, I was out of the grass. Two huge trees stood at my sides like natural gateposts, and I headed through them into the dim forest.

It was mysterious and eerie within the woods, with their velvety carpet of moss underfoot. The canopy of leaves far above blocked out nearly all the sunlight, so only the rare tendril of golden light reached the ground. The butterflies of the grass clearing were replaced with strange insects somewhere between dragonflies and moths that hovered and slid through the air in silence. Occasionally I heard the cry of some unfamiliar creature. It wasn't like any place I knew on Earth.

I walked for fifteen minutes, praying all the while that I didn't run into any large, hostile animals or monsters. Relief set in when an array of ample sunlight appeared in the distance ahead. Based on the increased volume of sound, I could tell there was a river nearby. My thirst spurred my legs into a quicker pace.

At the edge of the thick forest, there was a ten-foot buffer of grass, followed by the reflective silver of a water surface.

"W-waddah," I moaned piteously, crossing the final distance

to the riverside and its soft undergrass. "Whoa," I grunted as I stared into the water at point-blank range on hands and knees.

It was beautiful. The river was not very wide, but the water in its gentle curve was stunningly clear. It was absolutely colorless but for a drop of blue, the white sand of the riverbed clearly visible through the pure mountain water.

Given that, just a few seconds ago, I had been leaving room for the faint possibility that this was the real world, it might be dangerous to drink unfiltered natural water. But I could not resist the allure of a stream that looked like melted crystal in its pristine beauty. I gasped at the cutting chill of the water against my hand, but it did not stop me from scooping it up to my mouth.

It was practically nectar. The taste of such sweet, fresh, pure water made me never want to spend money on a bottle of mineral water at the store again. I scooped up the water over and over with both hands, until eventually I just lowered my mouth to drink directly from the stream.

With the intoxication of that life-water running through my veins, I finally eliminated from my mind the possibility that this was a standard full-dive VR world.

No existing unit, such as the AmuSphere, could model liquid perfectly. Polygons were just a set of coordinates connected by a plane and not well suited to depict the complex, random shifting of water. Yet the water that rippled and spilled over my hands was utterly natural in appearance.

It was tempting to dispel the notion that this was taking place in the real world, too. I sat up at last and surveyed the area. The beautiful stream; the fantastical forest that continued past the far bank; the odd, colorful fauna of the woods—none of it seemed to match up with a real-world location. After all, wasn't it true that the more untouched by human hands a place was, the more severe it was likely to be? How could I be walking around in this light clothing and not have been bitten by any bugs yet?

Thinking about that last question seemed likely to prompt the STL into summoning a cloud of poisonous insects, so I pushed it from my mind and got to my feet. I rounded down the likelihood of a real-world location to just 1 percent and looked around.

The river flowed from north to south, curving gently. Both ends visible from here vanished among the massive trees. But based on the state and temperature of the water, I felt certain that I had to be close to the source. I'd be more likely to find civilization following the river south.

I had just set off downriver, thinking it would be a much easier trip with a boat to ride, when the breeze shifted slightly, bringing a strange sound to my ears.

It was the sound of something large and tough being struck by something even harder. Not just once. It was happening at a steady pace of about once every four seconds.

It couldn't be an animal or a natural occurrence. It was a virtual certainty that a human was producing this noise. I imagined someone chopping down a tree, perhaps. Briefly, I wondered if it would be dangerous to approach them, then smirked at myself. This wasn't a kill-and-steal PvP MMORPG. My best option was clearly to make contact and gain information.

I turned around and headed back upstream in the direction of the sound.

Suddenly, I experienced a brief, strange vision.

A glittering river on the right. A deep forest on the left. Straight ahead, a green path advancing with no end in sight.

Three children walked down it abreast. A boy with black hair, another boy with flaxen blond hair, and between them, a girl wearing a straw hat with flowing golden locks. They threw off dazzling light from the setting summer sun.

Is this…a memory?

Long-distant days that would never return. Days he'd believed would continue forever, that he swore to protect and cherish, but that vanished as easily as ice left in the open sun…

Those nostalgic, heady days.

Sword Ar

The 4th Episode
Project "Alicization"

t Online

2

By the time I blinked again, the vision was gone, evaporating as quickly as it had come.

What *was* that? The image was gone, but the sensation of nostalgia it brought stayed with me, clutching my heart agonizingly tightly.

A memory of youth…In the vision of the three children walking along the riverside, I was absolutely certain that the boy with black hair on the right was…*me*.

But that was impossible. There were no forests this thick or rivers this pristine in Kawagoe, Saitama Prefecture, where I grew up. And I'd certainly never been friends with a blond boy and girl. Plus, all three of us in the image were wearing the same rustic fantasy clothes.

If this was the STL, did that mean the vision was a memory of my extended dive test last weekend? That seemed likely, but even with the fluctlight acceleration of the STL, I would have experienced only ten days at most. And the aching nostalgia that throbbed in my heart could not be caused by such a brief amount of time.

Things were truly turning in a bizarre direction. I glanced down into the nearby river, wondering if I was really myself, but the stream was too warped to recognize the finer features in its reflection.

I decided to forget about the prickling aftereffect and focused on that steady, repeating sound. This, too, had a familiar feel to it, but I still didn't know whether it was the sound of a woodcutter's ax. I shook my head to clear my mind and headed back upstream toward the noise.

By the time the steady pace of walking allowed me to enjoy the beauty of the scenery again, I noticed my path was taking me farther to the left. It seemed the source of the noise was not at the riverside but deeper in the forest.

As I walked, I counted on my fingers and realized that, oddly, the sound was not constant. After exactly fifty times, it would stop for three minutes or so, then resume for another fifty on the dot. It had to be coming from a human source.

I would walk with a vague sense of direction during each three-minute interval, then recalibrate when the sound returned. Soon I had left the water behind and ventured back among the trees. Silently I passed by the now-familiar dragonflies, blue lizards, and enormous mushrooms.

"…Forty-nine…fifty," I counted, just as it became noticeably brighter among the trees ahead. It could be the forest's exit or even a village. I quickened my pace toward the light.

Climbing a set of rising roots like stairs so I could peer around an ancient trunk without exposing myself, I was met with a sight that was nothing short of breathtaking.

It wasn't the end of the forest or a human settlement. But the scope of the sight was so jaw-dropping that I didn't have time to feel disappointed.

It was a circular clearing in the middle of the forest, far larger than the little patch of grass where I'd awoken—about a hundred feet across, I guessed. The ground was covered in that pale-green moss, but unlike what I'd been walking over all this time, there were no ferns, vines, or low bushes at all.

Just one thing, standing in the middle of the clearing, commanded my gaze:

What an enormous tree!

The trunk of the tree couldn't have been less than thirteen feet across. Unlike the gnarled, broad-leaved trees of the forest, this was a conifer that stood absolutely straight. The bark was so dark it was nearly black, and numerous layers of branches spread out far, far above. It reminded me of the ancient Jōmon Sugi tree on Yakushima or the giant redwoods of western America, but the sheer presence of this tree gave it an unnatural air. It towered imperiously over everything.

I slowly lowered my gaze from the impenetrable branches above to the roots of the tree. A lattice of massive roots thick as anacondas stretched in all directions, right up to the boundary of the rest of the forest. It seemed to me that the sheer life this tree sucked up was the reason for the clearing—nothing but moss could grow where the roots devoured all nutrients.

It was a bit nerve-racking to step into the garden of an emperor like this, but I couldn't resist the urge to touch such a tremendous thing. I made my way forward, tripping here and there over the mossy roots, because I couldn't stop gazing up.

Nearly every breath out of my mouth was a gasp. I had lost all caution for my surroundings, so enchanted was I at the sight. So, naturally, I didn't notice until it was far too late.

"_____?!"

When I dropped my gaze to ground level, I met the eyes of someone peering around the trunk. My breath caught in my throat, and I twitched, stumbled, and crouched. My hand started to reach over my back, but there was no sword there.

Fortunately, the first human I had seen in this world was not hostile or even cautious. He just stared at me, mystified.

He looked to be my age—about seventeen or eighteen. His ash-brown hair had just a hint of waviness. Like me, he wore a simple tunic and trousers. He was sitting on a root like a bench, holding something round in his right hand.

The odd part was his appearance. His skin was cream-colored, but he appeared neither fully Western nor Eastern. His features were fine and gentle, and his eyes looked dark green.

The moment I saw his face, something deep in my head itched again…deep in my soul. But the instant I tried to seize the feeling, it vanished. I pushed aside that odd hesitation and decided to speak, to make it clear I had no hostile intentions. But before I could do so, I needed to know what *language* to say it in. I stood there for so long with my mouth agape that the other boy spoke first.

"Who are you? Where did you come from?"

There was something just barely alien about his accent, but it was otherwise perfect Japanese.

I was just as stunned as when I'd first seen the pitch-black tree. For whatever reason, I hadn't expected to hear my mother tongue in this clearly foreign world. There was something unreal about hearing familiar words come from the mouth of an exotic, Middle-Ages-European boy, as if I were watching a dubbed version of a foreign film.

But I couldn't stand there dumbfounded. It was time to think. My brain had been getting rusty recently, and I needed to get it percolating.

If this was the STL's Underworld, that meant this boy was most likely either (1) another test player in a dive, with memories from the real world like me, (2) a test player, but with memory limitations that made him just another resident of this world, or (3) an NPC being run by the program itself.

The first possibility would make things easy. I'd just explain the abnormality happening to me, and he could tell me how to log out.

But the second or third possibilities would not be so simple. If I started listing off a bunch of incomprehensible jargon about Soul Translator anomalies and log-out methods to a human or NPC who was functioning as a resident of the Underworld, it would only put them on edge and make collecting information more difficult.

So I decided I needed to open a conversation using only safe terminology, until I could ascertain just who or what this boy was. I wiped my sweaty palms on my pants and tried to put on a reassuring smile.

"Umm...my name is..."

I paused. I wondered whether the names of people in this world were Japanese or European. I prayed that my own name could fit either case.

"...Kirito. I was coming here from that direction and wound up lost," I said, pointing to what I guessed was south. The boy's eyes bulged. He set down the round object in his hand and got to his feet, pointing in the same direction.

"You mean...from south of the forest? Did you come from Zakkaria?"

"Er, n-no," I said, fighting the instinct to let panic grip my features. "I, um...actually, I don't know where I came from, really... I just kind of woke up from being passed out in the forest..."

I was hoping for a response like, *Oh, an STL error? Hang on, I'll contact the operator,* but the boy merely gave me the same shocked response. He stared closely at me and said, "Wait...you don't know where you came from? Not even...what town you live in...?"

"Er, right...I don't know. All I remember is my name..."

"...I can't believe it...I've heard the stories about 'Vecta's lost children' but never thought I'd actually see one in person."

"V-Vecta's lost children...?"

"Don't they call them that, wherever you're from? When someone disappears one day or appears in the forest or fields all of a sudden, that's what the villagers call them. The God of Darkness, Vecta, kidnaps people as a prank, stealing their memories and placing them in a far-off land. In my village, an old lady vanished years and years ago, they say."

"Ohhh...Then maybe that's what I am..."

On the inside, I found this ominous. It no longer seemed likely that this boy was just a tester engaging in a bit of role-playing. Sensing that some walls might be closing in around me, I decided to test out a more direct tactic.

"Anyway…I'm in a bit of a bind, so I'd *like to leave*. But I don't know how…"

Silently, I was begging for him to pick up my hint, but the boy only looked at me with sympathy and said, "Yes, the forest is very deep. If you don't know the way, you're bound to get lost. But don't worry—there's a path out of here to the north."

"Er, no, I mean…"

I threw caution to the wind.

"…I want to log out."

My Hail Mary attempt was met by a curious tilt of the head. "L-log? What about a log? What did you say?"

That settled it.

Whether tester or NPC, he was a pure resident of the realm with no concept of a "virtual reality." I tried not to let the disappointment show as I hastened to clarify. "S-sorry, I think I slipped into my local slang for a moment. Um, what I meant to say was…I want to find a place I can stay in a nearby town or village."

I thought it was a very weak excuse, but if anything, the boy was impressed.

"Ohh…I've never heard those words before. And that black hair is uncommon in these parts…Perhaps you were born in the south."

"M-maybe you're right," I said with a stiff smile. He smiled back, all innocence, then crinkled his eyebrows with worry.

"Hmm, a place to stay. My village is just to the north, but we never get any travelers, so there's no inn. But…if I explain the situation, maybe Sister Azalia at the church can take you in."

"Oh…I see. That's good," I said with all honesty. If there was a village, a Rath staffer might be in a dive there or monitoring it from the outside. "In that case, I'll go to the village. Just north of here, you said?"

I glanced ahead and saw that in the opposite direction of the way I'd come, there was indeed a narrow trail. No sooner had

I started walking than the boy held out a hand to catch my attention.

"Oh, w-wait. There are guards in the village, so it might be difficult to explain the situation if you show up alone. I'll go with you and tell them what's going on."

"Thanks, that'll be a big help," I said. Inwardly, I was certain he *wasn't* just an NPC. His conversational skills were too fluid for him to be a low-level program with preset answers to general questions, and an NPC wouldn't elect to be so active in my affairs, either.

I didn't know whether I was diving from the Rath lab in Roppongi or their company headquarters at its undisclosed location in the Tokyo Bay area, but I could tell that whoever owned the fluctlight controlling this boy had a very helpful personality. Once I had safely escaped this test, I owed him some thanks.

Meanwhile, the boy's face clouded again. "Oh…but I can't right now…There's still work to be done…"

"Work?"

"Yes. I'm on my lunch break."

I glanced down at the bundle of cloth at the boy's feet, through which peeked two round rolls of bread. That was what I'd seen him holding at first. The only other object was a leather water pouch—a very meager excuse for a lunch.

"Oh, I didn't realize I was interrupting your meal," I said, but he only grinned back.

"If you can wait until I'm done working, I'll go to the church with you to ask Sister Azalia if she'll let you stay there. That'll be four hours from now, though."

I wanted to go to the boy's village as soon as possible and find someone who could explain the situation, but more important, I didn't want to be on thin ice with a bunch of conversations. Four hours was a long time, but with the STL's fluctlight acceleration, it was only an hour and change in real time.

And for some reason I didn't understand, I found that I wanted to talk more with the helpful young man. I told him, "It's fine, I can wait. I appreciate the help."

His smile grew a bit wider, and he replied, "I see. In that case, you can sit anywhere you like. Oh...I didn't give you my name yet, did I?"

He held out his right hand. "I'm Eugeo. Nice to meet you, Mr. Kirito."

His grip was much firmer than his skinny build would suggest. I rolled the name around in my head. I didn't recall hearing it before, and it didn't sound like it belonged to any language in particular, but the word was familiar on my tongue for some reason.

The boy named Eugeo let go and sat back down on the tree root, took the rolls out of the cloth, and handed one to me.

"Oh, I'm fine," I said, waving my hand, but he didn't withdraw the offer.

"Aren't you hungry, too, Mr. Kirito? You haven't eaten anything, I bet."

As soon as he said that, a pang of hunger hit my brain, and I unconsciously clutched my stomach. The river water was delicious, but it didn't fill the belly like food did.

"True, but..."

I hesitated again, and this time he pushed the roll into my hands. Eugeo grinned and shrugged.

"It's fine. I know it's ironic to say this after I just gave you one, but I'm not really a fan of them."

"In that case...thank you. As a matter of fact, I'm about to pass out from hunger."

Eugeo laughed and said that was what he figured. I sat down on the root across from him and added, "Plus, you can just call me Kirito."

"Really? Well, I'm just Eugeo, too, then...Oh, hang on," he noted, holding up a hand to stop me from taking a bite of the bread.

"...?"

"Well, that bread's only good point is how long it lasts, but it never hurts to be sure."

Eugeo put his left hand above the piece of bread he held in the other. With his index and middle fingers, he traced a curvy figure in the air that was like a combination of an *S* and a *C*.

To my astonishment, he tapped the roll, and with a strange sound like vibrating metal, a glowing, translucent light-purple rectangle appeared. It was about six inches wide and three inches tall. From a distance, I could make out the familiar letters of the alphabet and Arabic numerals. It was a status window.

With my mouth wide open, I told myself, *That settles it. This isn't real life or a true alternate world. It's virtual reality.*

That confirmation brought a wave of relief to my mind, and my body suddenly felt lighter. I had been 99 percent certain before, but that last little bit of blank uncertainty had been weighing on me, I realized now.

Of course, the circumstances of my dive were still unknown, but with the reassurance that I was within the familiar embrace of a virtual world came a bit of comfort and confidence. I held out two left fingers to call up my own window.

I copied the symbol and tapped the bread. A purple window appeared with a bell chime. I leaned in for a closer look.

The contents were very simple: just a single line that said *Durability: 7.* It was clearly the life span of the bread. When that fell to zero, what exactly would happen to it, though?

Eugeo asked, "Kirito, you're not going to tell me it's your first time seeing the sacred art of a Stacia Window, are you?"

I looked up and saw him staring at me suspiciously, holding his bread. I tried to put on a reassuring smile and brushed away the window, which vanished in a little spray of light. It was a relief that I'd demonstrated some familiarity.

Fortunately, Eugeo seemed satisfied with that. "There's plenty of life left, so no need to gobble it down. There wouldn't be nearly as much left if it were summer, though."

I guessed that the "life" he mentioned was the durability of the item. "Stacia Window" was the name for the status window. Based on how he'd described the act of calling up the window as a "sacred art," Eugeo understood this not within the context of a computer system but as a religious or magical phenomenon.

There was a lot still to process, but I set that aside for the more pressing concern of my hunger.

"Okay, here we go."

I opened my mouth wide and bit down. The toughness of the bread was astonishing, but I couldn't just spit it out; I had to keep chewing. The sensation was more real than any virtual food I'd ever tasted, which I marveled at even as my teeth felt ready to loosen in their sockets.

It was similar to the whole-wheat bread that Suguha liked to buy, but harder and firmer. The effort necessary to chew it was a bit much, but there was a rustic flavor to it, and I was hungry enough to keep my jaw moving. If I just had some butter and a slice of cheese—even having it freshly baked would be a considerable improvement, I thought, rather rudely for one who was getting a free meal. I glanced over and saw Eugeo smirking as he himself struggled to chew.

"It's not very good, is it?" he said.

I shook my head. "N-no, I didn't say that."

"Don't try to hide it. I buy some from the baker as I leave every morning, but it's so early that the only bread left is from the day before. And I don't have time to go back to the village for lunch, so..."

"Ohh...Couldn't you just bring lunch from home...?" I wondered idly. Eugeo looked down, bread still in his hand. I winced, realizing it was none of my business, but fortunately, he looked back up and smiled.

"A long time ago...there was someone to bring lunch fresh from the village. Not anymore..."

His green eyes wavered, brimming with the deep sadness of loss, and I was so absorbed in it that I forgot this whole world was a creation.

"What happened to them…?"

Eugeo looked up at the branches far, far above in silence. Eventually, he began to tell the story.

"…She was my childhood friend. A girl my age…When we were little, we played together from sunup to sundown. Even after receiving our Callings, she brought me lunch every day. But then, six years ago…in my eleventh summer, an Integrity Knight came to the village…and took her away to the central city…"

Integrity Knight. Central city.

The terms were unfamiliar, but the context of his statement suggested an agent for maintaining order and the capital of this virtual world. I held my silence, urging him on.

"It was…my fault. On a day of rest, the two of us went spelunking in the northern cave…and we got lost on the way back and wound up leaving through the other side of the End Mountains. You know what the Taboo Index says—the land of darkness that we cannot set foot in. I didn't venture out of the cave, but she tripped, and her hand landed on the ground of the other side… And just for doing that, an Integrity Knight came to the village, tied her up in chains in front of everyone…"

The half-eaten bread crumbled in Eugeo's hand.

"…I tried to save her. I didn't care if he arrested me, too. I was going to attack him with the ax…but my hands and feet wouldn't move. All I could do was stand there and watch as she was taken away…"

Eugeo continued to stare at the sky, his face devoid of emotion. Eventually, his lips curled into a self-deprecating sneer. He tossed the smooshed bread into his mouth and chewed it viciously as he lowered his face.

I didn't know how to respond. I took my own bite of bread and chewed it as best I could as I considered the information.

The existence of status windows meant this was a virtual world created with modern technology, and that this had to be a test of some kind. But if that was the case, why was this story event occurring? I swallowed my bread and asked, "Do you know... what happened to her...?"

Eugeo didn't look up. He shook his head weakly. "The Integrity Knight said she would be questioned and sentenced...but I have no idea what sentence she was given. I tried asking her father, Elder Gasfut, once...and he told me to assume that she was dead. But I still have faith, Kirito. I know she's alive."

He paused.

"Alice is alive, somewhere in the city..."

I sucked in a sharp breath as soon as I heard that name.

Again, an odd sensation raced through my brain. Panic. Desolation. And most of all, a soul-shaking nostalgia...

It was an illusion. I told myself that and waited for the shock to pass. I had no personal connection to this Alice, Eugeo's old friend. My mind must have reacted to the generic name, that was all. In fact, hadn't Asuna just been talking about it at Dicey Café yesterday? Rath, the developers of the STL, the Underworld virtual realm—they were all taken from *Alice's Adventures in Wonderland*.

The coincidence of the names repeating was startling but probably meaningless. More important was another piece of information contained in Eugeo's story.

He said he was eleven years old as of six years ago. Which meant he was seventeen now, and as far as I could tell, he had full memory of all that time—about the same length of time that I'd been alive.

But that was impossible. If the FLA's factor of time was three, it would take nearly six years of real time to simulate seventeen years' worth of time for this world. But as far as I knew, it had been only three months since the STL's test unit was set up.

How should I take this information?

If this was not the STL but some other, unknown full-dive machine, then it had been functioning for seventeen years. Or perhaps the time factor of three for the FLA was a lie, and they could run it over thirty times the speed of normal time. Neither case was believable in the least.

Anxiety and curiosity welled up within me in equal measure. Part of me wanted to log out at once and ask a human being what had happened, while another part of me wanted to stay on the inside and track down the answers to my doubts directly.

I swallowed the last bit of bread and hesitantly asked, "Then... why don't you go search for her? In this central city."

As soon as I said the words, I realized I had made a mistake. The suggestion was too far outside of Eugeo's regular expectations. The flaxen-haired boy stared at me for several seconds without reaction, then whispered incredulously, "Rulid Village is at the very northern end of the Norlangarth Empire. To get to Centoria at the very southern end of the empire, it would take an entire week with the fleetest of horses. I mean, it takes two days just to walk to Zakkaria, the nearest town. You couldn't even get there in a day if you left at sunrise on a day of rest."

"Then if you prepared for a proper journey..."

"Listen, Kirito. You're about my age—didn't you get a Calling where you grew up? You know I can't just abandon my Calling and go on a journey."

"...Oh, g-good point," I said, scratching my head. I watched Eugeo's reaction carefully.

The boy was clearly not just a regular old NPC. His wealth of expression and natural conversation skills were absolutely human in nature.

But at the same time, his actions appeared to be bound by some limiting force far more effective and absolute than the laws of the real world. Just like a VRMMO NPC, forbidden to act outside his approved boundaries.

Eugeo claimed he wasn't arrested because he didn't venture into this area defined by what he called the "Taboo Index." So that was the absolute standard he had to follow—probably hard-coded through his fluctlight. I didn't know what Eugeo's

Calling (his job) was, but it was hard to believe that it could be more important than the life or death of the girl he grew up with.

Deciding to get to the bottom of this, I chose my words carefully as Eugeo put the waterskin to his mouth.

"So in your village, are there others besides Alice who broke the Taboo…Index and got taken to the city?"

His eyes widened again. He wiped his mouth and shook his head vigorously. "Oh, no. In three hundred years of Rulid history, the only time an Integrity Knight has ever come was that one time, six years ago. According to Old Man Garitta."

He tossed me the water. I caught it, thanked him, and pulled out the stopper, which looked like a cork. The water wasn't cold, but there was a pleasant aroma to it, something like a mix of lemon and herbs. I took three mouthfuls and handed it back to Eugeo.

While I wiped my mouth in feigned self-control, on the inside another storm of shock buffeted me.

Three hundred years?!

If that wasn't just a piece of background writing but indicated three whole centuries of fully simulated time, then the fluctlight acceleration factor would have to be hundreds…over a thousand, even. If that was how quickly they had accelerated my personal time when I went on that recent continual-dive test, how long had I actually been inside the machine? I felt a belated chill crawl across my forearms, and I was too preoccupied to even marvel at how real it felt.

The more information I gleaned, the deeper the mysteries got. Was Eugeo a human being or a program? Why was this world built?

To learn more, I'd have to go to Eugeo's home of Rulid and contact other people. Hopefully I would run into someone from Rath who could fill me in…

I managed to put on something resembling a smile and said, "Thanks for the bread. And sorry about taking half your lunch."

"No, don't worry. I'm sick of that stuff anyway," he said with a much more natural smile, and quickly folded up the cloth. "Sorry about forcing you to wait. I've just got to finish my afternoon work first."

Eugeo stood up easily in preparation for his duty. I asked him, "By the way, what is your job…I mean, your Calling?"

"Oh, right…You can't see it from over there." He smiled and beckoned to me. I got up, curious, and followed him around to the other side of the tree trunk.

Once again, my mouth fell open as I registered a different kind of shock.

Carved into the midnight-black trunk of the enormous cedar tree was a cut about 20 percent deep—nearly three feet. The inside of the trunk was as black as charcoal, too, and there was a metallic gleam among the dense growth rings.

Then I noticed that there was an ax standing against the tree, just below the cut. The blade was simple, clearly not designed for battle, but it was striking how both the large head and long handle were made of the same ash-white material. It looked kind of like stainless steel with a matte finish. As I stared at its strange, shining surface, it dawned on me that the entire ax was carved down from a single mass of whatever its material was.

The handle was wrapped with shining black leather, which Eugeo grabbed with one hand, lifting it onto his shoulder. He walked over to the left edge of the five-foot-wide cut, spread his legs and lowered his stance, then squeezed the ax with both hands.

His slender body tensed and spun, the ax thrust backward, and after a momentary pause, it shot through the air. The heavy-looking head landed firmly in the center of the cut with a dry *krakk!* It was indeed the very sound I had followed to this place. My instinct that it had come from a woodcutter was correct.

Eugeo continued his chopping with mechanical precision and speed while I watched his smooth form in total wonder. Two seconds to pull back, one second to tense, one second to swing. The whole motion was so smooth and automatic that it made me wonder if this world had sword skills, too.

He made fifty chops at four seconds each in exactly two hundred seconds, then slowly pulled the ax out after the last one and heaved a deep breath. He stood the ax against the trunk again and sat down heavily on a nearby root. Based on the pace of his breathing and the beads of sweat glistening on his forehead, the swings were much more laborious than I had thought.

I waited for Eugeo's breathing to slow down then asked, "So your job...I mean, your Calling is a woodcutter? You cut down trees in this forest?"

Eugeo pulled a handkerchief out of his pocket to wipe his face, which bore a dubious expression. Eventually he answered, "Well, I guess you could say it like that. But in the seven years since I got this Calling, I haven't actually *cut down* a single tree."

"What?"

"This enormous tree is called the Gigas Cedar in the sacred tongue. But most of the villagers just call it the devil tree."

...Sacred tongue? Giga...Seeder?

A smile of a certain kind of understanding appeared on Eugeo's face in response to my confusion. He pointed up at the branches far, far above.

"The reason they call it that is because the tree sucks up all of Terraria's blessings from the land around it. That's why only moss grows beneath the reach of its branches, and all the trees where its shadow falls do not grow very tall."

I didn't know what Terraria was, but the first impression I got when I saw the giant tree and its clearing was largely correct. I nodded, prompting him to continue.

"The villagers want to clear the forest and plant new fields. But as long as this tree stands, no good barley will grow. So we want to cut it down, but, as the name suggests, the demon tree's trunk is wickedly tough. A single swing from a normal iron ax will chip the blade and ruin it. So they saved up a bunch of money to get this Dragonbone Ax carved from ancient dragon bone shipped from the center capital, and they designated a dedicated 'carver' to strike at the tree every day. That's me," he said without fanfare.

I looked back and forth between him and the cut, which was about a quarter of the way through the giant tree.

"So…you've been chopping away at this tree for seven whole years? And that's all you've managed in that time?"

Now it was Eugeo's turn to be stunned. He shook his head in disbelief. "Oh, hardly. If you could get this far in just seven years, I might feel a little better about it. I'm the seventh-generation carver. The carvers have come here to work every day for three hundred years, since the founding of Rulid. By the time I'm an old man and I have to hand the ax to the eighth carver, I might have gotten…"

He held his hands less than a foot apart. "This far."

All I could do was let out a long, whistling breath.

In fantasy-themed MMOs, it was a given that production classes like craftsmen or miners were doomed to a whole lot of tedious repetition, but spending an entire lifetime to not even cut down a single tree was taking it to a new extreme. Human hands created this world, so someone must have placed this tree here for a reason, but I couldn't begin to guess what it would be.

It still left a crawling sensation down my back.

Eugeo's three-minute break ended, and he stood up again and reached for the ax. On impulse, I asked, "Hey, Eugeo…mind if I try that?"

"What?"

"I mean, you gave me half your lunch. Doesn't it make sense for me to do half the work?"

Eugeo was stunned, as if no one had ever offered to help him at his work before in his life—which could very well be the case. Eventually, he offered a hesitant, "Well…there's no rule that you can't get someone's help with your Calling…but you'd be surprised how hard it is. When I was just starting out, I could barely land a hit."

"Never know until you try, right?"

I grinned, then thrust out my hand. Eugeo offered the handle of the Dragonbone Ax, looking reluctant. I grabbed it.

Despite being made of bone, the ax was tremendously heavy. I added a second hand to the grip and shook a bit as I tested my balance.

I'd never used an ax as my main weapon in either *SAO* or *ALO*, but I figured I would at least be good enough with it to hit a stationary target. I stood at the left end of the cut and tried to mimic Eugeo's form, spreading my feet and lowering my hips.

Eugeo stood at a safe distance, watching me with equal parts consternation and entertainment. I lifted the ax up to my shoulder, gritted my teeth, summoned all the strength I had, and swung for the cut in the trunk of the "Giga Seeder."

The ax head cracked on a spot about two inches away from the center of the slice. Orange sparks flew, and a terrific shock ran through my hands. I dropped the ax and cradled my numb wrists between my knees, groaning.

"Owww…"

Eugeo laughed heartily at the embarrassing spectacle I'd put on. I glared at him, and he waved in apology but continued laughing.

"…You don't have to laugh *that* hard…"

"Ha-ha-ha…No, no, I'm sorry. You put way too much tension into your shoulders and hips, Kirito. You've got to relax your whole body…Hmm, how to explain it…"

He awkwardly pantomimed swinging an ax, and I belatedly recognized my mistake. It was unlikely that this world was simulating muscle tension based on strict physical laws. It was a realistic dream the STL created, so the most important factor had to be the strength of the imagination.

The feeling was coming back to my hands, so I picked up the ax lying at my feet.

"Just wait, I'll hit it right on the mark this time…"

I held up the ax again, this time using as little muscle tension as possible. I envisioned all the movement of my body and slowly pulled back the tool. Imagining the motion of the Horizontal slashing sword skill I used so often in *SAO*, I shifted my weight forward, adding the energy to the rotation of my hips and shoulders down to the wrists and ax head, slamming it into the tree…

This time it missed the cut in the tree entirely and twanged off the tough bark. I didn't get the same numbing jolt in my wrists, but I'd been so focused on my own movement that I neglected to aim properly. I figured that Eugeo would laugh again, but this time he offered honest feedback.

"Whoa…that was pretty good, Kirito. But your problem was that you were looking at the ax. You've got to keep your eyes focused right on the center of the cut. Try it again, while you've got the hang of it!"

"O-okay."

My next attempt was also weak. But I kept trying, following Eugeo's advice, and somewhere a few dozen swings later, the ax finally struck true, producing that clear ring and sending a tiny little shard of black flying.

At that point, I switched with Eugeo and watched him execute fifty perfect strikes. Then he handed it off, and I attempted another fifty wheezing swings.

After a number of turns back and forth, I realized the sun was going down, and there was an orange tint to the light trickling into the forest clearing. I took the last swig of water from the large waterskin, and Eugeo set down the ax.

"There…that makes a thousand."

"We've already done that many?"

"Yep. I did five hundred; you did five hundred. My Calling is to strike the Gigas Cedar two thousand times a day, over the morning and afternoon."

"Two thousand…"

I stared at the large crevice cut into the massive black tree. It didn't look like any damage had been done to it at all since we'd started. What a thankless job.

Meanwhile, Eugeo said happily, "You've got talent for this,

Kirito. There were two or three good hits in that last set of fifty. And it made my job a whole lot easier today."

"I dunno…if you were doing it all yourself, you'd have been done sooner. I feel bad; I was hoping to help out, but I only held you back," I apologized, but Eugeo just laughed it off.

"I told you, I can't cut down this tree for as long as I live. And after all, it will regrow half of the depth that we carve out over the course of the night…Oh hey, I've got something to show you. You're not really supposed to look at it, though."

He approached the tree and held up his left hand, making the usual sign with his two fingers, then tapped the black bark.

I raced over to get a closer look, realizing that the tree itself must have a durability rating. The status—pardon me, Stacia Window—appeared with a chime, and we peered in at it.

"Ugh," I groaned. The number on the window was vast: over 232,000.

"Hmm. That's only about fifty lower than what it said when I checked last month," Eugeo noted, similarly disappointed. "So you see, Kirito…I could swing this ax for an entire year, and it would only reduce the life of the Gigas Cedar by about six hundred. I'll be lucky if the total is under 200,000 by the time I retire. Do you get it now? A little bit less progress over half a day doesn't make the least bit of difference. This isn't any ordinary tree; it's the giant god of cedars."

Suddenly, something clicked, and I understood the source of the name. It was a mix of Latin and English. The split wasn't after Giga, it was Gigas—there were two *S* sounds in a row. Gigas Cedar, the giant cedar.

Meaning that this boy spoke Japanese as his mother language, while English and other languages were treated as the "sacred tongue," like spells. If that was the case, he probably didn't even recognize that he was speaking Japanese. It was Underworldian. Or…Norlangarthian? But wait, when he talked about the bread, he had used the word *pan*, the Japanese word for it. But *pan* didn't originate from English…Wasn't it from Portuguese? Spanish?

My mind tumbled through a cavalcade of distractions, while Eugeo tidied up the things he'd brought.

"Thanks for waiting, Kirito. Let's go to the village."

As we walked to his village, Dragonbone Ax slung over his shoulder and empty waterskin hanging from his hand, Eugeo cheerfully told me about a variety of topics. His predecessor was an old man named Garitta, who was apparently quite a master woodcutter. The other children his age thought Eugeo's Calling was an easy one, an opinion he resented. I muttered and grunted to show that I was listening throughout his stories, but my mind was racing as it considered just one topic.

For what purpose was this world envisioned and put into practical use?

They didn't need to test the pneumonic visual system the STL used. It was already perfectly functional. I'd already experienced—to an unpleasant degree—just how indistinguishable from real life this world was.

And yet, the world had been internally simulated for at least three hundred years, and terrifyingly enough, extrapolating from the Gigas Cedar's durability and Eugeo's workflow, it was slated to continue running for at least a thousand more.

I didn't know what the upper limit of the fluctlight acceleration factor was, but a person who dove into this place with their memories blocked was at risk of spending an entire lifetime in the machine. True, there was no danger to the physical body, and if the memories were all blocked at the end of the dive, it would all be nothing but a "very long dream" to the user—but what happened to the soul, the fluctlight that experienced that dream? Was there a lifespan to the photon field that made up the human consciousness?

Clearly, what they were doing with this world was impractical, implausible, impossible.

Did that mean there was a goal worth so much risk? Like Sinon had said at Dicey Café, it couldn't be something the AmuSphere could already do, like making a realistic virtual world. Something created through a nearly infinite passage of time in a virtual world that was indistinguishable from reality...

I looked up and took stock of my surroundings. The forest was trailing off just ahead, replaced by a larger amount of orange sunlight. At the side of the trail close to the exit was a single building that looked like a storage shed. Eugeo walked over to it and pulled open the door. Over his back, I could see a number of normal metal axes, a smaller hatchet, various tools like ropes and buckets, and narrow leather packages with unknown contents, crammed messily into the shed.

Eugeo stood the Dragonbone Ax against the wall among them and shut the door. He immediately started back for the trail, so I hastily asked him, "Uh, shouldn't you lock it or something? That's a really important ax, right?"

He looked surprised. "Lock? Why?"

"Er, because...it might get stolen..."

Once I said my fear aloud, I realized where I went wrong. There *were* no thieves. No doubt in that Taboo Index there was an entry that said, "Thou shalt not steal," or something along those lines.

Sure enough, Eugeo gave me the exact answer I had just been anticipating.

"That would never happen. I'm the only one who's allowed to open this shed."

I figured as much. Then another question occurred to me. "But...didn't you say there were guards in the village, Eugeo? Why would that be a profession if there are no thieves or bandits?"

"Isn't that obvious? To protect the village from the forces of darkness."

"Forces of...darkness..."

"Look, you can see up there."

He held up his hand to point just as we crossed the last line of trees.

There was a full field of barley wheat ahead. The heads, still young and green and not yet expanding, swayed in the breeze. They caught the full light of the waning sun like a sea of grass. The path continued on through the field, winding toward a hill in the far distance. Atop the tree-dotted hill, as small as specks of sand to the eye, was a number of buildings and one taller tower among them. That had to be the village of Rulid, Eugeo's home.

But what Eugeo pointed at was far beyond the village—a range of pure-white mountains faded with distance. The line of peaks continued as far as the eye could see to the left and right, like the sharp teeth of a saw.

"Those are the End Mountains. On the other side is the land of darkness, beyond Solus's light. Black clouds cover the sky, even in the daytime, and the light of the heavens was red like blood. The ground and trees were all as black as coal..."

Eugeo's voice trembled as he recalled his experiences from the distant past.

"There are accursed humanoids in the land of darkness like goblins and orcs, and even more terrifying monsters...Not to mention knights of darkness who ride black dragons. Naturally, the Integrity Knights protect the mountain range, but every once in a while, some of them sneak in through the caves, from what I understand. I've never seen it happen myself. Plus, according to the Axiom Church, every thousand years, when the light of Solus weakens, the knights of darkness cross the mountains with a horde of enemies to attack. When that happens, the Integrity Knights will lead the village men-at-arms, the sentinels from larger towns, and even the imperial army in the fight against the monsters."

Eugeo paused, looked at me skeptically, and said, "Even the youngest children in the village know this story. Did you even forget *that* when you lost your memory?"

"Uh...y-yeah. It sounds familiar to me...but some of the details are different," I said, thinking quickly. Eugeo beamed in a way that made me wonder if he even understood the concept of doubt at all.

"Oh, I see…Maybe you really did come from one of the three other empires, outside of Norlangarth."

"M-maybe I did," I agreed, and pointed toward the approaching hill to steer the conversation away from this dangerous topic. "That must be Rulid. Which one's your house, Eugeo?"

"The thing in front is the south gate, and my house is near the west gate, so you can't see it from here."

"Ahh. And the building with the tower? Is that the church with Sister…Azalia?"

"That's right."

I squinted and made out a symbol at the tip of the narrow tower, a combination of cross and circle.

"It's actually…fancier than I expected. Are they really going to let someone like me stay there?"

"Of course. Sister Azalia is a very nice person."

I wasn't entirely convinced, but if Azalia was as much a personification of selfless virtue as Eugeo, then I could probably manage safely as long as I kept the conversation on sensible ground. Then again, I was totally in the dark when it came to knowing what passed for "common sense" here.

Ideally, Sister Azalia would be one of Rath's stationed observers. But I doubted that any staff members charged with monitoring the state of their world would take on a vital role like the village elder or nun. It was more likely they'd take the role of a simple villager, which meant I had to find them. And that was assuming they had an observer in this tiny village at all.

I followed Eugeo across a mossy stone bridge spanning a narrow waterway and set foot into the village of Rulid.

3

"Here you go, a pillow and blankets. There are more in the wardrobe in the back if you're cold. Morning prayer is at six, and breakfast is at seven. I'll come to check on you, but please do wake up on your own. There's a curfew once lights are out, so be mindful of that."

I accepted both the onslaught of words and the heavy pile of wool blankets with outstretched arms.

A girl of about twelve years was standing before me as I sat on the bed. She wore a black habit with a white collar, and her light brown hair hung long down her back. Her big, busy eyes held none of the downcast obedience she'd displayed in the presence of the sister.

Her name was Selka, and she was a sister-in-training, studying sacred arts at the church. She was also charged with watching over the other boys and girls living at the church, which was probably why she bossed me around like a big sister or mother, despite being several years my junior. It was hard to keep the grin off my face.

"Umm, is there anything else you need to know?"

"No, I think I've got it. Thanks for all the help," I said. For a brief moment, Selka's expression softened, and then it was back to fussy business as usual.

"Good night, then. Do you know how to put out the lamp?"

"…Yeah. Good night, Selka."

She nodded briskly and spun to leave the room, the hem of her slightly-too-large habit swaying. Once her quiet footsteps trailed away, I let out a long sigh.

They had put me in a little-used room on the second floor of the church. The room was about a hundred square feet, with a cast-iron bed, matching desk and chair, a small bookshelf, and a wardrobe next to it. I moved the blankets and pillow off my knees and onto the bed, then put my hands behind my head and rolled back onto the sheets. The flame in the lamp overhead briefly sizzled.

"What the hell…"

Is going on? I replayed all the events that had transpired between entering the village and now.

The first thing Eugeo had done was head for the guard station right next to the gate. There was another youngster in there named Zink, who glanced at me suspiciously at first but accepted Eugeo's story that I was a "lost child of Vecta" with almost laughable ease and granted me entry to the village.

The entire time Eugeo was giving the story, my eyes were locked onto the simple sword hanging from Zink's belt, so the specific words all went in one ear and out the other. I desperately wanted to borrow the aged sword to see if my skills—technically, the virtual swordsman Kirito's skills—would still function here, but I valiantly resisted that urge.

After leaving the station, we walked down the village's main street, attracting a slightly unnerving amount of attention. Several villagers asked who I was, and Eugeo stopped to explain each time, so it took us nearly thirty minutes to get to the small village square at the center of Rulid. One old lady carrying a large basket got teary-eyed when she saw me. "You poor thing!" she exclaimed, and pulled an apple (or something close to one) out of the basket for me. I felt a bit guilty about that.

By the time we got to the church standing on the small hill

overlooking the village, the sun was almost entirely gone. Sister Azalia, a nun whose picture ought to be in the dictionary under the word *stern*, answered Eugeo's knock on the door. She looked so much like Miss Minchin from *A Little Princess* that I was certain our plan would end in disaster. But at odds with her appearance, Sister Azalia welcomed me in almost instantly and offered me dinner to boot.

Eugeo promised to meet me in the morning, and thus left me at the church. Aside from Selka, the oldest, there were six children to meet, and we shared a quiet but peaceful meal of fried fish, boiled potatoes, and vegetable soup. As I feared, the children assaulted me with questions afterward, which I hoped I answered without dropping the ball. After that, I was sent to the bath with the three boys, and after undergoing all of these many trials, I was free at last to lie here, in the bed in the guest room.

The fatigue of the day rested heavily on me; I was certain that I'd fall asleep as soon as I closed my eyes, but the waves of confusion washing over me prevented that from happening.

What does all this mean? I asked myself silently.

In conclusion, there was not a single NPC, as I would define them, in the entire village.

From Zink the guard; to the passing villagers and the old lady with the apples; to the stern but kindly Sister Azalia and apprentice, Selka; to the six orphan children who'd lost their parents. Every one of them had realistic emotions, conversations, and subtly unique body movements, just as Eugeo did. They were all real people, as far as I could tell. At the very least, they were absolutely not the automated-response characters found in every VRMMO.

But that shouldn't be possible.

There was one Soul Translator at Rath's Roppongi office and three more almost ready for operation at their headquarters. That's what Higa told me, and he was one of the developers. Even if there were a few more than that in reality, it certainly wasn't enough capacity to create an entire village of this scale.

From what I could tell on our trip through town, there were at least three hundred residents of Rulid, and they couldn't mass-produce that enormous STL test unit on that kind of scale. If you actually factored in all the other villages, towns, and that center capital they talked about, there was no way they could hire tens of thousands of testers in secret, even if they had the capital to create and run that many machines.

"Or else..."

Were Eugeo and the others not real human beings—players with limited memories? Were they actually automated programs operating in a realm far beyond common sense, to a level of unfathomable perfection...?

The term *artificial intelligence* floated through my head.

The use of AI had been advancing rapidly in recent years, mostly in PCs, car navigation systems, and appliances. They would take the form of human or animal characters that could receive spoken commands or questions and perform actions or answer questions with remarkable accuracy. In a sense, the NPCs in the VR games I played were a kind of AI, too. Mostly they existed to provide information on quests and events, but if spoken to without a particular reason, they could give natural answers to a certain shallow extent. There were even people who exhibited what they called "NPC-moé," who followed around the pretty girl NPCs to talk with them all day long.

But that did not mean those AIs had true intelligence, of course. They were just a complex set of orders—"if they say this, answer that"—and could not provide real answers to questions outside of their parameters. If that happened, nearly all NPCs would offer a confused smile and say something along the lines of, "I don't understand your question."

Had Eugeo responded in that way even once throughout the entire day?

He reacted to my every question with natural displays of surprise, hesitation, laughter, and so on, and he gave me proper answers to everything. And not just Eugeo—Sister Azalia, Selka, and even the younger children never gave me a reaction that suggested what they heard wasn't "in their databank."

As far as I knew, the highest-level artificial intelligence of that sort was one named Yui, developed to be a mental counseling program for the old *SAO* and now considered a virtual "daughter" to Asuna and me. She had monitored countless player conversations for two years, collecting a vast amount of detailed data and compiling it into a complex database. She was perhaps the best current example of the boundary between automated program and true intelligence.

But even Yui wasn't perfect. Occasionally she would react to a statement by claiming that word wasn't in her database, and she sometimes mischaracterized more complex emotional expressions, like feigned anger or acting grumpy to hide embarrassed pleasure. All it took was a brief moment in a conversation for her "AI-ness" to show itself.

Yet I saw none of that in Eugeo or Selka. If human hands programmed all the people of Rulid into boy AIs, girl AIs, elderly AIs, adult AIs...it would be an even more preposterous case of super-advanced tech than the STL itself. It was impossible to take seriously...

I paused my roiling thoughts there and sat up so I could put my feet on the floor.

Fixed onto the wall behind the head of the bed was a cast-iron oil lamp that emitted a wavering orange light and a faint burning smell. I'd never touched one in the real world, of course, but there had been a similar lamp in the place where Asuna and I stayed in Alfheim, so I did what came naturally and tapped the surface.

When no control window appeared, I realized my mistake and made the two-fingered gesture—the "sigil of Stacia." When I tapped the lamp after that, the purple window appeared as expected. But all it displayed was the durability of the lamp itself and no buttons to turn it off or on.

I felt a rush of panic when I realized that I'd dismissed Selka's offer to teach me how to put out the lamp, but that vanished when I noticed the small dial on the bottom of the lamp. I gave it a clockwise twist. The metal squeaked, and the flame narrowed until it died out, leaving a brief line of smoke. Now the room was shrouded in darkness, with the only light coming from the faint moonlight streaming through the gap in the curtains.

With that surprisingly difficult task out of the way, I turned back to the bed, placed the pillow where I liked it, and lay down again. It was a bit chilly, so I pulled Selka's thick blankets up to my shoulders and felt sleep closing in.

They're not human, and they're not AIs. So what are they?

In a corner of my mind, an answer was already forming. But it was too terrifying to put into words. If what I was thinking was even possible, then this Rath company had plunged its hands deep into the realm of God. Compared to that, reading people's souls with the STL was as harmless as prodding the key to open Pandora's box with one's fingertips.

As I fell asleep, I heard my own voice rising from the depths of my mind.

This wasn't the time to be searching left and right for an escape route. I had to go to the city. I had to find out the reason this world existed…

Clang.

Somewhere far off, I heard what sounded like a bell ringing.

No sooner had my dreaming brain processed that than something prodded my shoulder. I wriggled deeper into the blankets and groaned, "Urr, ten minutes…just five more minutes…"

"No, it's time to get up."

"Three…just three minnis…"

The prodding continued, sending a signal of confusion through the sleep clouding my brain. My sister, Suguha, wouldn't wake me up in such a timid way. She'd scream at me, pull my hair, pinch my nose, or even use the cruel nuclear option: yanking the covers off the bed.

At last I remembered I wasn't in the real world or Alfheim, and I popped my head out from under the blankets. Through parted eyelids, I saw Selka, already in her nun's habit. The apprentice sister looked at me in exasperation.

"It's already five thirty. All the children have risen and washed up. If you don't hurry, you'll be late for worship."

"…Okay, I'm getting up…"

I sat up slowly, lamenting the loss of the bed's warmth and the comfort of peaceful sleep. Just as I remembered it from last night, I was in the guest room on the second floor of the church in Rulid. Or within the Underworld created by the Soul Translator, if you preferred it that way. My odd experience would not end as a brief one-night dream, it seemed.

"So it's a dream, but it wasn't a dream."

"What was that?" Selka asked, catching the statement I hadn't meant to say out loud.

I shook my head in a mild panic. "N-nothing. I'll just change and get ready. In the chapel downstairs, right?"

"Yes. You might be our guest and a lost child of Vecta, but if you're going to sleep in the church, you must pray to Stacia. Sister Azalia always says, even a cup of water contains the goddess's blessing and must be appreciated…"

I slipped quickly out of bed before her lecture could start dragging on. I lifted the hem of the thin shirt they gave me as nightwear, and this time it was Selka who called out in a panic, "Uh, y-you only have twenty minutes, so don't be late! Make sure you wash your face at the well outside!"

She trotted off and quickly opened the door to disappear through it. That was definitely not an NPC reaction…

I took off the shirt and reached for my "starter equipment"— the blue tunic draped over the back of the chair. Out of curiosity, I lifted it to my nose but didn't smell any sweat. Surely they

weren't simulating the bacteria that produced odors. Perhaps the measure of item degradation, like when something gets filthy or starts fraying, was summarized by the durability counter they called *life*.

I opened the tunic's window just to check, and it listed the value at 44/45. It would still be good for a while yet, but the longer I stayed here, the more likely I'd need to change at some point, and that meant looking into a means to earn money.

Pretty soon I had changed back into my original clothes, and I left the room.

Down the stairs and out the back door next to the kitchen, there was a brilliant sunrise overhead. She had said it was before six o'clock, which made me wonder how the people in this world told time. I hadn't seen any clocks in the dining room or guest room.

I puzzled over that one as I walked down faded paving stones. Very soon I saw a stone well ahead. The grass around it was wet, probably from the children using it. I removed the lid and lowered the wooden bucket until it made a satisfying *kerplunk* at the bottom. When I pulled the bucket up on its rope, it was full of crystal clear water, which I transferred to the nearby basin.

It was bitingly cold, but I slapped it onto my face anyway, then scooped up another cup and drank it down, feeling the last remnants of sleep wash away. I had probably gone to sleep before nine o'clock last night, which was why it felt like I'd had a solid eight hours, despite being up so early…but that raised another question.

If this was the Underworld, then the FLA function had to be in effect. If the acceleration factor was three, that meant I had less than three actual hours of sleep, and if my vague theories from last night about a thousand-fold accelerator were right, that would mean less than thirty seconds of sleep. Could so little rest actually refresh my mind the way it felt now?

It was all incomprehensible. I had to get out of here as soon as possible to figure out the situation…and yet that whisper in my ears from last night refused to go away.

Didn't I, Kazuto Kirigaya—regardless of whether my awakening in this world was the act of an error or the intentions of someone else—have a role to fulfill here? I didn't necessarily believe in fate, but I couldn't deny that I often believed that everything held a meaning. Because if not, then what was the reason for all those lives that vanished in *SAO*…?

I splashed another douse of cold water on my face to snap me out of my thoughts. I had two courses of action here: first, to look around the village to see if there were any Rath staffers who would know how to log out. The other was to travel to this "central city" they mentioned to learn the reason that this world existed in the first place.

The former didn't seem like it would be that hard. I couldn't say anything for sure without knowing the exact FLA factor, but if there were any Rath employees among the villagers, then they couldn't possibly be logged in for years or decades at a time. In other words, if any residents were traders or travelers who left home at times, it was highly likely that they would be company observers.

As far as the latter went, I had no plan for that. Eugeo said it would take a week to get to the city by horse, which meant at least three times that by foot. I wanted to ask for a horse, but I didn't know how to get one, and I had no money for the equipment and supplies necessary for the journey. I was missing too much basic knowledge about the world; clearly, I needed someone to act as a guide. Eugeo was the best suited for that, but he had a Calling that he needed to do for the rest of his life.

Would the quickest method be to violate that Taboo Index and have a whatever-knight come and arrest me? But that would probably get me taken straight to the cells of the city, and I wasn't cut out for years of hard prison labor. Not to mention the possibility that I would be executed outright.

I ought to ask Eugeo if there are any sacred arts that unlock doors or revive the dead, I noted to myself, when the church's back door opened and Selka popped her head out. When we locked eyes, she shouted, "How long does it take to wash your face, Kirito?! Worship is about to start!"

"Oh, r-right…Sorry, I'm coming," I said, waving. I put the lid, bucket, and basin back in their original places and quickly returned to the building.

After the austere worship service and a lively breakfast, the children engaged in their chores like cleaning and laundry, and Selka went with Sister Azalia into the study to practice and learn about the sacred arts. Feeling guilty that I was getting free food and board, I left through the large front doors of the church and headed to the middle of the square right out front to wait for Eugeo.

Within a few minutes, a familiar head of flaxen yellow hair appeared through the vanishing mist of the morning. Moments later, the bells atop the church pealed a simple but beautiful melody.

"Oh…now I get it."

Eugeo looked at me in surprise as he approached. "Good morning, Kirito. What do you get now?"

"Morning, Eugeo. Well…I just now realized the bells play a different melody for each hour. So that's how the people of the village know what time it is."

"Of course. It plays each of the twelve verses of the hymn 'By the Light of Solus.' And simple chimes mark each half hour. Unfortunately, the sound doesn't carry all the way to the Gigas Cedar, so I have to estimate the time by the angle of Solus."

"I see…So there are no clocks in this world," I muttered to myself. Eugeo looked confused.

"Kloks…? What is that?"

I panicked, having not realized that even the word itself was foreign here. "Uh, a clock is…a round board with numbers on it, with metal hands that spin around to tell you what time it is…"

To my surprise, Eugeo's face lit up with delight. "Oh, yes! I read about that in a storybook once. Long, long ago, a Divine Object of Time-Telling stood in the middle of the capital. But because the people spent so much time gazing at it rather than working, the gods destroyed it with a lightning bolt. Since then, the only thing that tells humanity the time is the bells."

"Ohh…Yeah, I get that. Sometimes you can't help but keep an eye on the time toward the end of class," I said carelessly, forgetting where I was again. Fortunately, he understood my meaning this time.

"Ha-ha-ha, indeed! When I had to study at the church, I kept my ears open for the lunch bells."

He glanced away, and I followed his gaze up to the church's bell tower. Gleaming bells of all sizes hung in a circular window on every side. Yet I didn't see anyone in the tower, despite the fact that the bells had just rung.

"How…do they ring the bells?"

"You really *have* forgotten everything, haven't you?" Eugeo said, half-dismayed and half-amused. He cleared his throat. "No one rings them at all. It's the only divine object in the village. They play the hymn on their own, at the exact same times, every single day. Of course, Rulid's isn't the only one. There's another in Zakkaria, and in the other villages and towns, too…Oh, although I guess that's not the only one now…"

I lifted an eyebrow in surprise. It was quite uncharacteristic of helpful Eugeo to trail off like that. But then he clapped, intent on changing the topic.

"Well, I've got to get to work. What will you do today, Kirito?"

"Umm…"

I gave it some thought. I wanted to go searching all over the village, but snooping around by myself was likely to get me into trouble. If I needed an idea of who might be an observer, I could ask Eugeo if anyone was out of the house a lot—and if I was going to lure Eugeo into this insane plan to travel to the capital, I'd need to learn a bit more about his Calling first.

"…If you don't mind, I'd like to help out with your work again today," I offered. He beamed.

"Of course, I'd love that. I had a feeling you'd say so; look, I brought twice the bread money today just in case."

He pulled two small copper coins from his trousers and jangled them in his palm.

"Ohh, no, I feel bad. I couldn't," I protested, but Eugeo just shrugged and smiled.

"Don't worry about it. All the payment I get from the village hall each month just piles up without anything meaningful to spend it on."

Oooh, perfect, that means a good stock of money for the trip to the city, I thought wickedly. Now I just needed to find a way to cut down that enormous tree so that Eugeo's Calling would be fulfilled.

Meanwhile, Eugeo's innocent smile made my heart hurt when I thought of the tricks I was playing. He said, "Let's go," and started walking south. As I followed, I looked over my shoulder one last time to the bells that rang automatically on the hour.

It really was a strange world. Around the edges of the ultrarealistic depiction of an agrarian village were little hints of VRMMO systems. Even in the old flying Aincrad, there were bell towers that rang out automatically on the hour in all the major cities.

Sacred arts. Axiom Church. Were these just the specific names for magic spells and the world-ordering system? If that were the case, what did the "land of darkness" outside the world mean? A system at odds with the system…

While I was lost in thought, Eugeo stopped to greet a woman in an apron outside of what looked like a bakery, where he bought four of those round bread rolls. Inside the store, I could see a man smacking and kneading a wad of dough, and a large oven emitting fragrant smells.

In another hour, perhaps half, we could buy fresh-baked bread, but I suspected that the fussy nature of the "Calling" system prevented us from doing that. Eugeo had a strict time when he had to be in the forest, swinging his ax, and it was not open to debate. I had to remind myself that my plan called for him to totally upend his way of life, and that overcoming this would not be easy.

But there was always a loophole, a shortcut. Such as me, the guy who showed up out of nowhere to help him do his work.

We passed through the southern arch and headed down the road, winding through green fields toward the heavy forest along the border. Even from here, the proud form of the Gigas Cedar was visible, jutting above all.

Eugeo and I took turns desperately swinging the Dragonbone Ax, until the sun he called Solus reached the sky directly overhead.

I summoned what little strength I had left into my numb, heavy arms, slamming my five-hundredth swing into the gut of the monstrous tree. It smacked heartily true, sending out a fleck of wood the size of a sand grain—a sign that I'd managed to inflict the tiniest bit of damage on the tree's preposterous durability rating.

"Aaagh, I can't swing one more time," I wailed, tossing aside the ax and wilting down onto the moss. Eugeo offered me a canteen of something he called siral water—I didn't know what language it was supposed to be—and I greedily sucked down the sweetly sour liquid.

He looked down at me with comfortable confidence and said in the tone of an instructor, "You know, you've got good fundamentals. I think you've really come a long way in just two days."

"…But I'm still…nowhere near as good as you…" I gasped, sitting up properly and leaning back against the Gigas Cedar.

Thanks to the heavy workout lasting all morning, I felt like I had a much better grasp on my own physical status in this new world.

For one thing, the superhuman strength and agility that *SAO* swordsman Kirito was blessed with were completely absent here, though I'd already surmised this. But my physique wasn't based on the frailty of the real-world Kazuto Kirigaya, either. If the real me tried swinging this heavy ax for an hour, I'd find myself bed-ridden from muscle pain the next day.

Which meant my current stamina must have been based on the average build of a seventeen- or eighteen-year-old boy. Eugeo seemed far tougher than me, which made sense if he'd been at this for seven years already.

Fortunately, the ability to use instinct and imagination to move my avatar was at least equally sensitive, if not even greater, than in the VRMMOs I'd been playing all this time. Thanks to attempting hundreds of swings with a focus on weight and trajectory, I felt confident I'd be able to control the ax to an acceptable degree, even with its high strength requirement.

Plus, repeated practice of the same actions was a specialty of mine; I'd cut down on my sleeping hours in Aincrad to do that very thing. When it came to patient perseverance, I was at least Eugeo's equal...

No...wait. There was something important in that thought just now...

"Here, Kirito," Eugeo said, tossing me a pair of rolls and interrupting my train of thought. I awkwardly reached out and grabbed a roll in each hand.

"...? Why the serious face?"

"Uh...nothing..."

I tried desperately to catch the tail of the slippery thought before it left my mind but was left with nothing but the irritating fugue of knowing that I'd just been thinking about something very important. I had no choice but to shrug it off and assume that if it was that important, it would occur to me again later.

"Thanks for the food, Eugeo."

"Sorry it's the same thing as yesterday."

"Don't worry about it."

I opened wide and bit down. The flavor was good—but the chewiness was a bit off the scale. Eugeo shared my opinion, scowling as he worked his jaw.

For several minutes we silently chewed away at our first rolls of bread, then shared an awkward smile when we finished together. Eugeo took a mouthful of siral water and gazed into the distance.

"...I wish you could have eaten one of Alice's pies, Kirito... The crust was crispy, and the insides were packed with juicy bits...With a cup of fresh milk, you couldn't imagine anything better..."

Oddly enough, I felt the taste of that pie register on my tongue, and a flood of saliva issued forth. I bit down on the second roll to hide my surprise, then asked, "Say, Eugeo...This Alice girl studied sacred arts at the church, right? In order to take over Sister Azalia's position one day."

"That's right. She was said to be the first true genius since the founding of the village. From the age of ten, she could use all kinds of arts," he answered proudly.

"Then...what about Selka, the girl studying at the church now?"

"Ah...After the Integrity Knight took Alice away, Sister Azalia was very depressed. She said she'd never take another apprentice, but Elder Gasfut convinced her that the teaching must go on, and so two years ago, she finally took in Selka as her new apprentice. She's Alice's little sister."

"Her sister...Ohh..."

That was funny, because if anything, Selka seemed like the bossy-older-sister type. If she was that girl's sister, then Alice must've been quite the busybody getting into everyone's business. She would have made a great team with Eugeo.

I glanced over at him and saw that he was pensive.

"...We're five years apart, so in fact, I haven't spent much time with Selka. On the occasions when I would visit Alice's home, Selka was usually hiding shyly behind her mother or grandmother...Her father, Gasfut; the other adults; and even Sister Azalia are all hoping that as Alice's sister, Selka will display the same talent for the sacred arts...but..."

"But Selka isn't quite the genius her sister was?" I asked rather bluntly. Eugeo grimaced a bit and shook his head.

"I wouldn't say that. Everyone is poor at their Calling right after they receive it. It took me over three years to learn how to swing the ax properly. No matter what Calling you have, if you treat it seriously, you can master it eventually, like the adults do. But in Selka's case...I think she's trying a little too hard for someone just twelve years old..."

"Trying too hard?"

"When Alice started studying the sacred arts, she wasn't actually living in the church. She studied in the mornings, brought me my lunch at noon, and helped around the house in the afternoon. But Selka left home, saying it wouldn't give her enough time to study. On the other hand, that was around the time that Jana and Arug came to the church, too, which was a little more than Sister Azalia could handle."

I thought of Selka, diligently watching after the younger children. It didn't seem like she was having that hard of a time with it, but doing a full day's study on top of taking care of six children had to be quite difficult for a girl only twelve years old.

"I see what you mean...And now they've got a 'lost child of Vecta' to add to the mix. I'd better be careful not to make extra trouble for Selka," I said, making a mental note to get up at five thirty on the dot tomorrow. "Oh, and did you say that all the kids aside from Selka living at the church lost their parents? Both parents? How are there six orphans in such a peaceful village?"

Eugeo glanced down at the moss at his feet, distress palpable in his features.

"Three years ago...there was a plague in the village. It hadn't swept through for over a century, they said, and it ultimately took the lives of over twenty villagers—adults and children. No matter how hard Sister Azalia and Miss Ivenda the herbs master tried, there was no help for those whose fever got bad enough. The children at the church lost their parents to the disease."

The revelation stunned me.

An epidemic? But this is a virtual world. There can't be actual germs or viruses here. Which means those who died of disease were meant to do so by the person or system in charge of managing this world. But why? Perhaps it was an intentional strain placed upon the village in the form of a natural disaster, but what was it meant to simulate?

Once again, it all came down to the same question: What was the reason this world existed?

Whether he recognized the meaning behind my expression or not, Eugeo continued, "It's not just the plague. A number of strange things have happened recently. Villagers attacked by wandering long-clawed bears and packs of black wolves, crops that refuse to bloom...Some months, the regular caravan from Zakkaria never shows up. They say it's because bands of goblins are attacking the road far to the south of us."

"Wh-what?" I said, stunned. "But wait...what did you say about goblins earlier? That the knights guard the border..."

"Of course. If the descendants of darkness approach the End Mountains, an Integrity Knight will defeat them at once. They have to—they're much, much worse than Alice, who merely brushed the ground of that place."

"Eugeo..."

I was surprised to hear a note of angry chagrin in Eugeo's normally placid voice, but a wan smile replaced it at once.

"...Which is why I think it's all just rumor. Still, it's true that there's been a rush of new graves out behind the church in the last few years. Grandpa says times like this come around."

I heard a little voice alerting me that this was the opportunity to ask one of those questions I'd been wondering.

"Say, Eugeo...Are there sacred arts that can, you know... bring people back to life?" I asked, expecting yet another of his wide-eyed stares, but to my surprise, he merely bit his lip and bobbed his head vaguely.

"I don't think many of the villagers know…but Alice once told me that among the highest sacred arts is the ability to increase life itself."

"Increase…life?"

"Yeah. We cannot increase the life of all people and things, including you and me, as you know. So a person's life grows and grows as we go from baby to child to adult, and in most cases, it maxes out at age twenty-five. After that point, it slowly drops, and at around seventy to eighty years of age, we are called back to Stacia's side. You remember all that, right?"

"Y-yeah."

It was all new to me, of course, but I put on an understanding face. What Eugeo said was essentially that one's max HP increased or decreased by age.

"But when you get sick or hurt, your life drops by a lot. Depending on the depth of the injury, it could lead right to death, which is why we use sacred arts and herbs to heal. In doing so, life can be restored, but never above the proper total. You cannot make the elderly as strong as their youthful peak with herbs or heal grievous wounds…"

"But you're saying there are arts that can do this?"

"Alice said she was surprised to read that in an old book at the church. When she asked Sister Azalia about it, the sister was ferociously stern, took the book away, and told her to forget what she'd read…So I don't know any more than that, but I'm sure that it's only usable by the highest priests of the Axiom Church. It works not on wounds or illnesses but on a person's life itself… from what she said. But I couldn't begin to guess how the arts themselves work, of course."

"Ohh…high priests, huh? So it's not like any old priest in the church can perform those sacred arts."

"Of course not. The arts get their strength from the sacred power that Solus and Terraria and the like pour into the air and earth. The bigger the art, the more sacred power necessary.

Manipulating human life is a tremendous art, so it might require more power than can be gathered from this entire forest. You won't find a single person able to wield so much power in all of Zakkaria, I bet."

Eugeo paused there, then continued in a quieter voice, "Plus… if Sister Azalia could do such a thing, she would never have allowed those parents and children to lose their loved ones to disease."

"Good point…"

That suggested that if I died on the spot, I would not be resurrected at a church altar to the sonorous tones of a pipe organ. Death would most likely result in my waking up in the STL in real life. If it didn't work like that, I had a problem. The STL didn't have the ability to destroy the user's fluctlight, unlike the NerveGear—I hoped.

But I preferred to save the "death as escape" option for desperate times. My expectation that this was the Underworld was not yet confirmed, and even if I knew that for a fact, there was a little voice deep down in my soul that warned it might not be best to disengage before I discovered the purpose of this living simulation.

If only I could instantly teleport to the capital, charge into this Axiom Church place, and grill the high priests for the answers. The lack of a teleportation feature was a major setback in terms of playability. Even *SAO* had teleport gates in almost every town.

It was an issue that I might complain about to the administrators, if this were a regular VRMMO. But without that capability, I just had to do my best within the confines of the system. The same way I racked my brain to figure out the best way to defeat bosses back in the old Aincrad.

I finished my second piece of bread and lifted Eugeo's canteen to my mouth, looking up at the impossibly massive trunk overhead.

Eugeo's assistance was vital to reach the city. But he was too responsible to abandon his Calling, not to mention that the Taboo Index no doubt forbade it.

That left one choice: figure out how to deal with this monstrous tree.

For his part, Eugeo was getting to his feet, patting his trousers clean. "Well, let's get started on the afternoon work. I'll go first—hand me the ax?"

"Sure," I said, leaning and grabbing the middle of the ax handle next to me so I could put it into his outstretched hand.

A bolt of lightning blasted through my head. The thing that had wriggled from my grasp before was back, and this time I squeezed tight and pulled, ensuring it did not slip away again.

Eugeo said it himself. A normal ax would easily chip on the tree, which was why they'd spent such an extravagant amount shipping this ax from the big city.

So what if we used an even stronger ax? One with a higher strength requirement, with even greater attack and durability?

"H-hey, Eugeo," I began, launching right into the pitch. "Are there any stronger axes than this in the village? Or if not here, then in Zakkaria…? It's been three centuries since you got this ax, right?"

But he merely shook his head. "Of course not. Dragon bones are the greatest possible material for a weapon. It's even harder than Damascus steel from the south and Tamahagane steel from the east. To get something stronger than this, you'd need an Integrity Knight's…divine weapon…"

His voice slowed and trailed off. I looked at him with equal parts patience and curiosity. Five seconds later, he spoke again softly, reaching blindly for his conclusion.

"…There's…no ax…but there is…a sword."

"Sword…?"

"Do you remember when I said there was another divine object in the village, aside from the Bells of Time-Tolling?"

"Er…yeah."

"It's actually quite close…And I'm the only one in the village who knows about it. I've kept it hidden for six whole years…Do you want to see it, Kirito?"

"O-of course! Please, please show it to me!" I said enthusiastically. Eugeo mulled it over a bit more and eventually decided he would do it. He handed me back the ax.

"Why don't you get started on this, then? I'll go get it, but it might take me a little while."

"Is it kept far away?"

"No, it's in the storage shed right over there. It's just…very heavy."

Sure enough, when he came back after I finished a full set of fifty swings, Eugeo's forehead was glistening with sweat.

"H-hey, you all right?" I asked, but all he could do was nod weakly and toss what he carried over his shoulder onto the ground. It landed with a loud, heavy thud and sank deep into the carpet of moss. Eugeo sat down, panting heavily, and I rushed to give him the siral water before I turned to look at what he'd brought.

I recognized the object—it was the narrow, nearly four-feet-long leather container I'd seen on the storage shed's floor when Eugeo put away the ax yesterday.

"Can I open it up?"

"Y-yeah…Just…be careful. If you drop it on your foot…you'll get worse than a scrape," he wheezed. I reached out for it.

The jolt of surprise I got was backbreaking—literally. If this was the real world, I probably would have popped a vertebra out of alignment, such was the weight of the leather case. I pulled with both hands, but it resisted my force as if it were nailed right into the ground.

My sister, Suguha, owing to her kendo skills and passion for muscle training, was heavier than you'd guess from her appearance—a fact I made sure *never* to say in her presence—and this leather bundle was at least as heavy as her, without exaggeration. I squared up my feet, bent my knees, and summoned all my strength into the process, like lifting a barbell.

"Hungh…!"

I thought I heard my joints creaking, but I did manage to lift the object. I rotated it ninety degrees to bring the part tied with string to the top, then set the bottom end onto the ground. With my left hand desperately holding it upright, I unwound the string with my right, and tugged down the leather wrapping.

It revealed a breathtakingly beautiful longsword.

The handle was finely decorated platinum, the grip neatly wrapped white leather. The knuckle guard was carved to look like leaves and vines. It wasn't hard to figure out what plant they were meant to represent. On the upper part of the handle and the white leather scabbard were decorative roses sparkling with blue jewels.

It gave off the impression of being quite old, but there was no grime or dirt on it at all. The austere grace and beauty of the sword told me that it had simply been sleeping for a very, very long time without a master.

"What's this…?" I asked, looking up. Eugeo's panting was under control at last, and he looked at the sword with both nostalgia and bitter sadness.

"The Blue Rose Sword. I don't know if that's its actual name, but it's what they call it in the fairy tale."

"Fairy tale…?"

"Every kid in Rulid knows it…every adult, too. Among the first inhabitants who founded this village three hundred years ago was a swordsman named Bercouli. There are plenty of stories about his adventures, but one of the most famous is called 'Bercouli and the Northern White Dragon'…"

His gaze traveled someplace far off, and emotion entered his voice. "To give you a basic version of the story, Bercouli went exploring in the End Mountains and wandered into the white dragon's lair, deep in a cave. The dragon, which protects the lands of humanity, was napping, thankfully, so Bercouli was going to leave at once—except he spotted a white sword among the piles of treasure that he simply had to have. He carefully picked it up without making any noise, but then blue roses grew around his feet and locked them in place. He fell over on the spot, and the dragon woke up...So goes the story."

"S-so what happened next?" I asked, eager.

Eugeo laughed and said it was a long story, so he summed it up by saying, "Basically, Bercouli managed to earn the dragon's forgiveness and escaped the cave with his life but no sword. The end. It's just a silly fairy tale. If only certain children weren't foolish enough to go see if it was true..."

The note of deep regret in his voice filled in the story for me. He was talking about himself—and his friend Alice. No other children in the village would have the agency to do such a thing.

After a long silence, Eugeo continued, "Six years ago, Alice and I went into the End Mountains in search of the white dragon. But there was no dragon. Only a mountain of bones with sword marks on them."

"W-wait...someone killed the dragon? Who would...?"

"I don't know. But whoever it was, they had no interest in treasure. There was a huge pile of coins and riches beneath the bones. And the Blue Rose Sword, too. Of course, it was too heavy for me to bring back when I was that young...And when Alice and I turned to leave, we went out the wrong exit and wound up going down the tunnel to the land of darkness instead. The rest is as I described yesterday."

"I see..." I looked away from Eugeo and down at the sword I held between my hands. "Then...how did the sword get here?"

"...Two summers ago, I went back to the cave and took it out. But I could only carry it a few kilors for every day of rest. I hid it in the forest each time...and it took me three months to move it all the way to that shed. As for *why* I would do that...I'm not really sure, to be honest..."

Because he didn't want to forget about Alice? Because he planned to take the sword and go off to rescue her?

A number of possibilities came to my mind, but a sense of respect for Eugeo kept me from turning them into words.

Instead, I summoned my energy again and attempted to pull the sword from its scabbard.

The resistance was tremendous. It felt like I was pulling a deep stake out of the ground, but once I had gotten it to budge, the blade flowed smoothly out of its sheath. It came free with a sweet *shaaang*, and my arm instantly felt like it was going to pop out of my shoulder. I had to drop the scabbard and use two hands to keep the sword up.

Even the leather scabbard was tremendously heavy; the prod end thudded and sank into the ground. It was a good thing it didn't crush my left foot, because it was all I could do to keep the sword aloft, and jumping back was out of the question.

Fortunately, without the scabbard, the sword was about a third lighter than before, which was just enough that I could keep it aloft. My gaze was stuck on the blade before me.

It was a strange material. The metal was thin, not even an inch and a half across, but it glittered a faint blue in the bits of sun that came through the leaves above. It refracted the light in a way that suggested it wasn't just bouncing off the surface but collecting on the inside as well—it was mildly translucent.

"This isn't ordinary steel. It's not silver, either, nor dragon bone. And it's certainly not glass," Eugeo said, his voice hushed with wonder. "In other words…I don't think this was crafted by human hands. Either a master of very high sacred arts made it with the power of the gods, or a god created it directly…We call such things Divine Objects. I'm certain the Blue Rose Sword is one of them."

Gods.

I'd noticed mention of "Solus" and "Terraria" in Eugeo's and Selka's stories, as well as Sister Azalia's prayers, but up to this point I'd considered them nothing more than typical artifacts of fantasy storytelling and ignored them accordingly.

But the appearance of an item purportedly created by the gods might be cause to rethink that attitude. Were the gods of a virtual world the humans who managed it from the real world? Or did that refer to the main program that ran the entire simulation?

It wasn't the kind of question that could be answered just by mulling it over. I'd have to consider that topic part of the "central system," if you will, along with the Axiom Church.

At any rate, the sword was clearly a high-priority item within the system. But was its priority higher than the Gigas Cedar? The answer would determine whether I could get Eugeo to go to the city with me or not.

"Eugeo, can you check on the Gigas Cedar's life for me?" I asked, still holding the sword. He looked dubious.

"Kirito…don't tell me you're going to hit the Gigas Cedar with that sword."

"What other reason would I have for asking you to bring it?"

"Uhh…but…"

Eugeo thought it over, clearly reluctant—I gave him no room to think any further.

"Or is there an entry in the Taboo Index that says you can't hit the Gigas Cedar with a sword?"

"Um…well, there's no rule against that…"

"Or did the village elder or, um…Old Man Garitta tell you that you couldn't use anything besides the Dragonbone Ax?"

"No…not that, either…But…I feel like something like this happened once before…" Eugeo mumbled, and he got up and approached the cedar. He made the sigil and tapped the trunk, checking on the window that appeared.

"It looks like 232,315."

"Okay, keep that exact number in mind."

"But Kirito, I don't think you'll be able to swing that sword. Look, you're wobbling just trying to hold it up."

"Just watch. You don't swing a heavy sword with strength. The key is how you shift your weight."

In the distant past of the old *SAO*, I had eagerly sought out the heaviest swords. I was enthralled by the idea of a single pulverizing blow to finish the fight, as opposed to a weapon meant for speed. Because my strength increased with each level, thus lowering the perceived weight of the weapon, I switched out for heavier and heavier blades. My final partners were about as heavy as this Blue Rose Sword when I first got them, if my memory was accurate. And I'd been able to swing one of those beasts with each hand at the same time.

Naturally, the fundamental systems of the worlds were different, so I couldn't compare them directly, but I could at least make use of that mental muscle movement. Once Eugeo was a safe distance away, I set up at the left edge of the tree, lowered my stance, and held the sword low, feeling like my arms were about to fall off.

I didn't need a combo, just a simple midlevel swipe. To use the *SAO* sword skill terminology, a Horizontal—the most basic of basic skills you learned at the start of the game.

I drew a breath and shifted my weight to my right foot, pulling back the sword. The inertia of the blade pulled my left foot off the ground. I nearly toppled back onto my rear, but as the point of the sword reached its peak, I struggled against it, pushing hard with my right foot to shift my weight back to the left. As I did so, the rotation of my legs and hips carried through my arm to the sword, beginning its swing.

The sword didn't glow or automatically speed up, but my body did trace the movement for the sword skill in perfect rhythm. My left foot rocked the earth with its impact, sending the massive weight hurtling forward along its prescribed, ideal path...

But my perfect execution ended there. My legs couldn't hold the weight and buckled, and the sword smacked against the bark, far from the intended target.

Giiing! It made an ear-piercing ringing that sent the birds above scattering in all directions. I didn't see them go, as I lost my handle on the grip and plunged face-first into the moss.

"See, what did I tell you!" Eugeo raced over to help me up. I spit out the green moss that had gotten stuck in my mouth. In addition to my face, which took the brunt of the fall, my wrists, back, and knees were all screaming in pain, too. I lay on the ground for a while, moaning, until I could finally produce a coherent statement.

"...This isn't going to work...My stats are all red..."

Naturally, Eugeo wouldn't understand a reference to what the menu displayed in *SAO* when the player attempted to equip a weapon with an STR requirement beyond his level. Before the concerned look on his face could deepen, I hastened to add, "Er, I mean...I think I was just a bit short on stamina. For that matter—someone was actually able to equip that monster...?"

"I told you, it's too much for us. You'd need to have the swordsman's Calling...and enough skill to join a big town's sentinel garrison."

I slumped and rubbed my right wrist, turning to get the sword. Eugeo looked over his shoulder in turn.

We both stopped still.

The Blue Rose Sword's beautiful blade was half wedged into the Gigas Cedar's bark, hanging there in midair.

"...You're joking...Just from one hit...?" Eugeo gasped, staggering to his feet. He reached out timidly, tracing the seam where sword met tree. "It didn't chip the blade...It really took two cens out of the Gigas Cedar..."

I got up, too, wincing in pain and patting my dirty clothes. "See? It was worth trying out. That sword has more...well, attack power than the ax. Check the life of the Gigas Cedar again."

"O-okay," he said, making the sigil and tapping the tree trunk. He stared eagerly at the window that appeared.

"...232,314."

"Wh-what?" Now it was my turn to be surprised. "It only went down by one? But I cut it so deep...What does it mean? Do you have to use the ax after all...?"

"No, that's not true," Eugeo said, crossing his arms. "You hit it in the wrong spot. If you got it inside the cut, not against the bark, it would have taken down more life, I think. You might be right that this sword can carve down the tree much faster than the Dragonbone Ax. Fast enough that I might be able to finish my Calling…But…"

I turned to him. He was biting his lip, looking pensive.

"But that's only if we can properly wield the sword. You hurt yourself pretty badly making just one swing, and you didn't even hit the target. At that rate, it might still be faster using the ax."

"Maybe I can't do it, but what about you, Eugeo? You're stronger than I am, I think. You should try giving it a swing," I insisted, and while Eugeo was reluctant, he did give in and admit he'd try it just once.

He grabbed the handle of the Blue Rose Sword and tried wrenching it loose from the tree. When it finally came free, Eugeo's upper half swayed and the end of the sword dropped until its point hit the ground.

"Wh-whoa! It really is too heavy. I can't do this, Kirito."

"I swung it; you can, too, Eugeo. The concept is the same as with the ax. Just make more use of your weight and capitalize on the momentum of your whole body, not just your arms."

I wasn't sure how much of that made sense to him, but thanks to his ample experience swinging the ax, Eugeo figured it out very quickly. His naive face tensed with determination, and he crouched down to lift up the sword.

He drew it back, paused, then hissed a quick breath and began a ferociously quick swing. The way his toe slid forward in a perfect line took even me by surprise. A vision of blue light hung in the air as the tip of the sword plunged straight for the cut in the tree.

But at the very last instant, his left foot was unable to bear all the weight. The end of the sword struck the upper side of the V-shaped cut, thudding dully. Unlike me, Eugeo was thrown behind. His back slammed against a thick root.

"*Urrgh…*"

"H-hey, you okay?" I asked, hurrying over, but he held up a hand as he grimaced. It was at that point that I belatedly realized that this world did, in fact, simulate pain.

In the current VRMMO model with games like *SAO* and *ALO*,

the pain that the brain was supposed to feel when the player's avatar was injured was nullified by a function called the Pain Absorber. Without it, no one would bother to delve into bloody physical battles with HP down to single digits.

But this world did not seem to be at all constructed for the purpose of entertainment. The pain was much duller than before, but still—my wrists and shoulders were throbbing. And that was just from twisting and striking. How much pain would I feel from an actual weapon wound?

If I was going to get into any sword battles here in the Underworld, I'd need to make a commitment I hadn't needed to face until now. In all my battles up to this point, I'd never had to imagine the pain of actually having a heavy blade slice my flesh.

Eugeo had a higher tolerance for pain than I did, clearly, as the grimace left his face after just thirty seconds. He hopped to his feet. "I don't think this will work, Kirito. We're going to start losing life before we ever hit it right on the sweet spot."

Next to the tree, the point of the Blue Rose Sword was sunken into the ground after it deflected off the top of the cut in the trunk.

"I was sure we were on the right track," I lamented, but Eugeo gave me an expression of admonishment, so I gave up and scooped the white leather scabbard off the mossy ground. Eugeo lifted the sword and carefully placed it inside the sheath I was holding steady. He wrapped the weapon in the leather again, tied it up with the rope, and placed it a safe distance away.

He exhaled after that task was over, then reached for the Dragonbone Ax resting against the trunk of the tree and exclaimed, "Wow, this ax feels as light as a bird's feather now! Well, we lost a lot of time on that, so let's get on with the afternoon shift."

"Yeah…Sorry about wasting your time on that whim, Eugeo…"

The other boy, the very image of the term *pure-hearted*, just smiled. "It's fine, Kirito. I had fun with it, too. Well…I'll take the first fifty swings."

He began the rhythmic chopping motion. I looked away,

walked over to where the sword lay, and caressed the sheath through the leather wrap.

I knew I had the right idea. We could absolutely cut down the Gigas Cedar with this sword. But Eugeo was right, too; just swinging it wildly wasn't going to work.

The existence of the sword meant that there must be some person in this world capable of wielding it. Eugeo and I simply hadn't reached the requirements yet.

So what *were* those requirements? Class? Level? Stats? How could we find out…?

"…"

My mouth fell open. I couldn't believe how dense I was.

I just had to look at its status window. The same way Eugeo checked the window of the bread yesterday…and the way I popped up the lamp's window in the church. Why hadn't I thought of that earlier?

I reached out with my left hand, made the symbol, then, after a brief moment of consideration, tapped the back of my right hand. Sure enough, a purple rectangle chimed into existence above it.

Unlike the bread's pop-up, this one had several lines of text. I tried looking for a log-out button out of habit, but there was none to be found.

The very first line read *UNIT ID: NND7-6355*. The mechanical sound of "unit ID" gave me a bit of a shiver, but I didn't dwell on it. The number was probably just a reference code that all people in this world had.

Beneath that, like with the bread and Gigas Cedar, was a *Durability* rating, which Eugeo called "life." It read *3280/3289*. Common sense suggested the first number was my current value and the second was my maximum. The little drop was probably from falling during my swing.

The second line said *Object Control Authority: 38*. Below that, it said *System Control Authority: 1*.

That was all. No RPG experience points, level, or statistics. I bit my lip and mulled it over.

"Hmm…Object Control Authority. I wonder if that's it…"

Based on the sound of the words, I expected it was a parameter that controlled usage of items. But there was no way to guess what exactly the number thirty-eight meant in that context.

I sighed and looked up. There was Eugeo, dutifully absorbed in swinging his ax. A thought occurred to me, and I closed my own window to examine the Blue Rose Sword's instead. I loosened the end of the package, pulled the hilt out a little bit, made the sign, and tapped it.

In addition to the sword's durability, which was nearly as high as the Gigas Cedar's at 197,700, it showed me what I was looking for. Right below was a line reading *Class 45 Object*, which likely corresponded to the control authority from my window. My authority was thirty-eight—not enough.

I closed the sword's window, tied it back up, and lay down on the spot. Through the branches of the Gigas Cedar, I could see little tiny patches of blue sky. I exhaled a long breath. The information was valuable, but it also confirmed in inarguable numerical values that I couldn't use the Blue Rose Sword. If I could raise my authority level to forty-five, that problem was solved, but I didn't know how to go about doing that.

Assuming this world operated on a rough approximation of VRMMO rules, and I wanted to raise some parameter of mine, it would probably involve either extensive, repetitive practice or going out and killing monsters to earn experience. I didn't have the time or inclination to do the former, and I hadn't seen hide nor hair of any monsters for the latter. Normally coming across a legendary weapon that was above my equip level was the source of motivation to keep grinding levels, but without a clear means of doing that, all I had left was frustration.

Hardcore MMO fans always said the most fun stage of a game was right at the start, when there were no wiki sites compiling information yet and you had to figure everything out yourself. When I got back to the real world, I was never going to say that

again, I swore to myself, albeit pointlessly. Meanwhile, Eugeo finished his fifty whacks and turned to me, wiping away his sweat.

"How do you feel, Kirito? Can you swing the ax?"

"Yeah…the pain's gone."

I swung my legs to rock myself up to my feet and reached out
for the ax. He was right; the Dragonbone Ax was almost laugh-
ably light compared to the Blue Rose Sword.

All I could do was pray that the act of swinging the ax somehow raised that particular statistic. I clenched the handle in both
hands and pulled it back for a swing.

"Aaahh…Now, this is paradise…" I moaned, the instant I hit
the hot water. A bath was just the trick after the rare experience
of hard physical labor.

The bathroom in Rulid's church had a large copper tub
installed next to a ceramic tile floor, with an oven on the outside
of the building that burned logs to heat the water. I didn't think
medieval Europe had baths like this, but whether it was installed
by the world creators' design or was the evolutionary result of
three centuries of simulation, it was nothing short of a blessing
to me.

After dinner, Sister Azalia took Selka and the two other girls
into the bath first. After that, the four boys and I got our turn,
and the rowdy kids had just gotten out after satisfying their natural desire to cavort. Somehow, the water filling the large tub was
not the least bit cloudy. I scooped up a handful of the clear liquid, splashed it on my face, and let out another relaxed, satisfied
moan.

Thirty-three hours had passed since I had been abandoned in
this world.

I couldn't guess how much time that was in the real world
without knowing how fast the fluctlight acceleration was, but if
it was working in real time and my absence was unexplained, my
family and Asuna would be very worried by now.

The very thought of it made me want to leap from my luxurious bath and race to find an escape from this place. But at the same time, I couldn't pretend that I didn't want to stay here and get to the bottom of the world's mysteries.

The fact that I was mentally present as Kazuto Kirigaya, complete with real-world memories, had to be an irregular occurrence. I was sure of it. It meant I was capable of wreaking undue havoc on the delicate simulation taking place. They did not simulate three centuries of incredibly in-depth history just so someone could come along and contaminate it.

That meant that I was both standing at the edge of a terrible precipice and also in possession of a once-in-a-lifetime opportunity. This was my first and last chance to figure out the true goal of Rath, the mysterious start-up with inexplicably vast and secretive funding.

"No...that's just another excuse..." I said beneath the surface of the water, the words emerging as bubbles.

Perhaps I was just being driven by simple desire as a VRMMO player: I wanted to "conquer" the world—to make my way through without a player manual, relying on nothing but my mind and instincts—as I improved my sword skill and defeated countless worthy foes, until at last I had seized the glory of being the strongest alive. It was the stupidest, most infantile desire.

Strength in the virtual world was an illusion of numbers. I'd come to reckon with that on several occasions. When Heathcliff stopped my elite Dual Blades skill, when the Fairy King Oberon laid me low, when I fled for my life from the pursuing Death Gun—each time left me with painful regret and the determination never to make the same mistake again.

But once again, the embers smoldering in the very root of my soul were lighting that fire under me. How many people in this world could lift the Blue Rose Sword with ease, unlike me? How powerful were the Integrity Knights that upheld the law and the knights of darkness who opposed them? Who sat in the highest seat of the Axiom Church, the structure that ruled this world...?

Without realizing it, I swung my hand up, and my fingers broke the surface of the water, throwing droplets against the far wall.

Meanwhile, a voice beyond the changing room door brought me to my senses.

"Huh? Is someone still in there?"

I sat upright when I recognized Selka's voice.

"Y-yeah, it's me—Kirito. Sorry, I'm coming out."

"Oh…n-no, it's fine, take your time. Just make sure you unplug the tub and put out the lamp when you're done. I'm going back to my room now…Good night."

I heard her start to scurry away, and an idea occurred to me. "Oh…Selka, I wanted to ask you something. Do you have any time tonight?"

The footsteps stopped, replaced by a hesitant silence. Eventually she responded, just loud enough for me to hear. "I have…a bit of time. But the kids are already sleeping in my chamber, so I'll wait for you in your room."

She trotted off without waiting for a reply. I stood up in a hurry, pulled out the wooden stopper at the base of the tub, extinguished the lamp on the wall, and exited to the changing room. The water dried up without needing a towel, which helped me get into my clothes faster, and I raced down the quiet hall and up the stairs.

Selka looked up from the bed, dangling her feet, when I opened the door. Unlike last night, she wore a simple cotton shift with her brown hair tied in a braid.

She picked up a large glass from the bedside table and offered it to me.

"Oh, thanks," I said, sitting down next to her on the bed and drinking the chilled well water. It felt like moisture was permeating my dried body from head to toe.

"Ahh, nectar, nectar."

"Necktar? What is that?" Selka asked, looking confused. I panicked, realizing that the word must not exist in this world.

"Umm…it's something you say about water that's extremely delicious and feels like it's healing you…I guess."

"Ohh...So like elixir, then."

"Wh-what is that?"

"It's holy water that a monk has blessed. I've never seen it myself, but they say that drinking a little bottle of it will bring back the life decreased by injury or illness."

"Ohhh..."

It made me wonder how they'd lost so many people to disease if such a thing existed, but I decided it was probably better not to ask. At the very least, this world and the stately Axiom Church that ruled over it were not quite the benevolent paradise I first took them to be.

Selka accepted the empty glass from me and prompted, "If you have more questions, make them quick. I'm only forbidden to enter the boys' room after the bath, not the guest room, but I feel like Sister Azalia will give me a scolding anyway if she finds out."

"Um...sorry about that. I'll make it quick. I wanted to ask... about your sister."

Her delicate shoulders twitched under her white gown.

"...I don't have a sister."

"Not anymore, right? Eugeo told me that you had an older sister named Alice, and—"

Before I could finish my sentence, Selka's head jerked up, startling me.

"Eugeo did? He told you about Alice? How much did he say?"

"Err...well...that Alice studied the sacred arts here at the church...and that an Integrity Knight took her away to some big city several years ago..."

"...Ahh..." She dropped her glance to the floor and continued, "So Eugeo didn't forget...about Alice..."

"Huh...?"

"The people of the village—Father, Mother, Sister Azalia—none of them will ever talk about her. Her room was tidied up and emptied years ago...like she was never there to begin with. So I thought everyone had just forgotten all about her...even Eugeo..."

"As a matter of fact, not only does he remember her, he still seems to be quite concerned for her. So much that if he didn't have his Calling to keep him busy, he would rush down to that city to find her," I said.

Selka was quiet for a few moments. She eventually mumbled, "I see...So the reason Eugeo doesn't smile anymore...is because of Alice."

"Eugeo...doesn't smile?"

"Yes. When my sister was around, he was always beaming. It was hard to find him *not* looking happy. I was still young, so I don't remember it that well...but ever since she was taken away, I feel like I never see Eugeo smiling anymore. In fact...even on his days off, whether he stays inside or goes into the forest, he's always alone..."

I found this statement to be a bit strange. Eugeo was rather reserved, it was true, but he didn't seem to be hiding his emotions from me. During our chats coming to and from the forest and on our break times, he had even laughed, and more than a few times.

If he wasn't smiling around Selka or the villagers anymore, was it...out of guilt? Guilt that he was the reason beloved Alice, the future Sister at the church, was taken away, and that he hadn't been able to save her? And he could stand to be himself around only me, an outsider who didn't know what happened back then?

If that was true, Eugeo's soul could not be a simple program. He had the same level of intelligence and humanity as I did... He had a fluctlight. And he had lived through six whole years of self-torment.

I had to go to the central city, I realized again. Not just for my own sake but to get Eugeo out of this village so he could find Alice and the two could be reunited. And the Gigas Cedar had to be eliminated for that to happen...

"...What are you thinking?" Selka asked, rousing me out of my thoughts.

"Oh…just thinking, like you said, Eugeo must still care a whole lot about Alice right now."

As soon as the thought tumbled out of my mouth, Selka's face seemed to warp a bit. Those clear eyebrows and big eyes clouded with loneliness.

"Yes…I suppose you're right."

Her shoulders slumped. Even I, hardly the most intuitive toward feelings, could tell what this meant.

"Selka…do you like Eugeo?"

"Wha…that's not true!" she protested hotly, then turned away, red down to her neck. She looked down for a while, and when she spoke again, her voice was suddenly tense. "I just…can't take this…Father and Mother never say it, but I can tell they always compared me to her and were disappointed. Same with the other adults. That's why I left home to live at the church. And yet…even as she teaches me the sacred arts, all Sister Azalia thinks about is how my sister learned them all on the first attempt! Eugeo doesn't treat me like them…but he avoids me. Because every time he sees me, he thinks of Alice. And that's not my fault! I…I don't even remember what she looked like anymore…"

Watching the little girl tremble in her pajamas stunned me to my core. Somewhere in my brain, I'd told myself that this was all a simulation, and while these people might not be pure programs, they were something less than real. But sitting next to a crying twelve-year-old girl was not something I was prepared to handle. Eventually Selka rubbed the moisture out of her eyes.

"I'm sorry for losing control."

"N-no…it's fine. I think you should cry when you need to," I said, a pretty weak excuse at consolation, but as Selka wasn't spoiled by the ever-present entertainment media of twenty-first-century Japan, she smiled and took it to heart.

"…Yeah. You're right. I think I feel a bit better now. It's been a really long time since I cried in front of anyone."

"That's really brave of you, Selka. Even at my age, I cry in front

of people all the time," I said, thinking of this scene and that, involving Asuna and Suguha. Selka's eyes went wide.

"Wait…you have your memory back, Kirito?"

"Er…N-no, not in that sense…I guess I just feel that way…A-at any rate, I'm only me, I can't be anyone else…so you should focus only on what *you* can do, Selka."

Again, it might as well have been ripped from a book of clichés, but Selka thought it over and took it to heart. "You're right… Maybe I've just been averting my eyes from myself…and my sister…"

The realization that I was actively trying to pull Eugeo away from this sweet, poor girl filled me with guilt. But just then, a pleasing melody came down from the bell tower above.

"Oh…it's already nine. I need to get back now. Oh…what was it you wanted to ask, again?" she wondered, but I said that I'd already figured out enough. "Well, in that case, I'm going back to my room."

She hopped down to the floor and took a few steps to the door, then turned back.

"Hey…did you hear the reason why the Integrity Knight took my sister away?"

"Uh…yeah. Why?"

"I don't know it. My parents won't say anything…and I asked Eugeo once, years ago, but he wouldn't tell me. Why was she taken?"

I hesitated a bit, but the answer tumbled out of my mouth before I could reconsider.

"Well…I think he said they went up the river to a cave that goes through the End Mountains, and then she put her hand on the ground of the land of darkness…"

"…I see…Past the End Mountains…" she mumbled, lost in thought. But soon she bobbed her head and chirped, "Tomorrow's a day of rest, but prayer is at the usual hour, so make sure you get up. I won't be coming to rouse you this time."

"I-I'll try my best."

Selka grinned briefly, opened the door, and disappeared through it.

As her tiny footsteps pattered into the distance, I flopped down on the bed. I was hoping to get more information on this mysterious Alice, but her sister had been too young at the time to retain much memory of her. All I had learned was just how deep Eugeo's feelings for Alice went.

I shut my eyes and tried to imagine the girl named Alice.

But of course, no face floated into my mind. The only thing I thought I caught a glimpse of on the backs of my eyelids was a glint of golden light.

The next morning, I would come to a very nasty realization of just how naive my plans were.

4

My eyes opened at the clanging of the five-thirty bell and I leaped out of bed, emboldened by the realization that I *could* do it on my own after all.

I threw open the eastern window, stretched, and sucked in a lungful of the cold daybreak air. The more I breathed in, the more it wiped away the last cobwebs of sleep clinging to the back of my mind.

In the room across the hall, I could hear the children starting to wake. I slipped on my clothes, determined to get down to the well to wash up before they did.

The tunic and cotton pants that served as my "starting gear" had no visible stains yet, but according to Eugeo, their life dropped faster and faster the less you washed them. So it was probably time to think about acquiring another outfit. That would be one of the things to ask Eugeo about today, I decided as I headed out the back door to the well.

I transferred a few cups of water from the bucket to the basin, splashed some on my face, and heard someone coming up behind me at last. I straightened, shaking the water from my hands, expecting to see Selka.

"Oh…good morning, Sister."

It was Sister Azalia, wearing her pristine nun's habit. I bowed hastily, and she returned the gesture and said hello. The perpetual frown tightening her lips seemed especially harsh today, which raised my hackles a bit.

"Um...Sister...is something...?" I asked.

She blinked, hesitating momentarily, then said, "I cannot find Selka."

"Uh..."

"Do you know anything about this, Kirito? She seemed to have taken a liking to you..."

For a second I panicked, thinking that she might be suspecting that I'd done something to the girl, but I soon realized that this could not be the case. The ironclad Taboo Index that none dared to violate governed this world; Azalia would not imagine in her wildest dreams that someone would actually kidnap a child. She assumed that Selka had vanished of her own volition and was simply asking me if there was any information I might possess about it.

"Umm...No, I haven't heard anything. Today is a day of rest, correct? She hasn't gone back to her family?" I suggested, trying to kick-start my recently awakened mind, but she immediately shook her head.

"In the two years since Selka came to the church, she has not once returned home. Even if that was the case, I cannot believe that she would go there without attending prayer or saying anything to me. Even if there are no laws against it..."

"Then...maybe she's out shopping. How do you get the ingredients for breakfast every day?"

"We bought two days' worth of food yesterday evening. All the stores in the village are closed today."

"Oh...of course." That emptied my meager stock of imagination. "...I'm sure she had something important to do. She'll be back very soon."

"...I certainly hope so..." Sister Azalia murmured, her brow furrowed with concern. She sighed and said, "In that case, I will wait until midday, and then pay a visit to the village hall if she is not back yet. Forgive me for interrupting you. I must prepare for the morning prayer now."

"It's all right…I'll check around the area afterward," I told her as she inclined her head and left. A faint, nasty tinge of worry welled up within me as I dumped out the remaining water in the basin. I recalled something troublesome in my conversation with Selka last night but couldn't remember what it was. Had I said something that would prompt her to slip out of the church?

Morning prayer passed with this concern gripping my chest, and at the end of breakfast, where the children all wondered where Selka was, she still had not returned. I helped clean up the dishes and went out the front door of the church.

We hadn't explicitly made the same agreement as yesterday, but it was nonetheless a relief when I saw that flaxen hair coming from the northern path at the eight o'clock bell.

"Good morning, Kirito."

"Morning, Eugeo."

He showed up with the same smile as ever. I followed up with, "You get the entire day off, right?"

"That's right. So I figured I would show you around the village today."

"That'd be great, but I need you to help with something else first. Selka hasn't been seen all morning…so I thought we could go look for her…"

"What?!" he exclaimed, his green eyes wide and worried. "She walked out of the church without telling Sister Azalia first?"

"That's what it sounds like. Sister Azalia said it was the first time this has ever happened. Can you think of anywhere she might have gone?"

"Might have gone? I don't know…"

"Last night I talked with Selka about Alice for a little bit. So I was wondering if she might be someplace that reminds her of Alice…"

Only once I had said the words aloud did I finally, belatedly, *ashamedly* realize the source of my unease.

"Ah…"

"What is it, Kirito?"

"No way…Say, Eugeo. When Selka asked you why the Integrity Knight took Alice away years ago, I hear you didn't tell her the reason. Why not?"

He blinked rapidly and, after a few moments, bobbed his head. "That's right…she did ask that. So…why didn't I tell her? I didn't have a very solid reason…Perhaps I was just uneasy about the possibility that Selka would try to go after Alice…"

"That's it," I grunted. "I told Selka last night. I told her how Alice touched the ground of the land of darkness…She must have gone to the End Mountains."

"What?!" Eugeo paled. "That's bad. We have to track her down and bring her back before the villagers realize…When did she leave?"

"I don't know. She was gone by the time I woke at five thirty…"

"In this season, the sky starts to lighten up around five. She couldn't walk through the forest before that point. Which means she left three hours ago," Eugeo said, looking up at the sky. "When Alice and I went to the cave, it only took us about five hours to get there, and we were kids. Selka's got to be over half the way there by now. I don't know that we can overtake her in time…"

"Let's hurry. We'll go right now," I insisted. He agreed at once.

"We don't have time to prepare. Fortunately the path is along the river, so we won't lack for water. Okay…it's this way."

Eugeo and I started walking north, just slowly enough that no passing villagers would be suspicious of us. As the shops trickled away, so did the foot traffic, and we were soon racing down the paved road. Within five minutes, we reached a bridge over the river and snuck out of the village without drawing the posted men-at-arms' notice.

Unlike the wide barley fields of the southern end, the north end of the village ran right up to dense forest. The river that wound around the hills of Rulid in the form of a canal split the forest as it ran north to south, and there was a small path on its bank covered in short grass.

Eugeo plunged down the riverside path without hesitation, then came to a halt about ten steps in. He held out his hand to stop me and crouched, touching a patch of grass with his other hand.

"Right here...It's been stepped on," he murmured, and made the sigil to bring up the grass's window. "Its life is a bit down. It would be more if an adult had stepped on it, so that certifies that a child walked here a little while ago. Let's hurry."

"Uh...right," I said, and picked up my pace to follow after him.

For as long as we walked, the river stayed on the right, and the forest stayed on the left. The only change to the scenery was one large pond and a brief elevation change. It almost made me wonder if we'd fallen into the RPG trope of the "looping dungeon." We were out of hearing range of the town's bell, so the only way to tell time was the slow progress of the sun.

Eugeo and I continued to trace the river's path at a trot just below a run. I would absolutely have run out of steam going at this pace for thirty minutes in the real world. Fortunately, the average male my age in this world was much healthier, and I felt it more as a pleasurable activity than fatigue. I proposed speeding up to Eugeo, but he said that if we ran any faster, our life would drop too much and force us to take a long break to recover.

We'd been following the path at this precise speed for two whole hours but hadn't seen the girl yet. In fact, she would probably have arrived at the cave by now. Fear and haste mingled in my mouth with a metallic tang.

"Hey...Eugeo," I called out, taking care to keep my breathing steady. A step ahead and to my right, he looked over his shoulder.

"What?"

"Just to be sure...If Selka goes into the land of darkness, will the Integrity Knight immediately come to take her away?"

His eyes unfocused as he consulted distant memories. "No...I think the Integrity Knight will fly to the village the next morning. That's what happened six years ago."

"I see...Then even in a worst-case scenario, we'll still have a chance to save Selka."

"...What are you thinking, Kirito?"

"It's simple. If we can take Selka out of the village before the end of the day, we might be able to run away from the knight."

"..."

He faced forward again, mulled it over, then muttered, "We can't...do that. I have my Calling..."

"I didn't say *you* had to come with us," I noted forcefully. "I'll take Selka and go on the run. This was my fault for running my mouth, anyway. It's my responsibility."

"...Kirito..."

I caught sight of the wounded expression on Eugeo's face and felt a prickle in my heart. But this was necessary to challenge his subservient nature. I felt guilty using Selka's peril for my own purposes, but I needed to ascertain whether the Taboo Index was simply a list of ethical and moral taboos or if it was an absolutely enforced set of rules for the residents of this world.

After a few seconds, Eugeo slowly shook his head side to side.

"You can't...You just can't, Kirito. Selka has her own Calling. Even if the knight comes to take her away, she won't agree to go with you. And I don't think it will come to that in the first place. Selka would never violate the serious taboo of setting foot in the land of darkness."

"But Alice did," I pointed out. He winced and bit his lip but argued more forcefully this time.

"Alice...Alice was special. She wasn't like anyone in the village. Not like me...and not like Selka."

He picked up speed, suggesting that he wasn't going to talk about it any further. As I followed, a silent question echoed in my heart to that mysterious girl.

Alice...who are *you?*

To Eugeo, Selka, and the other people of this world, the Taboo Index was clearly something they could not break, even if they wanted to—the same way that you could not break the physical laws that kept a human being from flying in the real world. That seemed to line up with my suspicion that they had true fluctlights but were not human beings in the same sense as I was.

But what did that make Alice, who broke—was *able* to break—that terrible taboo? Was she another tester diving in with the STL like I was? Or…

My brain seized upon different fragmented thoughts one after the other as my legs moved automatically. Eventually, Eugeo broke the silence.

"There it is, Kirito."

I came to my senses and looked up. The forest was clearing out up ahead, and I could see a wall of ashy gray rock beyond it.

With a last spurt of energy, we sprinted across the remaining few hundred yards and came to a stop where the ground underfoot turned from grass to gravel. I stared at the sight before me in shock, panting at last.

It was nothing short of a transition space between area maps, a sure sign of artificiality if I'd ever seen one. The thick green of the forest hit a brief neutral zone, then abruptly turned into a nearly vertical rock cliff. To my surprise, a light snow dusted the surface close enough nearly to touch. However high the altitude was, the peaks of the mountains were pure white.

Those peaks continued to the left and right as far as the eye could see, perfectly splitting the world between this side and that. If someone had designed this world, I could practically scold them for the lazy way they'd drawn this border.

"These are…the End Mountains? And just on the other side is the land of darkness…?" I muttered in disbelief. Eugeo nodded.

"I was surprised the first time I came here, too. That the end of the world…"

"…Was so close," I finished, unconsciously craning my neck in confusion. It was close enough that we'd reached it in just two and a half hours, without any impediments on the way. It was as if…it was tempting the villagers to come and trespass into the forbidden land. Or on the flip side, allowing the residents of the land of darkness to attack…

I stood there, mulling it over blank-faced, which prompted Eugeo to say, "Let's hurry. We must've closed the gap with Selka to thirty minutes by now. If we drag her back as soon as we find her, we can still be back to the village during daylight."

"Y-yeah…good point."

He was pointing ahead, where the little brook we were following got sucked into a hole in the rock face—technically, it was flowing out from there, not going in.

"So that's it…"

I trotted closer. The cave was quite tall and wide, with a rock shelf jutting from the wall to the side of the fierce creek. It was totally dark on the inside, and the occasional breeze brought a freezing chill with it.

"Wait, Eugeo…What are we going to do about light?" I asked. I had totally forgotten about the most important item for a good dungeon spelunking, but Eugeo said he had it under control. He lifted a stalk of grass that he had picked up along the way. I wondered what he was going to do with the fuzzy cattail—until he started chanting in English.

"System Call! Lit Small Rod!"

System Call?! I thought, shocked.

The tip of the stalk of grass in Eugeo's hand started to glow. It had enough pale bluish light to illuminate a few yards ahead. He headed farther into the cave.

I raced to catch up alongside him, the shock still racing through my veins. "Eu-Eugeo…what was that?"

He squinted sternly at me, but there was a hint of pride tugging at his mouth as he said, "A sacred art—a very easy one. I had to practice it a whole lot two years ago when I decided to come and get the Blue Rose Sword."

"Sacred art...But...do you know the meaning of those words? Like *system* and *rod*..."

"Meaning? There's no meaning; they're just spellwords. They're words you say to beseech God and receive a miraculous blessing. The higher sacred arts have many times more spellwords, I hear."

That made sense to me. They didn't know the meaning of the system terminology—it was all treated like mystical magic words. Still, that was a very practical spell. Whoever designed this world was clearly quite pragmatic.

"Say...do you think I can do it, too?" I wondered, excited despite the circumstances.

Eugeo wasn't sure. "It took me about two months to use this art, practicing between my work shifts every single day. According to Alice, people with the talent for it can use it in a day, and others might never be capable of it their entire lives. I don't know where your talent level lies, but I doubt you could do it right away..."

Did that mean that using magic—sacred arts—required some amount of skill training through repetition? If so, he was probably right that it couldn't be mastered in a day. I gave up on the idea for now and stared into the darkness ahead.

The wet gray walls turned right and left and seemed to continue on forever. A chilling wind assaulted my skin at all times, and even with a partner at my side, the lack of any sword, or even a sturdy stick, was starting to make me feel helpless and uneasy.

"Hey...are you *sure* Selka came down here?" I wondered aloud. Eugeo pointed the glowing cattail toward the ground at our feet.

"Oh..."

Within the ring of the impromptu lantern's glow was a shallow, frozen puddle. It had been stepped on in the middle, and there were cracks extending in all directions from that spot.

I tried stepping on it myself. The ice cracked loudly and split further—which meant that before me, someone lighter had been the perpetrator of the first cracks.

"I see...That settles it, then. I don't know if she's reckless or fearless..."

Eugeo found that statement to be curious. "There's nothing to be afraid of. No white dragon in this cave anymore—not even a mouse or a bat to contend with."

"Oh, r-right," I replied, reminding myself that there were animals in this world but no actively aggressive monsters to worry about. At the very least, I could consider this side of the End Mountains to be the equivalent of a VRMMO protected area.

I exhaled, trying to let the tension drain out of my spine—when from the darkness ahead came an odd sound on the breeze. We looked at each other. It sounded like the screeching of a bird or wild animal of some kind.

"Hey...what was that?"

"...I don't know...I've never heard that sound before...Ah!"

"Wh-what is it now?"

"Do you...smell something, Kirito?"

I drew in a deep breath of the cave air through my nostrils.

"Oh...it's kind of a burning smell...and..."

Mixed with the scent of burning tree sap was just a hint of something raw and bestial. I grimaced; it wasn't a reassuring smell.

"What is that...?" I wondered when a new sound came, and I held my breath.

It was the long, trailing sound of a girl screaming.

"Oh no!"

"Selka!"

We both leaped into action, our feet sliding a bit on the frozen rock.

The blood in my veins froze, and my limbs felt numb. It was the first true, palpable sense of danger I'd felt since I showed up in this world—even more than I'd felt when I originally didn't know where I was.

So the Underworld wasn't a paradise after all. It was a thin layer of peace stretched over a core of evil. That was the only explanation. This world was an enormous vise meant to trap all kinds of people in its grasp. Someone had spent centuries slowly, methodically screwing it tighter. To see if the residents would band together and fight back or be crushed under its weight.

Rulid Village was one of the places closest to the vise's jaws. As the final moment of reckoning approached, the souls in the village would slowly disappear, one by one.

But under no circumstances could I allow Selka to be the first. It was my fault she came to this cave in the first place. For toying with her fate, I had a responsibility to see her home safely…

Eugeo and I raced through the cave by the weak light of the grass stem. With each desperate gasp of air, my chest hurt. I slipped numerous times, the elbows and wrists that whacked against walls of ice throbbing constantly. It was easy to imagine our "life" dropping throughout the process, but that wasn't going to slow us down now.

The farther we went, the stronger the odor of burning wood and animal stink. Mixed in with the screeching voices was the constant shuffling of metal. I didn't know what awaited us ahead, but it was hard to imagine it being friendly.

My gamer's instincts told me that with a single knife on hand, we had to come up with a plan and tread lightly, but even louder in my head was the knowledge that we had no time to waste. Plus, Eugeo's panicked face was even paler than mine, and I knew he wouldn't be convinced to turn back anyway.

Suddenly, I saw orange light flickering on the rock walls ahead. Based on the way it was reflecting, there seemed to be a very large dome in the distance. I could feel the antagonism ahead, prickling against my skin. There was more than one of them—many, in fact. Eugeo and I plunged into the dome together, praying for Selka's safety.

Take in everything and execute the most efficient choice of action, as quickly as possible.

Following the guidelines burned into me from experience, my attention darted around, absorbing the images like a wide-angle camera.

The circular dome had to be nearly a hundred and fifty feet across. The floor was covered with thick ice, but there was a stretch toward the middle that was cracked open, exposing water nearly dark enough to be black.

The source of the orange light was a pair of fires lit around the impromptu pond. Firewood snapped and crackled within black iron braziers.

And surrounding the fires sat grouped figures, humanoid in shape but clearly neither human nor animal. There were over thirty of them.

Individually, they were not that big. Standing at full height, their heads might reach my chest. But their hunched frames were stout and stocky, and their abnormally long arms and gleaming claws looked strong enough to tear anything to shreds. They sported gleaming leather armor on their wide chests and dangled small furs, bones, and pouches from their waists. In addition, some held crude but deadly machetes.

Their skin was a dull grayish-green with patches of bristling hair. Each head was clean and bald; the only hair there proved to be needlelike clumps protruding from their ears. They had no eyebrows, either, just jutting foreheads hanging over bizarrely large eyes that threw off a cloudy yellow light.

The creatures were alien in appearance and yet completely familiar to me from over the years.

They were undeniably goblins, those low-level monsters that appeared in nearly every single fantasy RPG. My recognition brought a certain amount of relief, too: Goblins were usually designed for novice players to practice their skills on and earn experience, and they were almost always weak pushovers.

But my relief lasted for only the brief moment until the nearest one to me and Eugeo noticed us.

The look I caught in its yellow eyes froze me down to the marrow. I saw a bit of suspicion and surprise, then cruel delight, and, lastly, boundless hunger. There was enough malice there to make me feel as helpless as a fly trapped in a spiderweb.

The goblins weren't programs, either.

This realization hit me with an overwhelming terror.

They had souls, too. Just like Eugeo and me—up to a point—they had the same kind of intelligence shaped by fluctlights.

But why...? How could such a thing be?

In the two days I'd been in this world, I had come to a rough estimation of exactly what Eugeo, Selka, and the other people who lived here were—artificial fluctlights controlled not by the brains of flesh-and-blood people but by saved images of such, stored on man-made media. I couldn't begin to imagine what sort of media it was that could record a human soul, but if the STL could read one, it stood to reason that it could also copy it.

Chillingly, I similarly surmised that the source of the copies was an infant's fluctlight; that archetype soul was then copied countless times so they could be raised in this world as babies. This was the only hypothesis that could explain the contradiction inherent in the Underworld's residents: They possessed true intelligence, and yet there were far more of them than actual STL units. Rath's true goal, their blasphemous attempt at playing God, was to create true AI—actual human intelligence. And they were doing it by using the human soul as a mold.

That goal seemed to be 90 percent complete by now. The depth of Eugeo's thoughts surpassed mine, and the complexity of his emotional urges was profound. In other words, Rath's vast, arrogant experiment might as well be complete.

But if the simulation was still running, that meant Rath was still unhappy about something in the project. I couldn't begin to guess what that would be, but perhaps it had something to do with that Taboo Index, the set of rules that these people were fundamentally incapable of breaking.

At any rate, this theory did put a rough explanation to Eugeo's existence. He and his kind were just as human as us, with their own souls and everything—they simply existed on a different physical plane.

But then…what were these goblins? What was the stinging malice that sprayed from those yellow eyes…?

I couldn't believe—didn't want to believe—that their souls were based on a human's. Perhaps Rath had caught real goblins in the real world and put them in the STL seat, I thought bizarrely.

The goblin and I shared a look for not even a second, but it was enough to terrify me to my core. I stood stock-still, unsure of what to do, and then it unleashed a screech that might have been a laugh. It got to its feet.

And then the goblin spoke.

"Hey, look! What's going on today? It's another two fresh little White Ium younglings!"

Instantly, the dome was full of high-pitched screeching. One after another, the goblins got to their feet, brandishing machetes and looking at us hungrily.

"What now? Shall we capture them, too?" the first goblin cried. From the back came a ferocious roar, and all the goblins stopped laughing. They spread apart in two directions to clear a path for a much larger individual, one who seemed to be some level of leader.

This one wore metal scale armor and a headpiece around its forehead sporting bright feathers. Under that, its reddened eyes were full of an overwhelmingly evil and icy intelligence. Ugly yellow teeth jutted from its leering mouth. The goblin captain rasped, "You can't sell the male Iums for beans. Just kill them for their meat."

For a moment, I wasn't sure at which level the word *kill* should be taken.

I ought to be able to rule out actual death: a fatal wound to my real-life physical body. My body was sitting in an STL in real life, far from the danger posed by these goblins.

But I couldn't assume that death here was just a bad outcome, a minor setback like in any other VRMMO. Outside of the exception of the Axiom Church elites, there was no resurrection magic or items here. If they killed me here, that was probably game over for this Kirito.

So if I died, what happened to my consciousness?

Would I wake up in Rath's Roppongi office to a greeting from Takeru Higa, the operator, and a fresh cup of water? Would I just wake up in another forest, all alone, to start from scratch? Or would I float through the world as an immaterial ghost, fated to watch its outcome?

And if that happened, what fate awaited Eugeo and Selka, who were sure to be killed with me?

Unlike the self-owned storage media that was my physical brain, their fluctlights were probably stored on some kind of massively high-capacity memory system. Was it possible that when they died...they were simply deleted?

Though...Selka. *Where is Selka?*

I shut off my existential line of thought and focused on the scene before me.

At the goblin captain's orders, four followers began to walk toward us, machetes in hand. Their steady pace and toothy, sadistic smiles said that they meant to kill us long and slow.

The twenty-something goblins left around the pond screeched the others on, excitement in their eyes. In the back, I finally spotted what I sought: Hard to see against the gloom was the black nun's habit of Selka's, lying on a crude cart. She was tied down with rough ropes and her eyes were shut, but from the color of her face, she was only unconscious, not dead.

I thought back to what the captain said: the male "Iums"—that probably meant "human" to them—couldn't be sold, *so kill them here.*

That meant that the women *could* be sold. They were going to take Selka with them back to the land of darkness and sell her. And if we didn't do anything about the state of affairs, Eugeo and I would die. But in a way, Selka's fate was crueler than death. I couldn't just chalk this up to being part of the simulation. I just couldn't. She was a person just like me. A girl, only twelve years old.

That meant...

"There's only one thing to do," I muttered. Next to me, Eugeo's frozen body twitched.

I would save Selka, even if it meant paying the price of this temporary life.

It wouldn't be easy. They far outnumbered us, thirty goblins with machetes and armor, and we didn't even have sticks. But I had no other choice. It was my careless comment that had brought about this situation.

"Eugeo," I said under my breath, keeping my gaze forward, "we have to save Selka. Can you do this?"

I heard him murmur in the affirmative. As I expected, reserved and gentle Eugeo had a strong core.

"When I count to three, we'll rush the front four with a body slam. We're bigger than them, so we can win as long as we don't falter. Then I'll knock the left fire into the pond, and you do the right. Don't lose your glowing grass. When the fires are out, pick up a sword and guard my back. You don't have to beat them if you don't need to. I'll work on taking out the big guy."

"...I've never swung a sword."

"It's just like an ax. Here goes...one, two, three!"

We got a perfect start, racing down the ice without slipping. I could only pray that luck held out to the very end of this maneuver.

"Raaaaah!!" I bellowed.

A moment later, I heard Eugeo echo, "Waaah!" It was a bit more like a scream, but it did the trick. The four goblins stopped, their yellow eyes bulging. Then again, their surprise may have had more to do with the "Ium younglings" engaging in a suicide charge, rather than the ferocity of our yelling.

At the tenth step, I sank down, lowered my right shoulder, and charged like a football tackler for the gap between the leftmost goblin and the one next to him. Thanks to the size difference and element of surprise, I knocked both onto their backs, where they slid across the ice, arms wheeling. To the right, Eugeo's tackle was equally effective, sending the other two spinning like turtles in their shells.

We continued toward the goblin force, picking up momentum. Fortunately, their reaction time was poor, and most of them, including the captain, were still staring at us in shock.

That's right, keep gaping, I thought savagely, racing through the goblin ranks toward the final few yards.

Just then, the goblin captain showed off the intelligence that separated him from the others and snarled, "Don't let them near the—"

But he was just a bit too late. Eugeo and I leaped onto the fire braziers, kicking them over toward the water. The flames plunged into the black water, shooting up a cloud of sparks and emitting white steam where they fell.

For a moment, the dome was totally dark—until a faint white light pushed back the blackness. It was coming from the cattail in Eugeo's left hand.

Then the second stroke of luck occurred.

The crowd of goblins all around erupted into shrieks. Some covered their faces, while others turned away and cowered. Across the pond, even the goblin leader was leaning back, holding out his hand to shield his eyes.

"Kirito…What is this…?" Eugeo gasped, stunned.

"I think…they're weak to that light. Now's our chance!"

From the piles strewn around the pond, I picked up a crude longsword that was more like a flat sheet of metal, as well as a scimitar with a heavy tip. I pressed the latter of the two into Eugeo's free hand.

"That weapon should work the same way as an ax. Use the light to push them back, and swing that sword at any that venture too close."

"Wh-what about you?"

"I've got *him*."

I plunged forward at the goblin captain, who glared furiously through the slits of the fingers he held out to block the light. I tested the sword in my hands with a quick swing back and forth. It felt less sturdy than the appearance suggested, but it was certainly much easier to use than the Blue Rose Sword.

"Grurah! Filthy Ium brats…You think to challenge the great Ugachi the Lizard Killer?!" he roared, watching me close the distance toward him with one baleful eye. He drew an enormous machete from his waist with his other hand. The blackened blade was covered in menacing stains of blood and rust.

Can I win this fight?!

Although we were of equal height, he was clearly heavier and stronger than I was. But the next moment, I gritted my teeth and plunged onward. If I didn't defeat him and failed to save Selka, that would mean that all I'd accomplished in this world was setting her up for the most gruesome of fates. Size wasn't an issue. I had killed countless foes three or four times my size in the old Aincrad. And back then, I knew for a fact that death was permanent.

"I'm not going to challenge you—I'm going to *beat you!*" I yelled, half to him and half to myself as I closed the last stretch of distance.

My left foot plunged forward, and I swung the sword diagonally at his left shoulder.

I wasn't taking the foe lightly, but even then, his reaction was quicker than I had expected. He ignored my strike and swiped sideways with the machete, which I just barely evaded by hunching down. I felt a few hairs rip out as it passed. My own swing had struck true, but all it did was crush his metal shoulder pauldron.

Sensing that if my momentum died, he would overpower me, I stayed low and spun around the enemy, swinging horizontally at his exposed side. The feedback was solid again, but this time it merely broke five or six metal scales free without even piercing the crude armor.

I hissed a silent insult at the sword's owner to polish his weapon properly, as the counterattack just barely hurtled past my head. The heavy end of the machete drove deep into the ice underfoot, and another chill ran down my back as I was forced to know the goblin's strength.

Single attacks weren't going to do the trick. I strode in hard, intending to counter before the goblin captain recovered. My body moved largely on its own, repeating the movements I'd performed countless times in a different world: the special attacks known as sword skills.

The result was not in the least what I expected.

My sword took on a very faint red light. My body darted at a speed beyond the physical laws of the world. It was as if an unseen hand had just pushed me on the back.

The first slash rose from the lower right, clipping the enemy's left leg and arresting his movement.

The second swipe from left to right dug into the target's breastplate and lightly gouged his flesh.

The third slice from the upper right hit the enemy's left arm, raised in defense, and loudly severed it just below the elbow.

The spray of blood from the arm stump looked pitch-black in the pale glow. The severed limb spun through the air and landed in the pond on the left, splashing loudly.

I won! I thought, equal parts triumphant and shocked.

That attack wasn't just a mimicry of the three-part longsword combo Sharp Nail. It was the real thing. The blade took on a red light as it flew through the air, and an invisible force accelerated my movements. They were visual effects and system assistance by any other name.

Sword skills existed in the Underworld. They were written into the system that controlled the world. You couldn't explain this as a recreation based on the mind's imagination. I was barely even conscious of the movements as I executed them. The system read my first motion, activated the skill, and adjusted my movement accordingly. It couldn't happen any other way.

But that just led to a new question.

The day before, I'd tried to use the Horizontal skill on the Gigas Cedar with the Blue Rose Sword. That was an easier skill than Sharp Nail; it was nothing more than a flat swipe. But the system hadn't helped me then. The sword didn't shine, my body didn't speed up, and the weapon clumsily struck far from my intended target.

So why did it work *now*? Because this was a real battle? If so, how would the system determine if it was a "real" fight or not…?

All these thoughts ran through my head in the blink of an eye. In the old *SAO*, there would be no true window of opportunity. I'd be hit with my own post-skill delay, while the enemy suffered from a knock-back effect following huge damage.

But even with sword skills, the Underworld was not a VRMMO. I had very nearly forgotten that basic truth already.

Unlike a 3-D-modeled monster, the goblin captain did not stop moving whatsoever after I cut off his arm. The gleaming yellow eyes swam with no fear, no hesitation—just pure hatred. Black blood streamed from his wound as a roar shot from his mouth.

"Garruaah!!"

The machete in his other hand swept forward.

I wasn't able to cleanly evade the horizontal swipe of heavy metal. The end of it merely brushed my left shoulder, but it was enough force to knock me over six feet backward to slam onto the ice.

At last, the captain crouched, put the machete in his mouth, and squeezed the stump of his left arm with his remaining hand. A horrendous creaking emerged. He was stopping the flow of blood with sheer pressure. That was not the action of a straightforward AI. I should've realized this the moment he'd introduced himself with the name of Ugachi. This wasn't a battle between player and monster—it was a fight to the death between two armed warriors.

"Kirito! Are you down?!" Eugeo called from a distance, keeping the goblins at bay with the scimitar in one hand and the lit cattail in the other.

I tried to tell him that it was just a scratch, but my tongue was too stubborn to comply. I merely wheezed and nodded. I put my hand to the ice, trying to get up.

Instantly, a burning sensation like all the nerves in my left shoulder catching fire shot through my upper half, causing sparks to fly before my eyes. Unstoppable tears flooded from my eyes, and a groan tumbled from my throat.

What tremendous pain!

It was far beyond what I could stand. All I could do was curl up on the ice, panting quickly. Somehow, I managed to turn my head to look at the shoulder. The sleeve of the tunic was ripped, and an ugly wound gaped in the exposed skin. It looked more like I'd been gouged than sliced. The skin and the flesh beneath it was torn right out, replaced by gushing blood. My arm was equal parts numbness and burning, and my fingers were as immobile and unfeeling as if they belonged to someone else.

This can't be a virtual world, I wailed to myself.

A virtual world was supposed to eliminate all the pain, suffering, ugliness, and dirtiness of reality, providing an environment of sheer cleanliness and ease. What was the meaning of so thoroughly simulating pain this awful? In fact, it seemed worse than real life. In the real world, my brain would produce chemicals to knock me out as a defense mechanism against shock, right? No human being could withstand pain like this...

Maybe that's not quite right, I thought wryly to myself, trying to avert my eyes from the carnage.

Kazuto Kirigaya was completely unfamiliar with real pain. I'd never suffered a major injury in my life, and when Grandfather forced me to start kendo, I quit before long. The physical rehab after *SAO* was tough, but thanks to the high-tech training machines and supplemental drugs, I hardly had to deal with any pain.

And my virtual experience was even softer. With the pain-absorbing functions of the NerveGear and AmuSphere, I lived such a sheltered experience that wounds in battle meant nothing more than a loss of abstract HP. If pain like this existed in Aincrad, I would never have left the Town of Beginnings.

The Underworld might be built of dreams, but it was also built of reality's nightmares.

At last, I understood the meaning of the words I had said however many days ago in Agil's café: Reality was where true pain, suffering, and sadness existed. Only those who withstood and survived the endless repetition of those things could be strong here. Ugachi the goblin knew that, ages before I'd even considered the possibility.

Through tear-blotted eyes, I saw Ugachi finish staunching his bloody arm and turn to me. The fury exuding from his eyes seemed to set the air shimmering with heat. He moved the machete from his teeth to his remaining hand and swung it loudly.

"...Even tearing you to pieces and devouring your flesh will not remove this humiliation...but that doesn't mean I won't do it."

He swung the machete over his head as he approached. I tore my eyes away and glanced at Selka, trussed up in the far distance. I had to stand and fight, but my body wouldn't listen. It was as if the fright and hesitation in my heart took the form of physical shackles that bound me in place...

The heavy footsteps came to a stop before me. I sensed air moving, the approach of an enormous blade bearing down on me. It was too late to evade or counter. I gritted my teeth and waited for my last moment in this world.

But no matter how long I waited, the guillotine never struck.

Instead, I heard the sound of quick footsteps on ice and a familiar voice—

"Kiritoooo!!"

My eyes shot open and caught sight of Eugeo, leaping over me to attack Ugachi. He swung the scimitar wildly, driving the enemy back a few steps.

The goblin was initially startled, but he regained his poise quickly, nimbly reaching out with the machete to block Eugeo's attacks. For a moment, I forgot my pain and yelled, "Don't, Eugeo! Just run!!"

But he was bellowing and swinging the sword, apparently beside himself in the moment. Thanks to years of swinging that ax, the speed of his strikes was stunning, but they were on a predictable rhythm. Ugachi focused on defense, enjoying the resistance of his prey, and finally growled and swept Eugeo's support leg out from under him with a toe. As Eugeo lost balance and toppled, the monster confidently pulled back his machete.

"Nooooooo!!"

He swiped effortlessly before the scream left my lips.

The machete hit Eugeo in the stomach and threw him back to fall heavily at my side. I turned over to his direction, feeling a blinding pain in my shoulder but summoning the strength to ignore it.

Eugeo's wound was far worse than mine. A jagged line was carved straight across his torso, pulsing rivulets of blood. The piece of grass still clutched in his hand illuminated the vague sight of organs deep within the injury, moving irregularly.

He coughed and gurgled, producing a bloody froth. His green eyes were already losing focus, staring emptily into thin air.

But Eugeo did not stop trying to get up. He exhaled short bursts of misty red breath, willing strength into trembling arms.

"Eugeo…it's okay…just stop…" I mumbled. Eugeo had to be suffering far more than I was at this moment. He couldn't be in his right mind.

Just then, his unfocused eyes stared right at me, and he uttered blood-flecked words: "Wh…when we were…kids…we made a promise…You and I…and Alice…would be born on the same day…and die on the same day…This time…I'm going…to keep…"

The strength drained from his arms at last. I promptly reached out to support his frame with both hands. Eugeo's slender but muscular weight. The moment it sank into me—

A series of white flashes blinded my vision. Vague shadows floated onto that blank screen.

Beneath a vivid red sunset, walking down a road through barley fields. Holding my right hand was a young boy with flaxen hair. Holding my left, a girl with golden braids.

Yes…we believed the world would never change. We believed the three of us would always be together. And we failed to protect her. We were helpless. I would never forget that despair, that lack of power. This time…this time I would…

I didn't feel the pain in my shoulder anymore. I lay Eugeo's limp body down onto the ice, reached over, and grabbed the handle of the longsword.

When I lifted my head, Ugachi's machete was in the process of coming down on me. I swiped sideways and knocked it away.

"Grruah," he grunted in surprise, backing off a step, and I rose to my feet and tackled him. The goblin took a few more steps back.

I pointed the sword in my hand at the dead center of my target, took a deep breath, and exhaled.

Yes, I was an amateur when it came to physical pain. But I knew about anguish that was far more horrific than that. This wound was nothing compared to the pain of losing a loved one. This machine might manipulate memory, but the pain of loss never truly left.

Ugachi roared in fury and impatience. His screeching underlings fell silent around us.

"White Ium…Learn your place!!" he roared, rushing at me with the machete. I focused just on the point. My ears rang, and everything else on the outside of my vision disappeared. It was the speeding up of the senses, a sensation like brain cells blowing out that I hadn't experienced in a very long time. In this world, I guess it was more like my *soul* burning.

I lunged forward to avoid the diagonal swipe, bringing my sword up to slice off the enemy's remaining arm at the base. The massive limb and its machete spun through the air to land amid the goblins, who shrieked at the sight.

Ugachi, missing both arms now, locked me with yellow-eyed rage and even more shock as he faltered. Black liquid gushed from the fresh wound, landing in the water and sending up steam.

"…No…no Ium whelp could possibly…" he moaned. Before he could even finish his sentence, I was racing forward.

"No! My name is not 'Ium'!" I screamed, the words coming straight from my unconscious mind. My whole body whipped forward, from my toes through my fingers, to the end of the sword. It glowed again, light green this time. An invisible hand shoved my back. The charging skill, Sonic Leap.

"I am…Kirito the Swordsman!!"

The sound of air ripping hit my ears just after Ugachi's massive head floated high into the air.

It flew straight up, then spun in place as it fell into my left hand. I clutched the feathered headdress like a rooster comb and held up the bleeding trophy.

"I have taken your leader's head! If any of you still wish to fight, come now, or flee to your home of darkness!"

On the inside, I was urging Eugeo to hang in there, while outwardly, I glared at the goblins with all the malice I could muster. The death of their leader had made the group quite antsy. They looked at one another, screeching nervously.

Eventually, one stepped forward, a club bobbing on his shoulder.

"Ge-heh! If that's the case, then if Aburi kills you, he can be the next—"

I didn't have the patience to listen to his taunt all the way through. I raced forward, still holding the head, and used the same skill to sever him from right flank to left shoulder. Another spray of blood issued forth, and a moment later, his top half slid off the bottom to land on the ground.

That seemed to settle the issue at last. The remaining goblins let out high-pitched wails and breathlessly raced for the dome's exit on the far side from where we came in. They kicked and shoved one another in the hurry to escape through the tunnel and were soon gone from sight. The echoes of their footsteps and screeching faded away, and a cold silence fell within the icy dome. That prior heat might as well have never been there.

I took a deep breath to hold the returning pain in my shoulder at bay, and tossed aside the sword and severed head. The only thing that mattered now was getting to my fallen friend.

"Eugeo!! Hang in there!!" I called, but his pale eyelids didn't even twitch. Faint breath was going through his parted lips, but it might stop at any moment. Blood still oozed from the ghastly wound in his stomach, but I didn't know how to actually stop it from continuing.

With cramped fingers, I made the sigil and tapped Eugeo's shoulder, praying as I looked at the window that appeared.

His life power now read *244/3425*. Even worse, it was dropping a point every two seconds. That meant I had perhaps eight minutes left before Eugeo's life bled away forever.

"Hang in there; I'm going to save you! Don't die on me!" I pleaded, getting to my feet. I raced as fast as I could to the cart placed to the side of the dome.

It held barrels and boxes with unknown contents, a variety of weapons, and a trussed-up Selka. I grabbed a knife out of one of the boxes and quickly cut her ropes.

I lifted her light body and set her down on the floor for a quick examination—no noticeable wounds. Her breathing was much steadier than Eugeo's. I put my hands on the shoulders of her habit and shook her as firmly as I dared.

"Selka…Selka! Open your eyes!!"

Her long lashes twitched immediately and flipped open to reveal wide brown eyes. She started to shriek, not able to recognize me from the weak light of the cattail over at Eugeo's side.

"N-no…nooo…!"

She waved her arms, trying to push me off her, but I held tighter.

"Selka, it's me! Kirito! It's all right; the goblins are gone!"

She stopped struggling as soon as she heard my voice. Her hand reached out, trembling, to trace my cheek.

"Kirito…Is that you…?"

"Yeah, I came to save you. Are you all right? Are you hurt?"

"I…I'm fine…"

Selka's face scrunched up, and she flung herself desperately around my neck.

"Kirito, I…I…!"

I heard her suck in a fierce breath near my ear, about to begin bawling as only a child could—so I abruptly lifted her into my arms and spun around to run again.

"Sorry, hold back the tears for a bit! Eugeo's really hurt!!"

"Wha…?"

She tensed up in my arms. I raced back for Eugeo, kicking the chunks of ice and junk littered around by the goblins on the way.

"Normal measures aren't going to help him in time…You have to save him with your sacred arts, Selka! Hurry!" I urged, setting her down next to him. She held her breath and reached out a hesitant hand. When her fingers brushed the terrible wound on his torso, she shrank back.

A few seconds later, she shook her head, the braid waving back and forth.

"I can't…It's too deep…My sacred arts…aren't good enough…" she lamented, touching his pale cheek this time. "This can't be happening, Eugeo…You couldn't have done this…for me…"

Tears tracked down Selka's cheeks and landed softly in the pool of blood atop the ice. She pulled her hands back to her face and started to sob. I knew it was cruel, but I had no choice but to yell at her.

"Crying won't help Eugeo! I don't care if it doesn't work; just *try* it! You're going to be the next Sister for the village, remember? You're going to take over for Alice!"

Her shoulders twitched and slumped. "I…can't be like her… She mastered a sacred art in three days that I can't memorize over an entire month. The only thing I can heal…is the tiniest little scratch…"

"Eugeo…" I started to say, faltered, then allowed the emotion welling up within me to burst free. "Eugeo came to save you, Selka! He risked his life to come here and save *you*, not Alice!"

Her shoulders shook again, harder this time.

All the while, Eugeo's life was plunging toward zero. We had only two minutes, maybe one. An agonizingly long moment of silence passed.

And then, Selka abruptly looked up. The fear and hesitation in her eyes from just seconds earlier was no more.

"Normal healing arts won't work in time. I'll have to attempt a dangerous high-level art. I'm going to need your help, Kirito."

"A-all right. Just say the word—I'll do anything."

"Give me your left hand."

I reached out, and she gripped it with her right. Next, she used her other hand to hold Eugeo's where it lay atop the ice.

"If this art fails, both you and I might die. Just be aware of that."

"If it happens, make sure it only happens to me…Ready when you are!"

She nodded, gazing at me with powerful intent. Then she closed her eyes and sucked in a breath.

"System Call!"

A heavenly, pure sound filled the dome of ice.

"Transfer Human Unit Durability, Right to Left!!"

A high-pitched whir followed the echoes of the voice. It swelled—and then a pillar of blue light surrounded Selka.

It was blinding, far stronger than the cattail's light. Sky-blue filled the dome from end to end. I squinted a bit, but a strange sensation coming from the hand holding Selka's made me open my eyes wide again.

It felt like my body itself was melting into the light and flowing right out of my hand.

In fact, little motes of light *were* visibly passing from my body through my left arm and into Selka's hand. With blurred vision, I saw the trail of light pass through Selka, grow stronger, and funnel down through Eugeo's hand.

Transfer Durability. The sacred art must be designed to allow people to pass their life to another. I was certain that if I opened my window now, I would see my number sinking fast.

I don't care; use all of it, I prayed, focusing hard on my left hand. Selka was acting as a conduit and booster for all that energy, and it was taking its toll on her. It made me recall the enormity of what it meant for pain to be the payment in this world.

Pain, suffering, and sadness. Clearly these things, unnecessary in a virtual world, had some deep link to the very purpose of the Underworld's existence. If Rath's engineers were hoping to find a breakthrough by tormenting the resident' fluctlights, then my unexpected presence and salvation of Eugeo were unwanted interference with their project.

If that was the case, then they could eat shit for all I cared. Soul without a physical body or not, Eugeo was my friend. I would not let him die. Not like this.

As the life flowed out of me, a terrifying chill began to descend. My vision grew darker and darker, but I tried desperately to track Eugeo's condition. The wound across his belly was noticeably smaller than before we started. But it was not completely healed, not by a long shot. Even the bleeding was still ongoing.

"K-Kirito…can you…keep going…?" Selka said under her breath, pained.

"I'm fine…G-give Eugeo more!" I answered promptly, though I could barely see anymore. There was no feeling in my right hand or foot. My left hand was the only part of me that beat with a hot pulse.

If I lost my life in this world, it wouldn't bother me a bit. If I saved Eugeo's life, I could withstand twice the pain that I had earlier. The only regret I'd have would be failing to see what became of this world. What if those goblins were only the vanguard? What if the invasion from the land of darkness only intensified? I couldn't help but worry for Rulid, being situated right at the most vulnerable place. I knew I would lose my memory once I logged out, and it would be impossible to get back in.

But no. Even if I died…

Eugeo had seen and swung a sword at the goblins, too. He would do something about this. He would warn the elder, prompting more guards, and alert the neighboring towns and cities of the danger. I knew it with every fiber of my being.

For that reason as much as any other, I could not let him die here.

But on the other hand, my life was draining out of me. I could tell very clearly, despite my fading senses. Eugeo's eyes were still closed. Even the gift of my entire life would not be enough to heal his wounds and call him back from the brink of death?

"Oh, no…no…If we keep going, your life will run out…" Selka wailed, as if off from a distance.

I wanted to tell her not to stop, to keep going, but my mouth was frozen. It was getting hard even to think anymore.

Was this death? A pretend death of the soul within the Under-world…or could the death of my soul kill my physical body, too? It was cold enough to make that idea plausible to me. I felt so terribly alone…

Suddenly, hands touched my shoulders.

They were warm. My insides began to melt before they could freeze entirely.

I—I knew these hands. As delicate as birds' wings but powerful enough to seize the future when no one else would.

…Who…are you…?

The feeling of soft breath on my left ear met my silent question. Then I heard a voice so familiar and nostalgic that it made me want to cry.

"Kirito, Eugeo…I'll be waiting for you always…I am waiting for you at the top of Central Cathedral…"

A golden shine like starlight filled my insides. The surge of overwhelming energy permeated every last inch of my body and, looking for an exit, spilled forth from my left hand.

5

A light, percussive sound dispersed far above the spring haze.

Eugeo finished his fifty ax strikes and wiped the sweat from his brow, and I tossed him the flask of siral water.

"How's the wound feeling? Giving you pain?"

"After a whole day of rest, it's all the way better now. Just left a bit of a scar. In fact…maybe it's my imagination, but I feel like the Dragonbone Ax is way lighter now."

"I don't think it's your imagination. Forty-two of those fifty swings were right on the mark."

Eugeo's eyebrows shot up in surprise, and his face crinkled into a grin. "Really? Then I guess I'll win today's bet."

"We'll see about that." I laughed, took the Dragonbone Ax, and gave it a one-handed swing. It did seem to be much easier to control than I remembered.

Two nights had passed since the nightmare in the cave beneath the End Mountains. With Eugeo on my right shoulder—having been revived with Selka's sacred arts—and the head of the goblin captain slung over my left, we returned to Rulid far past sundown. The adults were gathered in the square, debating whether to form a search party, as we arrived. After the initial wave of relieved outcry, there came a thunderous scolding from Elder Gasfut and

Sister Azalia. The unthinkable situation of three youths breaking the village laws seemed to have thrown the adults into a panic.

But that lasted only until I thrust the severed head under their noses. When they saw Ugachi's hideous head—larger than ours, with yellowed eyes and ugly, jagged teeth—they fell silent at first, then erupted into greater shock.

After that, Eugeo and Selka explained about the goblin band camping out in the northern cave and how they were probably scouts from the land of darkness. The elders wanted to laugh it off as the overactive imagination of children, but the presence of the monstrous head the likes of which none of them had ever seen prevented them from dismissing our story. The discussion turned to the defense of the village, and we were released to drag our weary feet back home.

In my room at the church, Selka tended to my wounded shoulder, and then I collapsed into sleep. Both Eugeo and I were exempt from working the next day, and I took that opportunity to stay in bed. By the time I woke up after the second night in bed, the pain and fatigue were entirely gone.

After breakfast, the similarly hearty-looking Eugeo and I headed for the forest, where he had just finished his first set of fifty swings.

I looked at the ax in my hand while he sat down a short distance away.

"Say, Eugeo, do you remember...when the goblin in the cave slashed you...? You said something strange. That I was friends with you and Alice years ago..."

He didn't answer right away. After a long silence, a pleasant breeze rustled the nearby leaves, and his voice seemed to hang on to the tail end of the wind.

"...I remember. It's not possible...but for some reason, I remembered it very clearly then. You, Alice, and I were born and raised together in this village...and on the day Alice got taken away, you were with us..."

"…I see," I replied, and fell into brooding.

You might explain it as memory confusion in an extreme situation. If Eugeo's mind and personality were made of a fluctlight just like mine, it was possible that in the moment of life and death, his mental banks made a few mistaken connections.

But the problem was that I'd experienced the same memory confusion at the same moment in time. When I saw Eugeo dying before my eyes, I had a vivid sensation of growing up with him in Rulid Village—along with memories of Alice, the golden-haired girl whom I'd never met.

It was impossible. I had very clear and detailed memories of living in Kawagoe City of Saitama Prefecture as Kazuto Kirigaya, with a sister named Suguha, up until the day I woke up in this world. I couldn't believe that my background was fictional. I didn't want to.

Was this phenomenon just a kind of shared hallucination between Eugeo and me in that instant and nothing more?

But that left one thing without an explanation. While Selka's sacred art attempted to save Eugeo's life by transferring my life to his, I felt a fourth presence with my fading wits. Someone said, *Kirito, Eugeo, I'm waiting at the top of Central Cathedral.*

I couldn't simply claim that voice was the product of my exhausted mind. I had never heard the term *Central Cathedral* before this. I had never even heard of, much less been to, a place by that name in any world, real or virtual.

So the voice had to actually be coming from someone else, not me, Eugeo, or Selka. Was it a stretch to suggest that it was Alice, the girl taken from the village six years earlier? And if so, was this impossible past where I grew up with Eugeo and Alice in Rulid also real…?

I decided to stop thinking in circles about what had filled my head since yesterday morning and said, "Eugeo, when Selka used the sacred arts on you in the cave, did you hear someone's voice?"

This time, his reply was quick. "Nope, I was completely unconscious. Did you hear something, Kirito?"

"No…just my imagination. Forget it. Well, I've got to get to work. I'm shooting for at least forty-five hits."

I faced the Gigas Cedar, banishing the swirling thoughts that plagued me. My hands gripped the ax, and my mind dedicated all its concentration to the task at hand.

The ax followed the precise trajectory I envisioned, striking the exact middle of the crescent-shaped cut in the tree.

Our quota of a thousand swings for the morning session ended thirty minutes earlier than it usually did. We had barely any fatigue and required very little rest. The number of clean hits was far more than last week, and if it wasn't my imagination, it actually *looked* like the cut in the giant tree was deeper than before.

Eugeo stretched with palpable satisfaction and suggested that we take an early lunch, sitting down on his usual root. I joined him, and he pulled two of the same old rolls out of the cloth and tossed them to me.

I caught one in each hand, grimacing at the stony toughness of them, and said, "If only the bread had softened up, the way the ax is lighter now."

"Ha-ha-ha," Eugeo laughed, taking a big bite and shrugging. "Sadly, it seems to be the same as before. Anyway…I wonder *why* the ax seems so light all of a sudden."

"Who can say?" I replied, but truthfully, I had a good idea from when I'd checked out my own window last night. My Object Control Authority, System Control Authority, and maximum life were all much higher than before.

I was pretty sure I knew why. By driving off that goblin brigade—in other words, completing a difficult quest—I had undergone what a normal VRMMO would call a "level-up." I was not in any hurry to repeat the process, but at least I'd been rewarded for braving that dangerous battle.

This morning I'd asked Selka about it, and she, too, had claimed that, oddly enough, she was now much better at the sacred arts she'd struggled with just last week. Although she hadn't taken part in the battle, the level-up effect made sense if you presumed that the three of us were treated as a party.

I suspected that, like mine, Eugeo's Object Control Authority had risen to around forty-eight. There was no way I wasn't going to try my idea again.

I rushed to finish my two rolls of bread and got to my feet. I strode over to a large knot in the Gigas Cedar's trunk, feeling Eugeo's eyes on me as he chewed, and pulled out the Blue Rose Sword from where we'd left it the other day.

I grabbed the leather package and tried to lift it, half-certain I was right and half praying I was.

"Whoa…!"

I nearly tipped backward, and carefully steadied myself. The overloaded barbell weight that I remembered had now shrunk to that of a thick metal pipe instead.

It still put strain on my wrist. But if anything, that weight was now comforting, reminiscent of the swords that I used so lovingly in the later stages of old Aincrad.

I undid the string that bound the leather and squeezed the hilt of the beautiful sword. As Eugeo looked on with the bread stuck in his mouth, I gave him a little grin and drew the blade with a spine-tingling *shinng!*

Unlike its bucking bronco routine of the other day, the Blue Rose Sword settled into my palm with all the grace of a sheltered lady. It truly was a stunning weapon. The sticky texture of the white leather grip, the translucent cast of the blade that trapped the light in intoxicating patterns, the fine decoration of rose vines—these things could not be represented in the old-fashioned polygonal way. It made perfect sense that old Bercouli would have tested a dragon to steal a sword like this.

"W-wait, Kirito…You can lift that sword now?" Eugeo asked, stunned. I swiped it back and forth to show him.

"The bread isn't any softer, but it looks like this sword is lighter, at least. Watch this."

I faced the Gigas Cedar and crouched, drawing back my right

leg to face sideways and pulling the sword straight back at level height to maximize rotation. When I held it there, the sword began glowing a faint blue.

"*Seii!*"

I shot forward. The system added the velocity as I intended, hurtling the sword with tremendous speed and precision in the one-handed sword attack Horizontal.

The Blue Rose Sword flashed like sideways lightning, striking the target with pinpoint accuracy and tremendous impact. The Gigas Cedar's massive bulk rattled, and the birds gathered in the branches nearby all took flight.

It was so satisfying to indulge in the feeling of body and blade being one again. I followed the line of my right arm with my eyes, down to where the bluish-silver blade was stuck halfway into the blackened tree.

Eugeo's eyes and mouth bulged open. The half-eaten piece of bread fell from his hands and landed on the moss. But the wood-cutter boy wasn't even aware it had happened.

"…Kirito…was that…a sword art?"

Well, well. That suggested that the concept of sword techniques *did* exist here—though I didn't know if he was referring to system-designated "sword skills" or something more organic. I put the sword back into its sheath and chose my words carefully.

"Yeah…I think so."

"That means…before the god of darkness spirited you away, your Calling must have been a man-at-arms…or even a sentinel at a larger town. I mean, they only teach official sword arts to garrison sentinels."

Eugeo's green eyes sparkled with excitement as he spoke, chattering much faster than usual for him. In that instant, I realized that despite being a woodcutter and doing his Calling for six years without complaint, what Eugeo's soul cried out to be was a swordsman. His admiration for the sword and thirst to control it at will were etched into the deepest parts of his heart.

He approached me on stumbling feet and looked me in the eyes. His voice trembled.

"Kirito...what style of swordsmanship do you use? Have you forgotten the name...?"

I thought it over briefly, then shook my head. "No, I remember. My sword is the Aincrad Style."

The name just came to me, of course. But once I said it, I realized that it couldn't be called anything else. All my skill had been learned and honed in that flying fortress.

"Ain...crad...Style," he repeated, then nodded. "It's a strange name. I've never heard of it, but I suppose it might be the name of your teacher or the town where you lived...Kirito, will..."

He looked down and mumbled. But when his head rose again a few seconds later, there was powerful intent in his eyes.

"Will you teach me your Aincrad Style swordfighting? Of course, I'm not a soldier or even a village guard...so it might be breaking some rule somewhere..."

"Is there a verse in the Taboo Index or the Basic...Imperial Laws that forbids a non-soldier from training with a sword?" I asked quietly.

Eugeo bit his lip and muttered, "There's no verse like that...but holding multiple Callings at once is forbidden. It's only people with man-at-arms or sentinel Callings who train with swords. So if I start training...it might be seen as neglecting my own Calling..."

His shoulders fell, but his hands were balled into fists that trembled with the tension in his arms.

I could practically see the battle raging inside him. All these people living in the Underworld, these artificial fluctlights mass-produced somehow by Rath, all shared one trait that the people of the real world did not have.

It was my belief that they *could not disobey* the higher rules written into their consciousness. They were incapable of breaking the Axiom Church's Taboo Index, the Basic Imperial Law of the Norlangarth Empire tasked with managing the realm, and even the village standards of Rulid passed down through the years. They couldn't do it.

That was why Eugeo had to subdue for six long years his raging desire to rush to save his friend Alice. He suppressed his own feelings and swung his ax—against a tree that would never be felled so long as he lived.

But now, for the first time, he was attempting to carve his own path. Perhaps his request to learn how to use a sword was not just out of a childhood dream but something much deeper...A means to gain power in the pursuit of his ultimate goal: saving Alice from captivity.

I watched Eugeo tremble in silence and thought, *Hang in there, Eugeo. Don't give up—don't give in to what binds you. Take a step...take your first step. You're a swordsman.*

The blond-haired boy suddenly looked up as though he heard me. His pristine green eyes pierced my own, shining with intent. Through gritted teeth, he rasped, "But...but I...want to be... strong. So that...I never make...the same mistake again. To get back...what I've lost. Kirito...teach me how to use a sword."

Something powerful welled up in my chest, and I had to fight it down to maintain control. I grinned and told him, "All right. I'll teach you everything I know. But the training will be harsh."

I let my smile turn impish and held out a hand. Eugeo's mouth softened at last, and he clasped it.

"That's just what I'm hoping for. In fact...it really is what I've wanted...for ever and ever."

His head dipped again, and a few clear drops fell, catching the sunlight. He stepped forward before I could even register surprise and thudded his forehead against my shoulder. I felt his whisper through my body more than heard it.

"I just...figured it out. I've been waiting for you, Kirito. Waiting here in the forest for six long years for you to come..."

"...Yeah."

My own voice was barely audible. I reached around and

thumped him lightly on the back with my left hand, still holding the sword in it.

"I'm pretty sure that I woke in this forest...in order to meet you, Eugeo."

I hardly even recognized that I had said the words, but I was certain they were the truth.

The Gigas Cedar—steel giant, tyrant of the forest—toppled without much fanfare just five days after I began training Eugeo in the ways of the Aincrad School.

Mostly, it was because the tree made for the perfect practice dummy. With each demonstration of Horizontal and Eugeo's subsequent practice attempts, the slice in the tree's trunk grew visibly deeper. The momentous event occurred when the cut was about 80 percent of the way through the tree.

"*Seyaa!*"

Eugeo hit the trunk with a perfectly executed horizontal slice, and it let out an eerie creaking the likes of which it had never made before.

We looked at each other in shock, glanced up at the branches of the Gigas Cedar far overhead, and froze in place. It was falling, very slowly, toward us.

In fact, it produced the illusion that the tree was not falling on top of us but that the ground was tilting forward. Such was the unreality of the sight of a thirteen-foot-wide tree giving in to gravity and toppling over.

The two and a half feet of trunk still connected—eighty cens, in this world's measurement—was unable to bear the force of the rest, and it splintered and sprayed flecks like charcoal. The tree's dying wail was louder than the force of ten consecutive thunderbolts, and the sound carried through the center of town all the way to the guard outpost at the northern end of the village, from what we were told.

We screamed and split in different directions. Ever so slowly, the black mass split the orange of the late afternoon sky and finally crashed to earth. The thunderous impact threw me high into the air, and when I landed on my rump, my life went down by about fifty points.

"I'm amazed…I didn't realize there were so many people here," I mumbled, taking the mug of apple ale from Eugeo's outstretched hand.

Red fires ringed the center square of Rulid, illuminating the faces of the people gathered within it. Beside the fountain, an impromptu troupe of musicians played a jolly waltz with hide drums, very long flutes, and an instrument that looked like a set of bagpipes. The stomping and clapping of the people dancing along swirled up into the open sky.

I sat at a table off to the side, keeping time with my foot, possessed by a strange urge to leap into the midst of the people and join in the dancing.

"I don't think I've ever seen so many villagers in one place, either. There's even more people here than during the Great Solemnity prayer at the end of the year," Eugeo said, smiling. I held out my mug and we shared yet another toast. The bubbling cider-like drink was the weakest kind in the village, but downing a long swig of it was enough to make my face hot.

When the village elder and other dignitaries learned of the tree's fall, they had no choice but to convene a village meeting, right after the previous one last week. They came together and argued passionately about what should be done with Eugeo the Carver and me.

Frighteningly enough, many argued that we should actually be *punished* for completing the task of cutting down the tree a whole nine centuries ahead of schedule, but at the merciful suggestion of Elder Gasfut, a village-wide celebration was arranged, and Eugeo would be dealt with as the law dictated.

I couldn't actually tell *what* the law dictated in this particular case. I asked Eugeo what it meant, but he just laughed and said I would find out soon enough.

Based on that reaction, it seemed clear that he wasn't going to be persecuted. I drained my mug, picked up a meat skewer dripping with juices from a nearby plate, and took a massive bite.

In fact, all I'd eaten since coming to this world was that dreadful hard bread and the weak vegetable soup at the church—this was the first real meat I'd had. The tender beef substitute, slathered in its rich sauce, was so succulent, savory, and flavorful that I considered it worth cutting down the Gigas Cedar for this taste alone.

Of course, all was not well. In fact, I felt now that we had arrived only at the very start. I glanced over at the Blue Rose Sword, hanging proudly on Eugeo's belt.

Over the last five days, he had used the Gigas Cedar as a practice target for the basic One-Handed Sword skill Horizontal. As the impromptu "Aincrad Style" name would suggest, it was a system-recognized sword skill from the old *Sword Art Online* VRMMO.

It made sense that you could recreate the action. When I visited *Gun Gale Online*, which was based around gun-fighting, I managed to make my way through a few very sticky fights by using sword skills. But that was only by retracing my avatar movements—there were no flashes of light or system-assisted acceleration. It simply wasn't a gameplay system there.

But the Underworld fully facilitated sword skills. Make the designated motion and envision the movement of the entire skill, and then the sword would flash and speed away. On our first day of training, I was worried that I might be the only one capable of doing this, but by the second afternoon, Eugeo executed his first successful Horizontal, proving that any citizen could use sword skills if they fulfilled the requirements.

The problem was *why* it worked. There couldn't be any connection between Rath's STL virtual-reality Underworld and the late Argus's *SAO* game. If anything, perhaps the answer lay in the man who'd brought me this fishy job with Rath and had once been part of the government's *SAO* task force…

"That can't be," I muttered to myself as I took on a second skewer. If my imagination was correct, then he wasn't just a go-between but someone inextricably linked to the core of all these events.

But there was no way to figure out any of that from here. I'd have to leave Rulid and go to the central city, far to the south, to gain more information.

The biggest impediment to the plan had just been cut down. There was only one thing left to do.

I finished off the meat and vegetables on the skewer and called out to my partner, who was watching the villagers from his seat across the table.

"Hey, Eugeo..."

"Uh...what is it?"

"After this—"

But a high-pitched shout interrupted me.

"Aha, here you are! What is the star of the festival doing sitting over here?!"

It took some time for me to recognize that the girl with her hands on her hips was Selka. Instead of her usual braids and black sister's habit, she had her hair tucked behind a headband and wore a red vest and green skirt.

"Uh, well...I'm no good at dancing," Eugeo mumbled.

I shook my head and hand as well. "And I've got memory loss..."

"It will come back to you once you try it!"

Her little hands grabbed ours and launched us out of our seats. Selka dragged the two of us to the middle of the square and pushed us forward. A cheer erupted from the crowd, and we were swallowed into the midst of the dance.

Fortunately, it was no more complex than the dances at the school sports festivals, and by the time they'd switched through three partners, I was getting the hang of it. Moving my body to the simplistic rhythm started being fun, and my feet got into the act.

The more I danced with the laughing, red-cheeked girls with features somewhere between Eastern and Western, the more I fell under the strange suspicion that maybe I really was a wanderer who had lost his memory.

In fact, I had danced in a VR world before, with the sylph warrior Leafa, the Alfheim avatar of my sister, Suguha. I saw her smile on my dancing partner's face and felt something inside my nose sting.

A rush of keen homesickness overcame me. Meanwhile, the music sped up to a manic pace, then abruptly ended. I looked at the musicians and saw that the stage next to them now featured an imposing old man with a majestic beard. It was Gasfut, elder of Rulid and Selka's father.

He clapped his hands and spoke in a strong baritone.

"My fellows! Please forgive the interruption, but you must hear me!"

The villagers raised their mugs of ale and apple liquor in a cheer, quenched their dance-induced thirst, then fell silent. The elder looked out over the crowd.

"The deepest desire of our founding ancestors has been fulfilled at last! The devil tree that stole the blessings of Terraria and Solus in the fertile land to the south has been felled! We will have fresh new barley and bean fields and grazing pastures for our cattle and sheep!"

Cheers drowned out his speech. He held up his hands, waiting for quiet to return.

"I call forth the one who achieved this feat—Eugeo, son of Orick!"

He beckoned to a corner of the square, where a nervous-looking Eugeo stood. The short man next to him must have been his father, Orick. Aside from the hair color, they looked totally unalike, and he appeared more confused than proud.

Eugeo proceeded forward at the urging of the other villagers, not his father. He rose next to the elder and turned to the crowd.

The third and largest cheer yet erupted. I clapped, too, not to be outdone.

"In accordance with our rules," the elder began, and the village fell silent, "for completing his Calling, Eugeo is granted the right to choose his next Calling! He may continue as a woodcutter, or plow the fields after his father, or tend to cattle, or brew ale, or do business, or whatever he chooses!"

What was that?!

I felt the afterglow of the dance rapidly fading.

This was no time to be holding hands and dancing with girls. I should have been giving Eugeo one final pep talk. If he announced he would start growing grain, my plan would be completely ruined.

I watched him with bated breath. He looked down, uncomfortable, scratching his head with one hand and clenching and unclenching the other. I began to wonder if I should rush the stage, put an arm around his shoulders, and announce that we were off to see the big city—until I heard a small voice at my side.

"Eugeo's...going to leave the village..."

Selka had come to stand next to me at some point. There was a faint smile of both sadness and happiness on her lips.

"Y-you think so?"

"I know so. Why else would he hesitate to give his answer?"

As if he heard her, Eugeo's hand reached down to grip the hilt of the Blue Rose Sword at his waist. He looked up, first at the elder, then at the rest of the village, and stated clearly and loudly, "I'm going...to be a swordsman. I will join the garrison at Zakkaria, train my skills, and one day reach Centoria."

After a few moments of silence, little waves of murmuring broke out. It didn't seem to me to be adulation. The adults were craning their necks toward one another, muttering darkly. Eugeo's father and two other young men who I took to be his brothers looked more pained than anything.

Once again, it was Gasfut who brought order. He lifted a hand to silence the crowd, and with a stern expression, he said, "Eugeo, surely you don't…"

Then he paused and stroked his long beard. "No…I will not ask why. It is your church-given right to choose your next Calling. Very well—as elder of Rulid, I recognize that the new Calling for Eugeo, son of Orick, is a swordsman. If you wish, you may leave the village and train in the sword."

I heaved a long sigh of relief. Now I would be able to witness the core of this world with my own eyes. If Eugeo had chosen to remain a farmer, I was prepared to head out on my own, but with a lack of knowledge or resources, I couldn't say how many months or years my trip would take. A weight left my shoulders as my concerns of the last few days evaporated.

The villagers seemed to have accepted their elder's decision, and they began a hesitant round of applause. But before it could swell any louder, a sharp bellow cut across the night sky.

"Not so fast!"

A large young man strode through the crowd and leaped on the stage.

He had rough features and short hair the dull brown of dead leaves. But the simple longsword at his left side was what stuck out to me first. It was the guard who always stood watch at the southern waypoint of the village.

He puffed out his chest as a challenge to Eugeo and shouted, "It is my right first and foremost to seek employment in Zakkaria's garrison! Eugeo cannot be the first to leave the village ahead of me!"

"Yeah! He's right!" came a follow-up shout from a man behind him. He had the same color hair as the youngster but was much older and larger around the middle.

"Who's that?" I asked Selka. She made a face.

"That's Doik, the old head guard, and his son, Zink, who has the position now. Their family likes to claim they're the most experienced in the village."

"Ah, I see…"

I wondered what was going to happen now. Gasfut listened to Zink and his father and raised a hand to calm them down. "But Zink, you have only been at your man-at-arms Calling for six years. According to the laws, you cannot enter the dueling tournament in Zakkaria for another four."

"Then Eugeo should wait for four years, too! He's not as good at the sword as I am! It makes no sense that he should go first!"

"Mmm. Then how will you prove this claim that you are superior to Eugeo in skill?"

"Wha…!"

Zink and his father both went red in the face. The elder of the two was nearly steaming from the ears as he bellowed, "I won't stand for such an insult, even from the elder of Rulid! If you're telling me that a mere woodcutter can swing a faster sword than my son, then let's have them prove it right here and now!"

A few irresponsible villagers shouted, egging him on. Sensing that there was more entertainment to come from this impromptu festival, they raised their mugs and stomped their feet, crowing about a duel.

To my astonishment, within moments Zink had challenged Eugeo to a duel, which Eugeo could not very well refuse. A space before the stage was cleared away, and they faced off. In disbelief, I turned to whisper into Selka's ear, "I'll be right back."

"Wh-what are you going to do?"

I didn't answer. Instead, I made my way through the crowd in the direction of the fountain and raced up to Eugeo. While his opponent was as unruly and indignant as a bronco, Eugeo seemed more confused that it had come to this. His features relaxed when he saw me.

"Wh-what should I do, Kirito? Look what's happened!"

"I don't think you can get out of this with a simple apology at this point. Anyway, is this duel going to be a true sword battle?"

"Of course not. We have to stop before drawing blood."

"Ahh…but if you can't stop the sword in time and hit your target, that might end up killing your opponent. Listen—aim for Zink's sword, not Zink. Give him one Horizontal on the blade and that should do it."

"A-are you sure?"

"Absolutely. I guarantee it."

I pounded him on the back; gave a quick bow to Zink and his father, who were staring at me suspiciously; and returned to the line of spectators.

At the podium, Gasfut clapped and called for silence.

"And now, outside of the original plan, we have a duel between Zink, our head man-at-arms, and the carver…er, the swordsman Eugeo! You are not to lower your opponent's life through direct strikes. Is that understood?!"

Zink loudly drew his sword from his waist, and, a bit later, Eugeo reluctantly drew his. The gasp from the village crowd was no doubt due to the beauty of the Blue Rose Sword as it shone in the firelight.

Even Zink seemed to be overwhelmed by the aura of the sword. His head tilted back briefly before he regained his posture. With an even more hateful glare than before, the young guard jabbed a finger at Eugeo and said, to my surprise, "Does that sword really belong to you, Eugeo?! If it's borrowed, I have the right to force you to use a different—"

But Eugeo interrupted with righteous fury. "I got this sword in the northern cave, so it belongs to me now!"

The crowd murmured, and Zink seemed to be at a loss for words. I figured that he would demand proof of ownership from Eugeo, but he didn't. In a world without thievery, perhaps the simple act of stating that something was your own property was all the proof needed. Even doubting that statement might be seen as a violation of rights.

I had no idea if that was correct or not, but Zink didn't push the issue any further. He spat into his palms and held his sword up high.

Eugeo, meanwhile, held his blade perfectly still at eye level, drew his left side back, and crouched.

As hundreds of villagers watched in silence, Gasfut raised his hand high, then brought it down as he commanded, "Begin!"

"Raaaah!!"

As I expected, Zink was the first to charge. He bellowed and raced forward to deliver a vertical slice from overhead. It was so forceful that I feared he might really intend to hit Eugeo.

"…!!"

I gasped. Zink's sword changed directions in midair. He had gone from an overhead swing down to a sideways swipe from the right. As a feint, it was crude, but the timing was awful. I'd advised Eugeo to hit Zink's sword with a Horizontal, but it would be very hard to deflect a flat swing with a flat swing. He could easily miss and wind up losing…

"Y-yaaaah!!"

The shout was rather inferior to Zink's. And Eugeo's sword skill was *not* Horizontal.

He set his sword at the right shoulder. The blade glowed deep blue. He made one earth-shaking stomp and sliced at a sharp forty-five-degree arc. That was the diagonal sword skill Slant—but I had never taught him that.

Eugeo's attack, which came out a single pulse later, shot forward with lightning speed, striking Zink's sideways swing from above. Even in the moment that the steel blade shattered miserably, I couldn't help but question myself.

No doubt Eugeo had been practicing with a stick or something else when he went home at night. During that practice, he'd become aware of Slant—but there was nothing hesitant or amateur about that movement. If anything, the way he became one with the Blue Rose Sword was graceful, beautiful.

If he continued to build experience, learned a multitude of skills, and grew through actual battle, what sort of swordsman might he end up being? If…if I ever had to cross blades with him, would I actually emerge the victor?

The villagers marveled and applauded the flashy and unexpected conclusion, but it was the cold sweat running down my back that held my concentration.

Zink and his father retreated in stunned disbelief, and the music started up again. The festival was even more rousing than before, and it did not disperse until the church bell rang ten o'clock.

It took another three cups of the apple beverage for me to forget about my unease and rejoin the intoxicating dance circle. In the end, Selka had to drag me back to the church. At the door, Eugeo looked at me in mild exasperation but promised that we would begin our journey in the morning. I stumbled up to my room somehow and toppled onto the bed.

"Just because it's a festival doesn't mean you have to drink *that* much, Kirito. Here's some water," said Selka, offering me a cold cup fresh from the well. I downed it, feeling it cool off my brain, and exhaled. In Aincrad and Alfheim, the best you could do was pretend you were feeling drunk, but here in the Underworld, the alcohol was real. I made a mental note about that for next time. At my side, the young girl looked worried.

"Wh-what?" Selka asked suspiciously, noticing that I was staring at her. I tipped my head in embarrassment.

"I...I'm sorry. You probably wanted to speak more with Eugeo, huh?"

Selka's cheeks suddenly went cherry red. She was still dressed in her nicest outfit. "Why would you bring that up?"

"Because by tomorrow morning...Actually, I should apologize for that first. Now it looks like I'm pretty much taking Eugeo out of the village. If he had been a woodcutter here for the rest of his life, he might have, well...started a family with you, eventually..."

Selka sighed theatrically and sat down next to me on the bed.

"Honestly, what do I even say about that?" she wondered, shaking her head in utter exasperation. "Well...fine. Yes, I'm sad that Eugeo will be leaving the village...but I'm also happy. Ever since Alice went away, he's been living his life like he's given up on everything, but now he's smiling again. He made up his mind to go searching for my sister. I'm certain that on the inside, Father was happy, too…to learn that Eugeo hadn't forgotten about her."

"…I see…"

She bobbed her head and looked up at the full moon outside the window.

"Actually…I didn't go into the cave hoping to copy my sister and touch the soil of the land of darkness. I knew I wasn't capable of that. I knew…but I just wanted to get a bit closer to her. To go as far as I could…up to the point where I couldn't go any farther, and then I'd know for sure…that I can never be Alice's replacement."

I pondered the meaning of her statement, then shook my head. "No, you're really something. A normal girl would turn back at the bridge out of the village, or in the woods, or at the cave's entrance. But you went all the way down into that dark place and found a goblin scouting party. You did something that only you can do."

"Something that…only I can do…?" she asked, her eyes huge.

I nodded. "You aren't a replacement for Alice. You have your own unique talents, Selka. So focus on developing those."

In fact, I was certain that Selka's talent for the sacred arts was about to take a huge leap. She had helped defeat the goblins with Eugeo and me, so her system authority level had to be higher now.

But that wasn't the crux of the matter. She had sought the answer to who she was and found one. That, more than anything, would give her incredible energy. Belief in oneself was the truest power of the human soul.

It was time for me to find the answer to the question I'd been putting off.

Who or what was this sentient consciousness calling itself Kirito, or Kazuto Kirigaya? The fluctlight residing in a biological brain—the "real" me? Or a replica saved on storage media, read from my brain by the STL?

There was only one way to find out.

The Underworldians like Eugeo and Selka, with their artificial fluctlights, could not break the Taboo Index or Basic Imperial Law. But just because I could run afoul of this world's taboos was not proof that I wasn't an artificial fluctlight. I hardly knew any of the individual taboos in the index. The rules hadn't been written into my soul.

Instead, I had to find out if I could break my *own* rules that I lived by—my own set of personal morals. I'd been considering this topic for several days, but it was actually quite difficult. Attacking the villagers or stealing their possessions was out of the question, and I didn't feel right insulting someone just to confirm a personal suspicion. There was only one thing I could think of.

I turned and stared right into Selka's face.

"…What?" she asked, blinking. I put a hand on her cheek and silently apologized to Asuna and Yui. Then I audibly apologized to Selka, leaned closer, and placed a light kiss on her white forehead, just before the headband.

She twitched, then sat still. I pulled away after three seconds and saw that she was glaring at me, cheeks red all the way to the ears.

"What…did you just do…?"

"Let's call it…a swordsman's oath," I suggested weakly. On the inside, I savored a new factual certainty.

I had just carried out something that the real me would never do, thus proving that I was the real me. If I were a replica fluctlight, my body would have stopped automatically a few inches from Selka's forehead.

She continued staring at me, rubbed her forehead, and sighed.

"An oath…? I don't know if that's how you do things in your country, but if you had kissed my…instead of my forehead, an Integrity Knight would be coming for you right now. That's against the Taboo Index."

Her voice had gone quiet at one point, and I couldn't make out what she'd said, but I wasn't going to ask. Selka shook her head again, grinned in annoyance, and asked, "So…what did you swear?"

"Isn't it obvious? That I'll go with Eugeo, save Alice, and bring your sister back to this village. You have my word…"

I paused, then slowly said the words.

"…as Kirito the Swordsman."

6

The next morning was brilliantly clear.

Eugeo and I headed down a southern path we would not see again for quite some time, savoring the weight of the lunches that Selka had packed for us.

When we reached the split in the path that headed into the Gigas Cedar's woods, I noticed an elderly man standing there. His wrinkled face was covered in white hair, but his back was straight, and his eyes were sharp.

As soon as he saw the man, Eugeo burst into a dazzling smile and began to trot.

"Old Man Garitta! You came to see me off! I'm so happy—I didn't get to see you yesterday."

That name was familiar to me. If I recalled correctly, it was the previous carver of the Gigas Cedar.

Garitta smiled kindly under his heavy whiskers and placed his hands on Eugeo's shoulders. "Eugeo, in all my life, I only deepened the Cedar's cut by the length of a finger, and now you've toppled the beast…Tell me, how did you do it?"

"With this sword," Eugeo said, pulling the Blue Rose Sword from its sheath just an inch and letting it click back into place. Then he glanced at me. "And most of all, thanks to him…my friend. This is Kirito. He's really pretty crazy, actually."

I shook my head modestly, wondering what kind of introduction that was supposed to be. Garitta moved over to me and gave me a piercing, knowing stare—then beamed.

"So you are the lost child of Vecta I heard about. Yes, I see… You have the face of change."

No one had ever described me that way before, and I wondered what he meant by it. The old man gestured to the forest at his left and continued, "Well, I hate to delay your travels, but could you stand to help me? It won't take long."

"S-sure. You don't mind, Kirito?"

I couldn't see a reason to refuse. The old man smiled again and headed down the path into the forest, beckoning us onward.

I'd been walking down the path for only about a week, but it filled me with rich nostalgia now. After twenty minutes, we arrived at a wide opening.

The tyrannical tree that had split the heavens in the midst of this clearing for centuries was lying still on its side. Narrow vines were already climbing over its pitch-black bark, beginning the process that would one day, in the distant future, break down the tree and return it to the earth.

"What is it about the Gigas Cedar, Garitta?" Eugeo asked, as the elderly man proceeded toward the tip of the fallen tree. We followed after him, but the branches of the Gigas Cedar and the trunks of the other trees it had toppled in its fall were like a maze. I was stunned to find, on closer look, that no matter how narrow the Cedar's branches might get, every single one was still intact, even the ones stabbing into ground and rock. The toughness of that bark was simply astonishing.

With great difficulty, we made our way through the branches, picking up scratches on our exposed arms, and at last reached Garitta, who was standing calmly up ahead. Eugeo wiped his sweat with the palm of his hand and grumbled, "So what are we supposed to be looking at?"

"This," the old man said, pointing at a branch extending directly out of the very tip-top of the Gigas Cedar's trunk. It was very, very long, without a single side branch, and the end was pointed as sharp as a rapier.

"What about this branch?" I asked. He reached out his knotted hand and caressed the end, which was about two inches wide.

"Out of all the Gigas Cedar's branches, this one absorbed the most of Solus's blessings. Cut this loose with that sword. You must sever it in one strike. If you hack at it several times, it may break apart."

He made a chopping motion with his hand about four feet from the tip of the branch, then stood back.

Eugeo and I looked at each other and decided to follow his instructions. I took Eugeo's lunch from him and stepped back as well.

When he pulled the Blue Rose Sword from its scabbard to shine in the sunlight, the old man let out a muted gasp of wonder. There was a note of longing, it seemed, something that suggested that if he'd gotten his hands on that sword when *he* was younger, his life would have been different. But when I looked at his face in profile, it was placid, impossible to read.

Eugeo brandished the sword but didn't move after that. The tip quivered a bit, reflecting his inner indecision. Perhaps he wasn't confident that he could cut through a branch the width of his wrist in one swing.

"I'll do it, Eugeo," I offered, and reached out. Eugeo nodded and willingly handed me the hilt. I handed over the lunches, and we switched spots.

I didn't even think. I just looked at the black branch, lifted the sword, and brought it down. With no more than a slight crack and the briefest of sensations, the blade passed through my target spot. I used the flat of the blade to stop the long branch from falling and flipped it up into the air. It came down, spinning, and landed in my outstretched free hand. The weight pushing down against my wrist and the icy chill of it caused me to falter.

I gave Eugeo the sword back, then held out the black branch with both hands for Garitta to see.

"You should take this with you," he said, producing a heavy cloth and carefully wrapping the branch in it. When it was safely covered, he tied a rawhide cord around it.

"There you are. When you get to Centoria, take this branch to a craftsman in north District Seven named Sadore. He will be able to fashion it into a mighty sword—one that is every bit an equal to that beauty there."

"R-really, Old Man Garitta? That's wonderful! It was worrying only having one sword between the two of us. Right, Kirito?" said Eugeo excitedly. I nodded and agreed, but the branch was a bit too heavy for me to throw my hands into the air with exuberance.

We bowed to express our gratitude, but the old man only beamed.

"It's a meager parting gift. Take care on your travels. It is not only the benevolent gods who watch over these lands now...I think I will stay here and look at this tree some more. Farewell, Eugeo. Farewell, young traveler."

We headed back up the little path to the main road and found that where the sky had been clear blue earlier, there was now a storm cloud forming over the eastern edge.

"The wind's getting a bit damp. We should probably move on while we still have the chance."

"...Good idea. Let's hurry," I replied, and fastened the wrapped-up Gigas Cedar branch to my back with the cord. The rumble of thunder in the far distance resonated with the weight of the branch, casting a bit of gloom over my mind.

A pair of swords.

Was it a sign from the future, a portent of something?

I stopped in my tracks briefly, wondering if I should just bury the bundle deep in the forest somewhere. But I didn't know what I was afraid of or why.

"Come on, Kirito, let's go!"

I looked up and saw Eugeo's smiling face, dazzling with anticipation of the wider world ahead.

"Yeah...here I come."

I caught up with the other boy. He may have been someone I'd met just a week ago, but he felt like a friend I'd known all my life. Together, we headed south, our pace brisk—down the road leading to the center of the Underworld, where the answers to all the mysteries lay.

(*Alicization Beginning*—The End)

AFTERWORD

Hello, this is Reki Kawahara, and you've finished my first book of 2012, *Sword Art Online 9: Alicization Beginning*.

It was last August when Volume 8 came out, which means it's been half a year now. There are a number of excuses that may or may not apply to the situation, but I still wish to apologize for making you wait so long. I'm sorry! I'll do better next time!

...Well, I was planning on addressing the content of the book at this point, but where do I start...? I'd love to avoid spoilers for the sake of those readers who flip to the afterword ahead of time, but there's no way to get into it without spoiling! So I'm going to draw a spoiler warning line here. Beyond this line is the Dark Territory, where cruelty and unfairness reign! Wait...I just spoiled something there...

—————————SPOILER WARNING LINE—————————

So, after Asuna was the protagonist for Volume 7, and Volume 8 was a collection of short stories, we finally get to the beginning of Kirito's next journey in Volume 9. He's been through *SAO*, *ALO*, and *GGO*, and now, for the first time, he is tackling a virtual world from Level 1. No New Game+ this time! Or so it seemed...until he pulled out his trusty sword skills. I hope you'll forgive the familiar crutch...

I've been challenging myself as a writer to do unfamiliar things in this new Underworld setting. For example, it's not a girl who Kirito first runs across...Er, disregard that. What I mean is, I tried eliminating most of the online terminology to tell a traditional fantasy story, and I paid more attention to the AI NPC characters than usual, in the hopes of expanding my VRMMO setting to its limits. I can worry about bringing it all together later. This is going to be my mindset as I forge ahead into future volumes!

And now, much belated, I wish to touch upon the topic of *Sword Art Online*'s TV anime series. I began writing *SAO* in late 2001 and started quietly publishing it on the web the following year, and now the day has come that it turns animated...If you had told me back then, I would never have believed it. "What, like a GIF animation?" So to abec, the illustrator who helped this miracle come to life; to Mr. Miki, the editor who three years ago suggested, "Let's put this out, too!"; to the sub-editor Mr. Tsuchiya, whose HP bar was in the red due to the tightrope schedule; and to the many readers who have continued to support this series and its author: Thank you so much. The original novels will continue as always, of course!

Reki Kawahara—December 2011

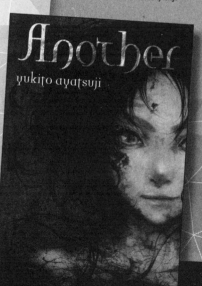